# Blue Feather's

# Frontier Life

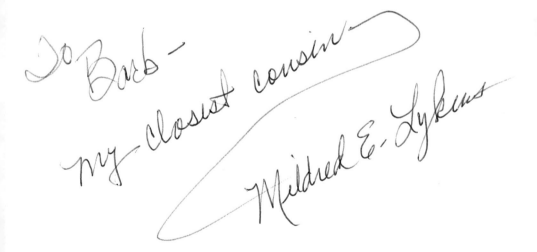

To Barb —
my closest cousin

Mildred E. Lykens

## by   Mildred E. Lykens

*Blue Feather's Frontier Life*

*Resources and acknowledgements:*
*Verbal history from living relatives and learned friends.*
*Bureau of Indian Affairs*
*Wikipedia.org*
*Google*

*U.S. Dept of Census Records 1890, 1900*
*Websites:*
*South Carolina*
*Arkansas*
*Oklahoma*
*Wikipedia*
*Google*


*ISBN# 978-0-359-94301-2*
*ID# 25259837*

*Dedication:*

*A grateful "Thank You" to my good friend*

*Linda Morehead*

*For making the story flow smoothly.*

# Chapter 1

Two couples left the office of Fort Wells' Commander Frederick J. Wadsworth, as newlyweds. One soldier and one trapper had just pledged their oaths to two Cherokee young women. Their first stop was to share the news with the other Cherokee clansmen being held captive at the fort, waiting for word from Washington as to their plight.

The clan gathered around their Chief Soaring Eagle to hear the news as the four entered the compound.

Blue Feather, now claiming an English name of Rebecca Blue, clung to her new trapper husband, William Hudson as did her best friend Squirrel, now renamed Ellen Squirrel hung onto her new soldier husband, Corporal Thomas Thorton.

The fort's jail had become overcrowded when the army soldiers brought the first half of the captives in, but even more so when the other half voluntarily surrendered.

Corporal Thorton had been placed in charge of the Indians due to his schooling in many of their languages and customs. He was also in charge of erecting another building that would house them all until news from Washington arrived. He and Squirrel had met as he guarded them and their attraction grew to trust and then to love.

The clan accepted the marriage news gladly because they knew the trapper, William, to be honest, trustworthy and brave, and the soldier, Thomas, to be friendly, caring and helpful; all noble characteristics in the Cherokee customs.

A few weeks earlier an older red-headed trapper, Gabriel Adams, had been summoned by the Commander to the fort and had also left with an Indian wife. Her name was recorded in his journal as Anita Sparrow. Her daughter Gigi had the same hair and eye color as this trapper. Surmising the situation, Wadsworth demanded the marriage, thinking he was answering his Christian duty; and yet unknowingly answering Gabe's prayers.

The clan had also accepted this white man because of his honorable actions. He had once released Blue's ankle from one of his snares, treated it, made her a crutch and carried her back to the outskirts of her clan's campsite.

The Ani-Tsiskwa, or Bird Clan, had divided when some surrendered and signed the Army's treaty, while others, like Soaring Eagle's group, had turned away and were hunted as renegades. Those who had surrendered had met with broken promises and had been driven from their homelands to small reservations, unable to live their previous lifestyle.

The capture of this small group had first left Rebecca Blue comatose; her mind could not accept witnessing her mother being murdered and her invalid father left senseless. The attack scattered the group and when the survivors reunited, they found themselves without their loved ones or their chief. Ellen's parents and brother Lame Elk were among this group who took a vote to voluntarily surrender.

When the four newlyweds returned to the captives they first spoke with the chief, then Squirrel took Thomas to her family. "Mother, Father, Lame Elk, I have chosen the English name of Ellen and will now lodge with my new husband, Tome-us Thor-ton. He is important to the white man's chief and has his own sleeping place, where I will now stay. Blue's new name is Rebecca and she married

William.  He is taking her to his new house in the woods next to Gabe, Sparrow and Gigi. Please be happy for us."

Her family, as well as the rest of the clan, came forward and patted the arms of each, showing their approval.

They all knew about Ellen's first husband, Snow Wolf, and how he mistreated her, almost killing her before Rebecca knocked his hands away from her throat. His infatuation with Rebecca caused him to believe she felt the same but was too proud to stop the marriage. But she didn't want him; and only tried to interfere with the marriage because of her friendship with Ellen.

Will and Rebecca said their goodbyes to the clan and later to Thomas and Ellen at the fort gate, "It will be hard to remember when we are called by our new names, but I love them." stated Rebecca.

"It will get easier as time goes by," said Thomas.

"And I learn more English each day," added Ellen.

"I want to know every little detail of my new bride," said Will as he pulled her up close. Looking deep into each other's eyes they could see the smoldering passion. "Let's go home, Bl…Rebecca."

The goodbyes were said with the girls hugging and the men shaking hands before one couple turned to go back to the corporal's quarters and the other to find their way to the cabin in the woods.

Will and Rebecca wanted to share their news with their dear friends, Gabe and Anita. But before he could knock, the door swung wide and little Gigi came rushing out all full of smiles and giggles, "I knew I heard something! It's Will and Blue! Come in, come in." Bouncing around the room she continued, "See our new house! Look at all the

6

things we have now. Beds and chairs, table and a st...stove. It cooks even better than the campfire."

Anita shushed the girl and pulled her close. "Blue! It's really you! I thought Gigi was seeing spirits. How? When? What happened?"

All of this was in their Cherokee tongue as the two men looked at each other and shook their heads. "Gabe, we've GOT to learn more Cherokee or they will be talking code about us." said Will.

"That they will, and probably already do," laughed Gabe. "I understood Anita's *how* and *when* so... *what*?"

"It went pretty much like you had planned before, only it was Corporal Thorton and Ellen who instigated it, making the Commander think that I had done more than sleep with Blue...by the way her new name is 'Rebecca'. She wanted an English name, so I thought hey, what was good enough for Daniel Boone is good enough for me, and you know what else? That Corporal Thorton got the commander to marry him and Squirrel while he had the book out! Her name is now Ellen. We had a double wedding just a few hours ago."

Gabe jumped to his feet and shook Will's hand, "Well congratulations, Will! We got our women and kept our scalps! Sparrow has a new name too. It's Anita, after the name of her original clan. She has been busy and after getting this cabin all spiffy, she tackled yours; so it's ready for you and your new bride. I can't keep that woman still. She is always cleaning; even got the outhouse swept out..."

Will was letting Gabe talk as he looked over at Rebecca. When he saw her smiling back, it was all he could do not to go to her and pull her in close. Interrupting everyone, he rose and went to her and said, "Excuse us folks, but I think it's time to show Rebecca her new home."

He guided her out the door and down the path toward the smaller cabin. Unknown to them, Gigi had snuck out to see if Gabe was telling the truth about the white man's custom, and was convinced when she saw Will scoop his new bride up into his arms, and carry her across the threshold.

# Chapter 2

Rebecca started her newly married life in wonderment. She marveled at the small rock fireplace that warmed the cabin in the winter and made evening lanterns or candles unnecessary. Wanting to know everything all at once, she stepped from one thing to another, holding an item up or pointing to it as Will named and demonstrated its use. She repeated each name until she got it right.

When she was satisfied with his explanations of everything inside, they ventured out. He took her to a long building with three doors, built against a nearby hillside.

Each room was self-explanatory as she entered. The one closest to the house had a stack of split wood, an axe imbedded into a chopping block and tools on the walls. The next held hooks on the rafter close to a blood-stained cutting table, and frames for stretching hides. The third room displayed meat hanging above a slightly smoking rock fire pit. In the back of this room was a door that showed a passageway leading to a dugout in the embankment. It was a root cellar, made with shelves to stock jars of canned goods, gunny sacks for vegetables and fruits with boxes along one wall that held previously preserved meat. But the small building farthest away from the house was different. It was quite small and odd-shaped. Inside she found a built-in bench with two holes cut in the seat; one larger than the other.

She was surprised to discover its use and he was surprised to find that Anita had replaced the old catalog with a woven basket full of tufts of moss and leaves with small bouquets of heather and mint hanging in the corners. He smiled at the ingenuity and nodded his approval; he thought *it needed a woman's touch for sure*.

At Gabe and Anita's door, Will showed her how to knock instead of scratch, as was the custom with teepees made of animal skins, and of course it was Gigi that opened the door and began to rattle off with her mixed languages, which no one was able to fully understand.

"Speak one language and translate. You know English fairly well, just as these ladies will before meeting the townspeople," Gabe corrected gently.

"But I get excited and forget."

"I know, Sugar, but it's important to learn proper English so the trade people won't try to cheat you or make fun of you…understand?"

"Yes, Papa, like the clan did Mama and me, before you came to take us away."

"Anita, do *you* understand?" He asked

"Some. Not all. But I learn fast."

Gabe smiled and hugged them both. "Yes, you do, and I'm so proud of each of you. Now we can all help Blue."

Will stated, "Although *Blue* and I chose her new name to be Rebecca; we decided to shorten it to, '*Becca*,'"

She smiled and patted her chest and repeated, "Bek-uh."

Everyone nodded, and in unison repeated, "Bek-uh."

"Anita, Gigi, are you satisfied with your English names?" asked Gabe.

Looking at each other for a couple of seconds, they both smiled, "Yes, Mama and me, we keep our names."

He nodded in agreement, "Now that that's settled, let's get some breakfast going. This morning we shall all feast together as one big happy family."

# Chapter 3

At the fort Ellen went to her new husband, Thomas, with a question. "What do soldiers do with hides from their kills? If they don't need them, it would be good for clan to make new clothes. I know about the cloth from the trading post, but our way is to use all pieces of the animal when it is killed. I believe the white chief knows that we can be trusted as he allows many outside the post with the soldiers to hunt and inside the fort to help with building."

Thomas took her in his arms, and holding her close he said, "That's my wife, always thinking of others. I will go to him and see what he has to say about it."

Upon getting the commander's approval, Ellen went to the area where the animals were skinned in preparation for the kitchen. The soldiers there were more than glad to hand over the skins and any other parts that she asked for. She took them immediately to the clan. Although the brig doors were no longer locked and the prisoners could come and go, they usually gathered there. When she explained the situation, the clan began preparations immediately. The men found scraps of wood from the building site, as well as strong limbs and vines from outside the fort for frames, as the women began to clean and stretch the hides. Now that they had something familiar to do, they were more content in their situation.

Knowing that Thomas could understand their language, Lame Elk spoke to him in Cheyenne, "This is a good thing you do for the clan."

Thomas smiled and answered, "It's the right thing to do, and you can thank your sister here for thinking of it."

"She has always been clever, even though she might be as flighty, as her name Squirrel says she is, he teased."

"Watch it, big brother, or I'll say you want to wash dishes in the fort kitchen," she countered, as they all laughed.

As the soldiers saw the women's handiwork and the different items being made, they became involved as well. They began offering beads purchased at the trading post, as well as items they found, such as small nut and snail shells, pinecones, and claws from various birds, wolves or bear. And when chopping down trees for lumber or firewood, they caught themselves pocketing items that could be used as decoration for the clothing and jewelry being made.

One of the carpenters used a fine hacksaw blade and cut deer antlers into thin slices, and using a tiny nail he made holes in each and presented the "buttons" to Ellen. She rewarded him with a broad smile and a pat on his arm.

As Commander Wadsworth stood at his window, observing the camaraderie formed by the intermingling of these two peoples, he wondered, *why is the government so scared of these people that they would want to eradicate them? Why can't we just live our separate lives and leave them be? There is no record of this clan ever harming anyone.* His thought was interrupted by a knock at his door,

"Enter." Turning, he saw his personal secretary, Sgt. Wilson, standing at attention. "What is it Sergeant?"

"Commander, Mrs. Thorton to see you, Sir,"

"Please, escort her in. Bring up a chair for her." After she was seated, he sat behind his desk and asked his visitor, "Now, to what do I owe the pleasure of your presence?"

"I see your tobacco pouch...old. I make you new one. I hope you like." With that she leaned forward and placed it on his desk.

He also leaned forward and picked it up. It was an eight-inch circle cut of leather with two thin leather laces woven around the outer edge that could be drawn to form a pouch. It was of the softest leather; decorated with a three- inch round patch of colored beads. The patch showed an outer circle of two rows of red beads, with a filling of blue. In the center of the blue were beads of white that formed the shape of an eagle, much like the one perched on top of the flagpole, standing in the corner of his office.

"Mrs. Thorton, this is a most beautiful gift, and truly a piece of art. I am humbled by your generosity. I feel I've no way to repay you."

"I pay *you* for gift of husband, Tome-us. You very kind and care for all people."

"Well, young lady, I try to be as fair and honest as my God wants me to be. Do you know about my God? Someday I would like for us to share each other's spiritual knowledge. It could probably help us both."

Seeing that some of the words were unfamiliar to her he added, "Bring your husband to see me one day soon and with his help we might be able to communicate even further. But in the meantime, thank you for this." He held it up and brought it to his chest.

She smiled and though not knowing all of his words, she understood his actions, and left.

On one of Thomas' visits to the trading post he ventured to take Ellen. He was apprehensive about how the white people would treat her, but was pleasantly surprised to find they seemed to ignore that she was native. As she wandered through the aisles and looked at the many items for sale, she called to him for explanations. He would go to her side and explain what it was and how it was used, using both languages so she could practice. She would nod and go on to examine something else. She came to a music box and when Thomas wound it, she was startled to hear the music. She smiled, closed her eyes and swayed to the tune.

Ellen touched very little until she came to the fabrics. The bright calicos and shiny satins drew her. She felt their texture and weight and thought how fine a dress she could make out of them. *I could look like a real English woman in a dress made of this. Like some of white ladies wear, maybe please Tome-us more.* She softly called to him and showed him the fabric and expressed what she thought.

"Squir...Ellen, I love you just the way you are. You don't need to dress like them to make me proud of you...I am already!" But seeing the dejected look in her eyes made him understand how much she wanted it.

"Ma'am, how much is the fabric?"

The storekeeper's wife came and said, "That is twenty-six cents a yard."

"How many yards would it take to make her a dress?"

"Well, that would depend on the style of the dress, and her size, of course."

"Do you have a catalog that she could look at and choose the style she would like?"

14

"Why, yes. We even have patterns. She looks to be about a size 10 or 12. She can look through these and see if she can find a dress she likes."

Taking Ellen by the hand, he followed the lady while he explained the conversation. Ellen began to browse through the patterns and shooed him away, but after awhile she called him back and showed him one, "You like?"

"That's real nice and would look wonderful on you. Do you know how to use a pattern?"

She shook her head and turned to the lady, "How hard to use a pat-tern?"

"You need to know how to read the directions, but most of them have diagrams that show how."

When he relayed the message, Ellen dropped her head and returned the pattern to the box.

He came to her and took her hand. Quietly he said, "We'll start your reading lessons when we get back to the fort and you will be able to make that dress real soon."

She gave him a sad smile and nodded. Her expression tore at him and he squeezed her hand and pulled her close. Patting his arm, she turned away and sought a chair near the potbellied stove in one corner of the shop, which gave him the opportunity to finish the fort's shopping list.

When Ellen saw his purchases being wrapped, she went to the wagon, and returning with two large woven baskets, began to load them. In answer to his questioning look, she said, "To make easy for carrying."

"Those are perfectly lovely baskets! Where on earth did you get them?" asked the lady.

"Ellen makes them. It's one of her many talents," Thomas boasted.

"Would she be interested in selling any of them? What I couldn't use, I'm sure I could sell," offered the clerk.

Understanding some of this, Ellen looked at both of them and nodded. "How many you want?"

The storekeeper's wife smiled at Ellen's knowledge of English and said, "Whatever you can bring me, I will buy. They are quite unique and would be very useful to the women in the area."

Thomas explained to Ellen the unfamiliar words and then said to the storekeeper's wife, "Well, then it looks like my wife will become an entrepreneur!" with a proud smile. He turned to Ellen and added, "Honey, you have some work cut out for you in the next few days."

# Chapter 4

Gabe and William kept busy with their trapping as their wives learned more about their new homes. When William took hides to the trading post he stopped by the livery and worked an hour or two cleaning stalls and greasing tack. "What price did you settle on for that horse, Smithy?"

"Wut one ya hankerin' to hav'? Gots a goodn' comin' in that yous mite like. She's real gen-tile and purty, wid hair most like ol' Red hisself," laughed the blacksmith.

"A sorrel...and a mare, you say? Hmmm, sounds good. How long in the tooth?" asked Will.

"Gettin' to bes a reel hoss trader now?" teased Smithy.

"Well, I'm not buying a pig-in-a-poke, that's for sure."

"Whal, ya markin' yer 'ours down an all, reckon we's 'bout evens up already. Yous ben workin' both here and trappin' out thar, I says ya's dun 'nuff. When she gets her', I'll hav'er redy fer ya next times ya comes in. I gots anudder tang frettin' me though. One of my custa'mers done paid me with a goat. I's knows he dun got no money, but he says he pay his debts, so's I take da goat. Will ya take 'im to yourn place cuz I got's no use of 'em here?"

"A goat now? Smithy you are so lenient with customers paying their bills. I've seen you accept chickens, or a side of pork, even a weaner pig...and now a goat?" Laughing he asked, "If you kept the pig and chickens, why can't you keep the goat?"

"Caus da udders, dey don' need no milkin', and I don' got no time for dat. You's got ta hep' me out, here. Think o' yo' missus. She mi be right pro'd ta hav' da milk for her cookin' and sech.'"

"How many more work hours you need for the goat?'"

"No way, No mo'. Jest do's me a fabor an tak' her offn my han's!'"

"Well, if you are certain that I've done my share, then I'd be much obliged, and the women will be glad to have her I'm sure. And as usual, it's been a pleasure doing business with you, Smithy!'"

Smithy's smile filled his whole face, "Plsure be's all mine, Will'yum. You's a good worker and a good frien'."

Once more they spit in their hands and slapped each other's palms, sealing the contract.

As Will left the man, his mind wandered, *Smithy's vocabulary brings back memories of when I spoke that way, in my younger years, before Gabe took me under his wing and later sent me off to that college back east. My first lessons were from Gabe himself as he convinced me to speak proper English in order to gain respect and stand equal to my peers and so as to not be cheated with the price of my hides. I found out that Gabe had, years before, been a professor at that same college. As fate would have it, we both became friends with, and tutored English to, the same black man; a janitor at the college named Jacob Lincoln Grant Lowry, who also spoke like Smithy. I wonder if Smithy would want to learn proper English. But I can't think of that now. Gabe and I already have our hands full teaching Sparrow, Gigi and Blue. No, Anita and Becca!*

With that in mind he stopped in at the trading post and purchased a dictionary, three tablets, pencils and a first grade reader.

Smithy was right…the women folk were thrilled with the goat, as well as having access to milk daily.

Lessons continued in the families, when the men were not out trapping or hunting. The students progressed at separate levels. Their favorite lesson became a game: mimicking animal sounds and learning the meaning of each. The men practiced those calls when nearing the cabin after a long day's trapping, and the girls would respond.

Gigi was remarkable in her learning and was insatiable to learn more. "Papa, read to me. Read from your big black book," she pleaded.

"Its name is the 'Bible'. But I think *you* should read to *me*! You and your mama are coming along nicely with your English lessons. That school book Will bought has been a blessing in teaching you two and Bl..*Becca* as well. Let me see what you learned today," Gabe asked.

"You promise to read story from the Bi…Bibul?"

"Yes, Pumpkin."

Pouting, she said, "I not pumpkin. I not fat and orange."

Gabe scrambled for an explanation, "That's just a term of endearment with white people. It means…you are as sweet as pumpkin pie!"

"What is that word, in-deer-mint?

"It means 'love'."

Accepting the explanation, she snuggled down beside him with the reader. When Anita finished her dinner chores, she sat with them to listen and learn.

After Gigi read her short chapter, she closed the book and said, "Now…you read."

He smiled, and picking up the Bible, he started, "In the beginning God created the heavens and the earth…"

Gigi interrupted, "Who is 'God'?"

He stopped and thought for a moment then said, "You know it's a hard question to answer, but maybe we can think of Him as the Clan's Great Spirit, Yowa."

"Why?"

"Well, much the same as you have your Clan name, 'Gigage Gitlu' and an English name, Gigi," and pointing to her mother, he added, "Sparrow is now Anita. And me? I go by many names: Gabe, Smithy calls me Red, your mama calls me husband, and now you call me Papa. One person can have many names."

"So this God could be Yowa?"

"Maybe, I don't have all the answers, Honey. We will link them together for now. The spirit world is something that we have to use faith in believing."

"What is *faith*?"

Taking a deep breath while he thought, he settled back and explained, "Faith is accepting something to be true, without having proof. We can't touch, see, smell or hear our Great Spirits, but we know they are there by using faith.  Here, let me show you. Stand on that chair…now turn around and fall backward and I will catch you." After she did, he said, "See? You had *faith* in my promise to catch you, even though you didn't *know* that I would."

"But I *did* know you would not let me fall."

Gabe sighed, "Maybe it's like, if you want something really bad, you ask Yowa for it and then you have *faith* that one day you will get it." Looking at Gigi and Anita he asked, "Do you understand?"

Anita smiled as her shoulders raised and dropped.

Gigi took a few seconds to mull it over, and then looking at him through her eyebrows with a sly smile, she said slowly, "So, maybe I have *faith* that I will get a puppy?"

Gabe burst out laughing, "Now, my little one, *that* is called manipulation. I think you understand faith enough, so let's get back to reading."

Rebecca was struggling to learn new words each day, plus keeping up with her daily chores. While working on her language, at times she became frustrated with words that seemed impossible to pronounce, let alone grasp their meaning, and most of the time the dictionary was with Gigi. The book seemed to be little or no use when not hearing how to pronounce each word, so her questions left her even more upset.

Since Will was often trapping, hunting or at the trading post, Becca would have to remember to ask when he came home. Although the cabins were a short distance apart, it seemed she was alone more than she preferred. In the clan there was always someone close by to talk to or help with problems. She missed her parents, but knew that if she went to see her father at the fort, he would not know her.

Gigi and Anita visited and helped her, and she was happy with Will, but she feared there was a reason that he was not at home as much as she had thought he would be.

One morning while Anita visited, Rebecca expressed her emotions, "I thought we would always be together."

"But he has to do his work and keep the food on the table just like in the clan. The men were not always at home with their women," answered Anita.

"I know. But the days are long when he is not here."

"But the nights…is he not with you every night? And does he still show you how much he loves you?"

"Yes, I know he loves me, but I wish he was here more. I miss him. I want to have him here to hold me…"

"I know. I miss my husband too, when he is away, but we must do our jobs, as they do theirs. Perhaps we could go to the trading post together, all three of us. We know the way, and it would be fun to see new things, and get out and move our bones," suggested Anita.

"That would be so good. And didn't you say Gigi has been making beaded goods? Maybe the store owner would like to see them. I heard from William that the clan was working well with the soldiers and all is good there. Maybe we could even visit them someday."

"I think we had better talk to the husbands about that. They will know if we are able to visit the clan. Let's try going to the trading post first. "

"Today? Now? Without the husbands?" asked Becca.

"Oh, Mother, let's go now! I can't wait to see the town!"

"Why not? It's early and we have finished our chores."

# Chapter 5

Soaring Eagle became restless and asked Thomas if there was something he could do. "Even in age, one must make himself useful, or there is no need for life."

Thomas nodded his understanding and asked, "Do you have anything in particular in mind?"

"I would love to work with the horses. Brush them and talk to them. I wish to visit Puma and see that he is well."

"I will go and speak with Commander Wadsworth and see if you can at least visit Puma once in awhile. The commander has decided that the new building is to be attached on the outside of the fort's north wall and will be the new stables. The building where the stables are now will be cleaned and extended to accommodate the clan."

"But how will the soldiers reach the horses?"

"There will be a doorway cut through the fort wall into one end of the stables. That way the horses will be safe from predators, and the new building will be safe for the clan and later visiting representatives," explained Thomas.

When he explained to Wadsworth Soaring Eagle's plea, the commander asked him to interpret their conversation.

"Soaring Eagle, can I trust you to not harm the remuda, nor try to escape if given the chance?"

"I treat all animals as the Great Spirit's gifts. When I surrendered, that was my oath to not escape."

"You did not surrender, you were captured,"

"If I had not surrendered you would not have taken me alive. My word is my honor."

Looking at the chief, the commander knew what it took for the man to humble himself by requesting a task. He then exchanged nods with first Thomas, then the chief.

The rest of the clan kept busy either working on the new building or in their quarters preparing the hides for articles that could be used in the fort or to clothe themselves.

Soldiers and braves worked side by side and when Thomas was there to interpret they exchanged friendly banter, sometimes making small contests of different chores to lessen their boredom. Each side pondered the idea of why they felt no ill will toward one another, and expressed due respect.

Soaring Eagle eagerly went to the stalls and directly to Puma. The horse reacted by snorting his happiness and stretched out his neck to reach his approaching friend. The man went to the horse and Puma arched his neck to place his head over the chief's shoulder and pulled him closer. Soaring Eagle hugged the neck of his friend and they stood embracing each other.

After awhile the chief found a brush and began to curry the horse while he spoke quietly and sang softly the tunes he had sung to the horse before. Puma turned his neck to reach Soaring Eagle and gently bumped his friend, nuzzling to grip a piece of his shirt and pull him back to his head. The chief placed their foreheads together. It was clear their feelings could not be denied.

The visit was not as long as both wished, but the chief had promised to help with the stable and began to clean the stalls and furnish with fresh hay. Untied, Puma followed the chief and kept nudging him and pushing him playfully.

When Soaring Eagle had finished he again turned to the horse and began testing Puma's memory.

Those who watched this exchange realized they were witnessing the close bond between man and animal.

They watched as Soaring Eagle easily mounted Puma bareback and started putting him through the different tricks he had taught the horse. When he softly said 'water' they were amazed to see the horse turn and go straight to the watering trough. Cheers went up and other soldiers joined in to watch. All the time they had the horse they had no idea what all he could do.

Word spread quickly to the Commander and he also came to watch. By this time the horse and rider had advanced from the stables and were in the center of the fort.

The horse and man were as one, side stepping, spinning turns, trotting, and galloping around the grounds, all without a halter, reins or saddle. The commands were made with just the touch of the chief's hand on the horse's neck or the pressure of his knees.

When the chief saw that Puma was tiring, he rode to the center of the arena and had the horse bow, then dismounted and stood, with the untethered horse beside him.

Whistles and applause filled the air as the audience expressed their admiration. Soaring Eagle beamed with pride. Puma placed his head on the chief's back and nudged him all the way back to the stables.

# Chapter 6

The girls had not ventured far from the cabins without the men, so several times they thought they were lost, only to have Becca's tracking skills get them back on the almost invisible path. As she did she gathered wisps of feathers and small straight twigs that caught her attention. When they crossed a creek she pulled her knife from its sheath and collected some large reeds. After measuring them to her satisfaction, she replaced the knife in its sheath and put the other items inside a pouch that hung from her belt.

Gigi asked, "Why do you gather these things?"

Becca answered, "I'm going to make each of us a new blow gun. I will teach you how to use it and we can bring in...maybe a bird or a rabbit to our cooking pots while doing our daily chores around the cabins."

"Oh, you always wanted to be a boy!" said Anita

Thinking of her life now, Becca smiled coyly, "Not any more. I love being a wife, and make my husband smile when he sees me bathing at the water."

"Becca! You should not talk that way in front of Gigi," scolded Anita.

"Mother, I'm almost woman now. I see many things and learn by what I see. I think it's good she is happy with husband. Someday I will find out too. And I want to learn about this blow gun. I think that would be good that we can help the men bring food to the table."

Changing the subject Becca asked, "Don't you think the trail should be well worn by now, as often as the husbands go this way?"

"Our men do *not* make a path that could lead others to our homes. They do not want others there," replied Anita.

Hours later they stood overlooking the town of Ft. Wells. It was laid out mostly in a straight line; stores faced each other across a dirt street. Just on the western outskirts the railroad tracks ran parallel to it as it followed the river on past the fort.

Excitedly Gigi pointed, "Look, some of the houses are bigger than others. There is one painted white with a tall pointed top."

In turn Becca pointed out, "And most of the buildings have a larger front than a back. Look, there is the fort, way over there; let's go and see all the white-man things."

As they entered the town, all three were in awe. They saw people walking on a path of wood attached to buildings, and men sat on benches against the stores. Children ran beside tall iron wheels, while propelling them with sticks.

One of the most amazing things was the glass windows. "I can see inside, all the way to the back!" Becca cried out as she pressed her nose to the glass, "This must be where Will comes to get our needs. I see some of the things inside like what he has brought home."

They saw horses tied to posts with their heads hung low as they shifted from foot to foot and flies converging on steamy piles of dung behind them.

"I hear strange sound. I think it comes from that place over there with the short doors. Sounds pretty. Let's go see," said Gigi.

As they neared the music, the doors flew open and a man came staggering out, then he froze as he faced them.

"He acts as though he has drunk from the white man's bottle that makes all men act stupid," hissed Anita.

"Let's go see that white building," pleaded Gigi.

"I want to go back to the store place. I want to see everything inside," argued Becca.

"Wait. Stop. Both of you, come here," beckoned Anita.

Ignoring her they began to head in different directions.

"I said come *here!*" urged Anita, through gritted teeth.

Both Becca and Gigi stopped and turned. Seeing the anxious look on Anita's face they came to her side.

"What's wrong? Why do you speak to us like that? We've done nothing wrong," stated Becca.

"Yes, I think we have. While you both have been busy seeing all the new things I've been watching the people. They are not happy that we are here. The mothers grab their children and pull them away. And the men glare at us. Do you realize that they do not know we are joined to white men in marriage? It is as if we left our clan and just walked into their world. We must go back quickly; before they decide we are a threat."

Looking around, Becca and Gigi saw for themselves. Women hid their children behind them and men reached for their guns, anxiously looking toward the timber line.

"We must head back to our homes, but just like facing a wild animal, do not show fear, lest they attack. Smile at them and nod. That's right. Good," assured Anita.

As they reached the forest she said, "I think we are safe now but we best hurry back to our cabins. We must make a new path. Becca, I'm counting on you to take us home."

Becca studied the woods and visualized in her mind their previous steps. She chose a parallel course, with Gigi and Anita close behind. After traveling for a distance, longer than they each thought necessary, Anita called a halt. "Are you sure we are going in the right direction, Becca?"

"No, but it's because we are not taking the same path,"

Gigi piped up, "Wait. See that tall tree over there, the one with the broken top? I saw it when we first started out, and its top was bent away from me and now it is facing me. Shouldn't we go to where it will be the way it was first?"

"Yes, my little pathfinder. I now remember it also. We *are* going in the right way and not far from our homes. It's good that you pay attention," praised Anita.

"I've learned many tracking and hunting skills from Papa and Will. They say, "Find a landmark…something that stands out from all the rest…and study it. When you see it again you will remember and know where you are.""

Anita became concerned and asked, "Have they taught you to shoot the gun or use the hunting knife?"

"No, mama, but I have used slingshot. Will made one for me. I haven't been successful yet, but I'm getting better. Soon I may kill a fine fat rabbit for dinner!"

Recalling the earlier height and position of the broken top, Gigi cut across, in front of it, which led them to their first path and they quickly retraced their steps to the cabins.

As they parted Becca called out, "I will make the blow guns and we will start our lessons tomorrow, after the men go off to hunt."

The two waved and shouted back their willingness to start a new project and surprise the men with their own kills.

Becca found all the essential parts to make the weapons and began by hollowing out a large reed to make it clean of any debris that could block the dart's flight. Then she made the darts. With tufts of feathers and porcupine quills she formed cones using pine pitch to adhere the parts together.

She then trimmed the feathers to fit the inside of the reed and tested it. Hitting the target she chose, she nodded to herself and decided it was acceptable until she found more suitable articles to use in creating them. Now all she had left to do was teach the others.

When Gabe and Will returned from a hunt with fresh kills, the families united to get the meat and the skins processed. The men took the carcasses and skinned them. Gabe worked on larger kills like the deer or elk, while Will took on the smaller ones such as beaver, rabbit and raccoon, Gigi took Will's animals to the creek behind the house and washed them thoroughly, then presented them to the women for cutting, cooking or preserving.

Different forms of preserving were used: either salting, smoking or drying.

Salt was used abundantly and rubbed into the meat, then it was placed in a cool area for about a month, all the while adding more salt. Finally it was wrapped in canvas fabric and set aside to age.

Smoking required a month-long exposure to smoke, drying the meat while flavoring it with favorite seasonings. Wood such as hickory or oak was used. The meat was then left to hang. The smoke deterred hungry insects and scavengers.

Drying the meat was similar to smoking, because it required the same procedure, but the meat was usually cut into smaller strips and threaded along a strand of sinew to hang in the smokehouse. It could be dried to use as a snack, add to a stew, or grind into a flavoring for a broth.

All of this was a lot of hard, time-consuming work.

# Chapter 7

The commander motioned to a chair across from his desk, "Corporal Thorton, please take a seat. Could I be so bold as to ask your wife and maybe some of her friends, to make my quarters presentable?" asked Commander Wadsworth. "My wife is coming for a visit next week on the train and I would hate for her to see what a messy housekeeper I am. She would scold me thoroughly."

"I can only ask her sir, but I'm sure she would be delighted to help. Our quarters are so clean that she hunts for things to do, although her hobbies help kept her busy."

"About those hobbies…she is very gifted, you know, as well as the rest of the clan with their diverse talents. I have seen the camaraderie between our soldiers and the clan. The clan trades finished art products for raw materials the soldiers bring. I see no animosity between the peoples and I am aware of the contented atmosphere around the fort. Clansmen and soldiers work side by side exchanging language and laughter…why can't it be like this all over? Why can't those in power see that these are gentle people who just want to be left alone?"

"I don't know sir. You see in all of them what I've found in my wife. She tries to make everyone happy and desires to please me most. I've never known anyone like her. She was mistreated by her first husband, whom she divorced, and fears that because of his abuse she will not be able to bear children. We are both devastated, but we are trying to accept it. We are prepared if it will be just the two of us."

"I'm sorry to hear that son, but you know the missus and I had only one child. She was lost to us during an Indian raid up north that also left my wife near death. You might think that it would prejudice us against the Indian, but we feel it was God's will and have accepted it as such. I think Olivia will be delighted to have your wife…Ellen…around to give her female company and to help her."

"Thank you, Commander. I'm sure Ellen will be happy to learn anything she can from your wife. She is learning to read right now so she can understand the dressmaking pattern she found at the store in town. She is determined to make what she calls a 'white-woman's dress.'"

"Well, that's right up my Olivia's alley. She was a dressmaker in Charlottesville, where we met. I needed my uniform mended and the locals sent me to her. I'll forever be in their debt. She is a remarkable woman and I'm glad that you will be able to meet her."

"Yes, sir, I'll tell Ellen the news. I know she will make sure your quarters are spotless and make your wife proud. She wanted me to ask if her friends, the ones you married to the trappers, could visit."

"Of course they can, anytime. And forgive me for rattling on. I seldom have someone to just chat with and the thought of Olivia's visit has me as excited as a schoolboy."

"No problem sir. It's nice to get to know each other. It makes life more interesting. Perhaps even friendships with superiors are possible."

"I may be your superior under army rules, but not under God's eyes. We are equal in His eyes and I hope I never have to use rank to have my men respect me."

"Sir, I've never heard a cross word about you from any of the men. They all respect you highly."

"I hope so, Corporal, and thank you…you are excused."

# Chapter 8

Gigi hesitated then asked, "Papa, are you sad about us?"

"What do you mean?"

"Are you sad about us to the white people?"

"I don't understand."

"Thomas take Ellen to town. To store, to shop. He is not sad about her to white people."

"You mean *ashamed*? Of course not! I'm not ashamed of either of you. I'm very proud that you are with me and we are a family."

"But you not take us to town. Only to fort."

"Oh, baby, come here." He gathered her in his arms and looked at Anita. "I'm so sorry that you think that I could ever be ashamed of you. I love you both very much. Maybe I've been too protective. I didn't want you hurt by the way town people may treat you."

"They act more scared of us than be bad."

"What do you mean?"

Gigi's eyes widened, knowing that she had just divulged the girls' secret. Anita busied herself at the stove.

Gabe let go of Gigi and stood with his hands on his hips, and tilting his head he looked from one to the other and asked softly, "Gigi? Anita? What does that mean 'they acted more scared than bad?'" The room became very quiet as he waited for an answer.

He repeated his question and went to Anita, turning her to face him. Her chin rested on her chest and she would not look up. He looked over her shoulder at Gigi who had sat on the edge of her bed, clutching her pillow; also not looking at him.

"Am I going to have to go ask Becca?" he asked.

Anita's head shot up and she shook her head, "No. No tell Will. It my fault. I tell them 'let's go.' We wanted to see."

Gigi jumped to defend her, "Nothing happened, Papa. We were careful not to use same path and everything. No one follow us. I use trick you show me of finding something to remember and it help find our way back."

"When did all this happen?"

"Last week. See? Nothing happen. We went, we see, and we come home," she answered quickly.

Gabe took a deep breath and dropped his head, letting it all sink in. Looking up again he asked, "So, you three went to town…by yourselves…shopped and came home?"

"No. We not shop. We not go into stores. No time. Mother saw looks on faces. They scared of us. We hurry and come home."

With distress in his voice, he said, "You could have all been shot! Those people don't know they have nothing to fear from you." Shifting from one foot to the other he sighed, "That settles it. We are all going down to talk to Will and Becca."

After hearing about the incident, Will took Becca by her elbows and looked her straight in the eyes, "Is this true? Do you also think I'm ashamed of you? Becca, that can't be further from the truth. I'm *proud* of you. You are my whole life. Gabe and I thought we needed to keep you away from town until you spoke English well enough that they would not make fun of you or treat you less than what you are. You are special in every way and I want to show you off to the world to let them see that I'm the luckiest man alive, just to have you. If we knew what you were thinking we would have taken you to town sooner."

Becca looked up at him and whispered, "You no tell me. I want to see everything and be part of your world, but you keep us here like hiding us. You not home with me. You want town more. Ellen gets many things, sees many things and tells us. I want also these things. Tome-us happy she his wife, show everyone."

Closing his eyes, Will inhaled deeply. Shaking his head slightly he exhaled, "Oh, Lord, what have I done? I've been so selfish not to realize." Taking Becca into his arms and raising her chin, he searched her tear-filled eyes, "Becca, Sweetheart, I'm so sorry that I've been so blind."

As tears welled up in his own eyes, he continued, "Gabe, dear friend, we have our work cut out for us. We have to show these beautiful women how much we care. I'm ready to take them to town and strut around like a proud peacock to show every person in that town how lucky I am."

"I'm with you, Buddy. Let's get up tomorrow and head out early. We've got a lot of making up to do to cure the ailment we afflicted on our lovelies." Turning to Anita and Gigi he asked, "Is that too soon for you ladies?"

Smiles filled their faces and Gigi jumped around clapping her hands.

# Chapter 9

Guards in their polished uniforms stood at attention and lined the depot as the train pulled in. Commander Wadsworth stepped forward and assisted his wife as she stepped onto the station's platform. After he gave her a quick kiss on the cheek, the guards moved in unison to form a security row to the waiting wagon. Designated soldiers gathered her luggage and followed the two, then joined the others as they lined each side of the wagon as it proceeded slowly to the fort.

The moment they were alone he took her in his arms, "Olivia, my beautiful darling, I'm so happy that you arrived here safely. The days are long without you. Do you know how dear you are to me, and how much I miss each minute we are apart?"

Blushing slightly she rested her head on his chest, "Frederick, you are the most loving and thoughtful husband. I too, long to see you when there are so many miles between us. We have so much to catch up on, but beautiful? I'm afraid I must look a fright with the long dusty trip here."

"Not to me. You are a sight that makes my eyes yearn for more. But knowing you, I knew you would feel this way so I have arranged a hot bath for you in my...*our* quarters."

Closing her eyes she sighed deeply, "Oh, my dear husband that sounds absolutely marvelous. If you don't mind I would love to enjoy that as soon as possible".

He smiled as he guided her toward the waiting, fragrant scented bath, "I'm ahead of you dear. It's here for you this minute and I have extra hot water standing by to keep it nice and warm. Go, relax and we will talk later."

When she rejoined him, still in her bathrobe, she found a candle lit table set with a freshly starched linen tablecloth. Matching folded napkins and highly polished silverware adorned each side of the plates and a small vase of wild flowers was placed in the center.

He turned and smiled as he filled one glass with vintage white wine and offered it to her.

As she stood taking it all in she tipped her head slightly, and coyly stated, "If I'm not mistaken, Frederick I would say you are trying to seduce me."

"You are not mistaken, my lady. I've yearned for this moment since the hour I knew you were coming and I want to savor every detail and make you know how very much I love you."

Accepting the glass and taking a sip she looked over its rim and locked eyes with him, "You know, Freddy…I think this dinner can wait just a wee bit longer, don't you?"

Setting his glass down he closed the distance between them and took her in his arms, "Yes, my little Buttercup, I think it can."

# Chapter 10

The first stop in town was to the livery so the men could introduce the girls to their friend, Smithy. He was unaware of them standing just inside the huge heavy doors, marveling at the many tools on the walls, the large anvil near the tall open fire place. They watched as he grasped forceps and pulled a red hot horseshoe from the embers and began to pound on it with a sledge hammer, forming it to his liking. When he was satisfied he plunged it into a vat of water standing nearby.

Gabe took this opportunity to get Smithy's attention. When he turned and saw Gabe and Will his face lit up with a huge tooth-filled smile. Understanding the situation immediately, he said, "Well, whos do we's hab here? Mighty fine lookin' ladies to be in da compny of these ragged ol' men."

Gabe was the first to step forward, bringing Anita and Gigi on each arm. "These are my girls, Smithy. The ones I've been bragging about all this time. I wanted them to meet the best friend we have in town first before showing them off to the rest." Looking to each he introduced Anita and Gigi, with Smithy slightly bending at the waist in a courtesy bow. "I's offer my hand, but it plumb dirty wit all dis soot. But I'm mighty proud to make yer acquaintance."

Will took this time to introduce Becca. Smithy smiled and nodded his head, "Wal, I sees why des mens keep you ladies to dem selves. You's all mighty nice to de eyes, fo sho." Then looking at Will he added, "Yer order dun cabe in ta day, mister Will. It be out back. Sees if'n it ta yer likin', sos we can settle up."

Will got excited and turned to Becca, "This is why I've been away so much. Not that I wanted to be away from you, but because I was working to buy you something I think you will like. Come, see." He took her by the hand and led her through a back door, with the others close behind. There was a small corral that held three horses. He took a rope from the wall and went through the gate, up to a sorrel filly with a blaze face. Looping the rope around her neck he led her over to Becca. "She's for you, Becca. I worked the hours away from you so I could buy her."

Becca could not believe her eyes as she slowly reached up and touched the velvet nose. The filly's nostrils flared as she gently nudged Becca's hand and stepped closer. Becca went forehead to forehead with the sorrel; as everyone stood in silence the animal and the girl accepted each other's scent. Then Becca turned and rushed into Will's arms, "I sorry. I sorry I think bad. Thank you. Thank you."

They gently rocked back and forth until Will looked up and made eye contact with Smithy, "Would it be ok if we left her here until we head for home?"

"Yo sho can. She be righ' here awaitin'."

"Now it's time to go see the rest of the town. Who's up for checking out the mercantile?" asked Gabe.

They entered the store and Gigi was immediately drawn to the beads and buttons and colorful ribbons. The men stayed near their wives, masking their apprehension with smiles and answering many questions.

The store proprietor approached Gigi. "I couldn't help noticing that necklace you are wearing."

Gigi suddenly realized what Gabe had been telling her all along. *I have to speak good English so she does not look bad of me.* She reached up and touched it, and said, "Thank you. You like?"

"Yes, very much. It's beautiful. Where did you get it?"

Gigi patted her chest, trying to recall the correct words she said, "I made it."

"You made this yourself? You are very talented. Do you have more of these?"

"Yes, at home."

"I'd be interested in seeing them and if you are willing, I would like to sell them here in the store."

Gigi's courage ran out and she searched for Gabe, "Let me ask… Papa!"

This exchange had not gone unnoticed by Gabe and he left Anita with Will and Becca and came to her side.

"Is there a problem, Gigi?"

"No, Papa. She like my necklace."

Understanding Gigi's dilemma he offered, "You will have to excuse my daughter; she's a bit slow in her speech, but coming along nicely."

"You can certainly tell she is your daughter, sir, with that hair and those eyes…my yes. You say she's slow in her speech. Is it mental or just from not learning?"

"I'm afraid I've held her back, being a trapper and living deep in the woods. She's had little chance of getting the proper schooling she needs. But I've been teaching her and she's coming along quite nicely."

"You certainly seem well educated and have a good grasp of the English language…for a trapper. I mean no offense, but most trappers lack in higher education."

"No offense taken ma'am, my education came before I became a trapper. Now, the concern about her necklace?"

"Oh, no. I was just asking if she might be interested in making more...to sell here in the store. I could either buy them from her outright, or I could put them on consignment and pay her as they sell. I'm sure they would have great appeal to the passengers on the train during regular stops."

"Well, that's entirely up to you, Gigi. Would you like to do that?" Gabe asked.

"Can Papa help until I understand?"

"Of course. And if I may be so bold, perhaps you could enroll her in school here...to advance her learning faster."

Gabe nodded, "We'll give it some thought and get back to you very soon. Thank you for the opportunity...and the advice, they are both appreciated."

Looking from one to the other she answered, "Excuse me, may I be even bolder and ask if she...you, Miss, would be willing to sell the one you are wearing?"

Gabe and Gigi looked at each other and Gabe said, "Again, that's entirely up to you, honey."

"How much you pay?"

Gabe had to turn to hide his smile. *She is smart. Damn, I'm proud of her!*

The woman said, "That's a good question. How would twenty cents a necklace sound?"

Gigi pulled Gabe away and whispered, "Papa? Is that good?"

"I think it's a fair price, Gigi. But this is your business venture and I will support any decision you make."

Gigi returned to the lady and said, "I will take twenty five cent price, for now. But some may cost more later."

"Excuse me for not introducing myself earlier, my name is Dorothy Hamilton. My husband Charles and I are the proprietors. And I understand your name to be… 'Gigi'?"

"Forgive us also. My name is Gabriel Adams and yes, this is my daughter Gigi."

"As for the price you quoted, it is acceptable. Do you want to sell the one you are wearing for twenty five cents?"

Taking off the necklace and handing it to the woman she said, "I take your offer."

Gabe wanted to dance a jig at seeing his daughter negotiate her first business deal.

In the midst of their discussion, a clerk approached Will with Becca and Anita. "May I be of assistance?"

Will smiled and shook his head, "No, thank you. We're just browsing…and waiting for our friends speaking to that lady over there," said Will.

"I see. Well, I couldn't help but notice the craftsmanship of the beaded belts and moccasins the ladies are wearing. They are exquisite and I was wondering if they hire out."

Will saw red, *Don't get angry. Stay calm.* "You might want to ask them yourself. I don't speak for my wife."

"Of course, pardon me, I meant no insult. It's just that we seldom get…uh…customers as talented in beadwork…" Clearing his throat, he continued, "Do either of you ladies sell your decorated footwear?"

Becca picked up more of the words than Anita, so spoke up, "That depends…which size, which pattern."

"I understand. What would you charge for the size and pattern you are wearing?" he asked.

Becca was now desperate for Will's help and turned to him. Seeing her anxiety, he said, "She'll have to get back to you on that. She will have to check her records and see the cost and profit margins first. Could she give you an answer on her next visit?"

Realizing what the situation was, he turned to Becca and Anita and answered, "My, yes. Ask for me, Mr. Hamilton. I am the owner. I will give a fair price."

When Gabe and Gigi returned to the others he could barely contain his enthusiasm. He whispered, "Wait until we get outside…this is going to floor you!"

"I think you are going to be surprised at our news too."

They continued to browse the store and made a few needed purchases before moving on with their tour.

When they got out of the storeowner's earshot, first Gabe relayed all that had happened while Gigi stood there, smiling, knowing that he was proud of her, "Where did you learn to barter like that, daughter?"

"You tell Will to say you want more for the price of hides and I listen. I learn. I did good?"

"You were terrific, sweetheart. And yes, I'm very proud!"

"Well grab yer britches, Gabe." Pointing to Becca and Anita he added, "*These* girls are in business too! The storeowner, Mr. Hamilton himself, wants the girls to make beaded belts and moccasins to sell in the store!"

"What? Oh, my goodness! What talented womenfolk we have here. You know, Will. We just might sit back and enjoy this empire the ladies are building! Yes sir, quite the empire!"

"What is the sound from that house there, the one with the short doors? We almost see before Mother call us back and we leave," asked Gigi

"That, my dear, is a bad place. They sell the drink that the wagon man sells to the clan that makes them fall down and act stupid. It does the same thing to white men. It is a dangerous place and you should never go near there."

"But the sound is pretty, Papa."

"It's called a piano; and you can hear that sound in other places, Gigi."

"What other places have pee-yan-o?"

"Well, church, and school, and some people even have them in their homes."

Anita was happy to just tag along and listen to them talk. She loved the sound of the questions and answers and was learning by their conversation. *Gigi is so happy now. and husband is so proud of her. One day I will make him proud of me too...somehow. It pleases me that we are a family.*

It was Will's nudging and eye shifting that brought Gabe back to Anita. He went to her and whispered, "What would you like to see, or do, here in town, my little Sparrow?"

She knew he used the term as an endearment, and she smiled. "I happy you show me town and show town to me."

"It is my pleasure and your word is my command. I am your obedient servant, here only for your pleasure."

She smiled, not understanding all of the words but content in knowing he loved her. "You say fancy words. You my husband and that all I want. Be with Gigi now".

When they came to the school the children were out playing on the grounds. Some were on the teeter-totter, some on the merry-go-round and others on the swing set. Gigi watched the children and turned with a questioning frown. "Why do they go round and round and go nowhere? And up and down, back and forth for no reason?"

"Because it's fun," offered Will.

"What is fun?"

"When you play with other children; run and play... games and such," offered Will.

"Clan children would not 'fun' with me."

"Oh, baby...I'm so sorry for your childhood. If I had only known..." began Gabe.

She interrupted, "I not sorry. I not miss fun. I have Mother...now Papa. I have Will and Becca...I have clan."

As they were standing there the teacher noticed them and started their way. Gabe had not spoken to Anita about the store owner's suggestion about school, and was apprehensive about her feelings, so he quickly recited the conversation before the teacher got there. Looking deeply into her eyes he asked, "How would you feel about Gigi going to school here and learning more?"

She first looked at her daughter, then Gabe. "Gigi big girl, she decide. I want best for her. Gigi, you want?"

"Yes Mother, I want to learn much. I want to know all I can learn."

Anita gave a sharp nod of approval and the group was ready before the teacher stopped just inside the fence surrounding the schoolyard.

"May I be of assistance to you?" she asked.

"Hello, Miss. My name is Gabriel Adams and this is my daughter Gigi. She has only received the level of education that I have given her as a trapper in the backwoods. The store owner suggested that she might be allowed to enroll at the school. Is there any chance of an opening for her?"

"Of course, I am the school teacher, Ms. Evans...Sara Evans. I'm able to accept applications on my own and I'm more than willing to have her join us. I will test her in the basics and place her in the grade I believe will give her the best opportunity to advance." Turning to Gigi she asked, "When would you like to start?"

Overwhelmed, Gigi looked anxiously toward Anita, then to Gabe. "It's up to you, baby. Want to start tomorrow?"

Will laughed, "Tomorrow is Saturday. She can wait until Monday, I'm thinking."

Gabe said, "Of course. What time does school begin?"

"Bell rings at eight o'clock sharp", Ms. Evans answered as she turned back to the schoolhouse and children.

"Now that she is enrolled in school, don't you think she will need some school clothes?" asked Will.

"Oh, wow, I never thought about that. I'm not sure what I have in the tin can at home, but I'll have to bring her back tomorrow to find a dress...and shoes...and Lord knows what all. What was I thinking?" Gabe stammered.

"That you want the best for your daughter and you want her to have all the opportunities that she deserves."

Sighing deeply Gabe said, "Yes, yes of course. But I sure got caught up in this whole trip to town with the girls. And you...you now have another mouth to feed."

Becca turned and stared, as Will asked, "What are you talking about?"

"The horse, what did you think I was talking about?"

"Oh, I plumb forgot about the horse. I made a deal with Smithy to work a couple hours a day for its feed and care."

Becca spoke up, "We go get horse now? I tired and think rest of town can wait for next time. You think, Anita?"

"Lot to think about. Lot to do. Best go home."

Gabe checked to see if everyone was in agreement then stated, "Well, let's go get that horse of yours and Becca can ride it back home…Come to think about it, we are going to have to make a regular trail to the cabin now, for the horse. It can't be crawling over logs and such… and Gigi will need a clear path to get to school easier. Yes, we do have a lot to think about and a lot to do,"

# Chapter 11

Days melted into weeks, like a whisper on the wind. Everyone was comfortable in their stations in life and the world seemed content to slip from one season to the next.

The commander had wooed his wife and showed her there was nothing to fear from the clan at the fort. He took her by the arm, under guarded escort, and introduced her to Soaring Eagle and Willow and those he knew by name.

She met Corporal Thorton's wife, Ellen, and heard the story of how they came to fall in love. When she found out that Ellen wanted desperately to learn to sew, Olivia became her mentor and began to nurture her in the finer art of being an officers' wife. Ellen gave Olivia a purpose; making it easier for the commander to convince his wife to stay longer, and how much life at the fort would be a happier place for them both.

"Frederick, what would you say to my moving here permanently?" she asked.

"That would make me the happiest man alive, my dear. But are you sure? You would be giving up the city life and the ladies' society that you love. Your friends…"

"That is all just pomp and circumstance, and has come to mean nothing to me. You said yourself that it is safer here now, and I want to be with you, and a part of your life. Here I feel I have a reason to greet the morning and know that I can be of use…and not lonely anymore."

He took her in his arms and whispered, "You never told me you were lonely. I would have demanded you come here to be with me. I love you my little Buttercup."

She looked into his eyes and melted into his arms, "Oh Freddy, my dear, dear, Freddy, my heart is full."

Back at the cabins life was also peaceful and full of bliss. Gigi had placed high in her grading and advanced rapidly, working daily at both her jewelry and homework.

Secretly she wore her new shoes until out of sight of the cabins, then slipped them off and carried them until nearing school. They fit well, but felt restrictive.

Will and Gabe had cleared a trail to town, and with the timber they felled, they not only stocked the woodshed but built a lightweight sled to carry hides to town and supplies back to the cabins. They sold their hides and the cured meat extras in town. Will regularly spent a few hours at Smithy's, in payment of necessary items for Becca's horse.

Anita needed very little to make her content. Helping with the hides, cooking, tidying the cabin or tending her garden was enough. She was proud of all the vegetables that she had nurtured from seed to the cooking pot, and fondly remembered that Gabe had surprised her with the seeds he had secretly bought during that first visit to town.

While Becca and Will visited the fort one day, Becca pulled Thomas aside and asked him the English word for "Adawehi". He repeatedly pronounced it until she could speak it correctly. When she rejoined Will she announced that her horse's name was "Angel."

The time between Becca and Angel was well spent, for they had formed a special bond. Angel trusted Becca and quickly accepted the bridle as well as a harness made by Smithy to pull the sled

What Commander Wadsworth had said was true. The clan and the soldiers had become friendly as they shared, traded and exchanged ideas on many levels.

Aware of the diverse articles that the clan created, the soldiers were drawn into helping by delivering their needed supplies with armloads of reeds brought from the river banks to create the hand-woven baskets as well as the trinkets to adorn them.

The train made Ft. Wells Station a regular two-hour stop for passengers to venture into town for a bite to eat at the hotel/restaurant, have a drink at the tavern or stretch their legs with a stroll around town.

Shopping was a favorite with the passengers and the Indian-made items, set in the front window, drew attention. Upon inquiry; they were well worth the price. The shelves inside held intricately woven mats, beaded leather purses, belts and moccasins which sold quickly; but the woven baskets with Ellen's elaborate patterns were preferred.

Gigi's handiwork was special and held a coveted place on the counter next to the cash register. She made the jewelry with beads and feathers, tiny stones and shells, as well as nuts and small woven vines or extra fine wire she ordered from the catalog.

"Tell me Little One, what are you going to do with all the money you have socked away?" asked Gabe.

"What is socked?"

"That means set aside, or placed somewhere special."

"I order more supplies."

"I *will* order more supplies," he corrected her, then added, "What about the extra left over?"

She knew it was for her sake and accepted his correcting as a loving gesture.

"I help with needs for the family."

"I *will* help with *the family needs*, You should be thinking about saving some of it to invest in your future."

"What is my future, Papa?"

"Whatever you want, Gigi. Opportunity's door will open wide for you. You could go to college, when the teacher thinks you are ready. They will guide you by your skills."

"How will they know my skills? My jewelry?"

"No, dear. They will test you like the school teacher did...on how well you read, write and do math. That's why I ask you to strive harder with your learning."

Anita added, "Listen to your Papa. He very smart. He once leader at big school."

Gabe turned to her and asked, "Who told you that?"

"Will tell me that you send him to same school you was leader," she answered.

"Why you not correct Mother?"Gigi interrupted.

"Why *don't* you correct Mother," he corrected.

"Is 'don't' the word for 'do not'?"

"Yes, it combines the two words, and is not perfect English, but acceptable," he explained.

"Then your sentence says, 'Why do not you correct Mother', right?"

Gabe closed his eyes and envisioned the sentence on a chalkboard. "You are right. It doesn't make sense that way, but...well...uh...I can't explain that one, honey. You might ask your teacher tomorrow."

"You have not answered my question. Why do you not correct Mother?" she spoke deliberately.

"Oh, boy. Now you are getting into an area that is very fragile. Usually a man does not correct his wife...if he

51

wants a happy home life. But if she wants to speak better English, I will. Anita? Step in here…anytime…do you?"

"I speak English good enough. I learn by listening."

"OK. Now that that is settled, where were we?"

"Something about you being a leader at a school?"

"First of all, I was a professor, a teacher at a university and I suppose one could say 'leader', but I had to go to school for many years before getting there."

"But you not teach now. What you do with learning?" Gigi asked.

Gabe decided to let the correcting go for now. Reflecting on his teaching he stated quietly, "I left that world because of a misunderstanding that could have cost me my life. One of my students, a young girl, was murdered and they blamed me. They would not believe my innocence so I escaped and came here to hide. It wasn't until Will came back from the university that I found out that I had been cleared of those charges because a man was caught in the process of repeating the same crime. And as for what I'm doing now with my teaching? I'm content in teaching the two most beautiful women in my life."

"You gentle and kind to everyone. Why they think you bad?" Asked Anita

"Most people are quick to judge negatively…bad…about others, because they believe they are superior…better. That's why I want you both to learn English well. I want you to be able to clearly express your mind and feelings so that *no one* can feel superior to you. Do you understand?"

As Anita nodded, Gigi answered quietly, "Yes, Papa."

# Chapter 12

Wading out into the river, Gabe was knee deep when his right moccasin slipped on a submerged log near one of his traps. He first felt the pain in his lower leg before the fear engulfed him. Lying on his back he took a few deep breaths and tried to stand, only to find nothing to support him. He could barely reach the bottom with his arms before the water flowed up, over his chest and to his chin. Knowing his entire body would plunge beneath the surface, he thought, *"I can push my body hard up and back with my arms and bounce my way back to shore."* On the first bounce he knew there was a problem. The piercing hot pain rushed throughout his body, nearly causing him to black out. *"This has always been my worst fear: out here all alone and no way to signal for help. It will be a long time before anyone becomes concerned and decides to search for me so, Ol'boy, you have to get out of this on your own."*

Although numbness was setting in, he realized his foot was wedged tight between a branch and the trunk and he could not free it. Trying to twist it was too excruciating and moving his body back and forth settled the log, and his leg, deeper into the silt. He tried using his left foot as leverage, but to no avail. *"I guess it's up to you Lord. Is this how I am to die, after all these years living in fear for my life, and just now finding the family I always dreamed of? I know enough to talk about what's fair; the whole world is not fair. But I'm hoping that you will give me a few years to enjoy my wife and daughter. You brought them to me and put them in my care. Anita, Gigi...We were just talking about their futures, but I didn't think it would be without me. I want to provide a good life for both of them. Have I failed you, Lord? OK, that's enough whining. It's not getting you out of this situation. I know you have a solution, Lord, so can you enlighten me?"*

Gabe searched the river's edge and bottom and realized that he was in line with the log, and that his arms, reaching backward had straddled it. He twisted his upper torso and reached down for a handhold and found other stubs. Knowing that by now the water had made his moccasins soft and pliable, and with his leg once again numb, he set his mind to ignore the pain he knew was coming. Taking another deep breath he pointed his toes as far as he could as he yanked on the handholds beneath him.

Whether it was the rotting branch, his slippery moccasin, or brutal strength, his foot was freed and his body surged close to the bank.

Letting the pain once again subside, he thought, *"I never knew a person could sweat submerged in water, but this ol' body did, screaming its protest to the pain it was submitted to. Now it's time to see about getting back home."*

He pushed with the good leg, dragging the broken one out of the water, onto the bank, and up to a tree where he pulled himself up to stand.

Remembering a time years earlier when he found a young Indian girl in one of his snares, he had treated her foot and made her a crutch out of a tree branch and hoisted her upon his shoulders until they were close to her village. *"I wish I had a ride back on someone's shoulders now. But a large tree branch will have to suffice and one step at a time will get me back to my loved ones. Thank You Lord, your blessings never cease to amaze me. Thank you that it's not winter, Thank you that the bone has not broken through the skin.*"

Darkness had settled around the forest as he slowly made his way toward home. With each step by hopping-step he endured the pain while relying on the crutch he had made from a Y-shaped tree branch. Struggling over fallen logs and foliage that he had paid little attention to before, he tried to determine how far away he was from home.

Sounds of the night brought back memories of the years of solitude he chose above living in the civilized world of those who are too quick to judge without question. He had time to think about the differences between those same people and those they called savages. His discovery of Soaring Eagle's Clan had been one of God's endless blessings. Even though his Anita had been a captive from another tribe and made a slave, she had become the wife of one of the clan. *He must have seen in her what I did...a very loving 'civilized' human being. In spite of the life thrust upon her, she has remained all that is good, and I am so happy to know she is waiting for me at the cabin.*

As the cold set in and the pain became unbearable he decided to rest. Sweat created from the pain reminded him of the time when he tangled with a cougar. He reached up and traced the scars on his chest where Will had had to stitch the gashes. Gabe had soaked that shirt too, until he passed out, relieving him of the pain. Then Will had known that Gabe would not feel the sting of each stitch.

Gabe's reflections brought to mind his age. He was nearing fifty and knew this was a sign, but pondered what it could mean. He had taken his old instincts for granted and they had kept him alive for the years of solitude, but now he wondered if they had abandoned him or whether he could still rely on them. *Are there creatures out here that I am not aware of? Are there any hostile Indians waiting in the darkness? I have no hair rising on my arms or neck, no buzzing in my ears. Is it because I am not in jeopardy of losing my scalp or being eaten for dinner? Relax Ol' boy; I'm sure the instincts are still there; they just haven't had to save your ornery hide.*

After starting again, each step caused excruciating pain but took him closer to home. He was getting weak and spells of dizziness came and went. When he came to a large fallen tree he wondered how far it was to each end of it, but couldn't see in the darkness. He decided to rest again and leaned against it, waiting to regain his breath and for the pain to subside and realized he was in trouble when neither happened. The last wave of dizziness brought darkness as he slid down the log and on to the forest floor.

The darkness was invaded by visions that would appear first vivid then fade to vague; he saw Will across branches high above the ground, a blue bird twittered near him before it flew away. Far below he saw soldiers leading his beloved Sparrow and his beautiful redheaded child. He cried out, but no one could hear him. Policemen surrounded him with people yelling and shaking their fists; he tried to tell them he was innocent. He stood near a chalk board with students at their desks; a black man was laughing and shaking hands; he lay in a teepee hearing the screams of a man being tortured and knew he could do nothing. Loved ones' faces towered above, but changed into forms of beasts that gnawed at his leg. Hides and skins floated, and then settled upon him with so much weight he struggled to breathe. Heat overwhelmed him to the point that he tore at his clothes, only to feel freezing cold. Thirsty, dry lips, cool water, choking, He felt weightless and soared with the eagles, only to have one attack and pierce his leg with its beak. He heard himself cry out each time the pain was too intense.

Gabe awoke in confusion. Anita was standing at the table peeling potatoes; Gigi was across from her stringing beads. He blinked. *Am I dreaming? Am I delusional?* He ventured a question, "Are you real?"

"Papa! You're awake! I'll go get Will and Becca"

Anita set down her knife and came to his side. "Yes, we are real, husband." She knelt down beside him and removed the towel from his forehead. Gabe saw the tears welling up in her eyes and reached out and pulled her up close as she added, "It good that William find you."

Will came bursting through the door with the girls close behind. Coming to a stop beside Anita he couldn't contain his relief at seeing his old friend awake. Letting out a burst of air he scolded, "You gave us all quite a scare, old man."

Gabe saw tears in the rest of their eyes, and then something else. "What is it? What's wrong? I'm here, I'm fine and will be back on my feet in no time. Now tell me, how did I get home?"

Gabe watched the exchange of glances but they all remained quiet. Softly he asked, "Are one of you going to tell me what's wrong?"

Anita rose from her knees and lifted the cover from his leg. When he raised himself on his elbows he couldn't believe his eyes. The leg was not his. This one was purple and swollen beyond recognition from the knee down, including his foot. It was unreal and he thought he must still be dreaming.

As he looked up, seeking confirmation as to what he saw, he found only concerned frowns.

Will broke the silence, "After you weren't home by dark we knew something was wrong so I took a lantern and went to find you. Gabe you were only yards away from our cabin. I came back and got the women and we brought blankets. After we got you on one, we each took a corner and carried you back here. You were in so much pain and cried out with every bump, When we got you here you were so delirious that we decided it best not to move you any further until we could rig something up to get you to the doctor in town. Gabe, it's not going to be a painless trip getting you there, but we can't wait any longer. We don't know what else to do…"

"I understand. How long have I been out?" Gabe asked.

"A day and a half," said Will.

"You have to get me to the doctor."

"We were barely able to carry you here. Town's too far."

"Get the sled hooked up to Angel, and get me on it."

"Oh, my Lord, why didn't I think of that? We could have done it while you were unconscious. It will be very painful now. The doctor in town or the fort?" warned Will.

"It doesn't matter. If I don't get to one of them I will lose this leg; if I haven't already."

"Quick, Gigi, harness Angel to the sled. Anita, bring blankets and pillows, Becca you will have to help me hold him down if he gets too wild with pain. I know. I've been with him before, after a cougar attack…Go NOW."

After weeks in the fort's infirmary, Gabe's frustration became too much and he called for the doctor, "Explain to me why my foot rolls off to the side when I try to walk. How was *it* affected when it was my *leg* that was broken?" Gabe demanded.

"First explain to me how the injury came about and how and what you did afterwards."

After Gabe had stated step by step what he could remember, the doctor nodded. "That explains why. When you jerked your foot free, you broke several bones in the top of your foot. Those broken bones were not noticed because of the swelling until it was too late to set them properly. They have begun to heal incorrectly and to undo the damage you will have to go to the hospital in Greenville, where they will have to re-break them to reset them. Even then, they won't break in the correct manner as to find the exact ends of each to mend properly. You see, when bones begin to mend they form a larger mass around the break, making it even stronger than before. It is impossible to break the bone in the exact place; on either side of it yes, but not the same place. I do not have the technology here that they have there. I'm sorry, Mr. Adams, but I did the best I could. I *did* save your leg."

"I meant on offense, doc. And yes, I remember my anatomy classes at the university. I'm just rattled at the fact that I have no way of supporting my family if I can't get back out into those woods and do my trapping. Who is going to feed my family?"

The doctor shook his head, "I have no answer for you, Mr. Adams, but it is certain, your trapping days *are* over."

# Chapter 13

School was out for the day and Gigi was on her way to the fort to check on Gabe, but seeing the train at the station and then Ellen through the store window, she decided to say hello before inquiring if any new jewelry-making items arrived. She found Ellen near the fabrics and patterns but she was with an older white woman.

Ms. Evans was working hard on Gigi's English, but with Gabe now away from the house, not correcting her, she sometimes slipped back and into the more familiar way of talking with her mother.

She recalled her father's lecture and did not want to embarrass herself and have the stranger think less of her. She carefully chose her words, "Hello, Ellen. It's good to see you. Are you delivering more baskets?"

Ellen was trying hard to remember the lessons that Thomas, and now Olivia, were teaching her, as she introduced the two, "Hello, Gigi. Yes, I brought a few. Have you met Commander Wadsworth's wife yet? Her name is Olivia. This is Gigi, Gabriel and Anita Adams' daughter. By the way how is your Papa?"

The two ladies exchanged nods, with Olivia trying hard not to stare at Gigi's beauty. "I'm glad to meet you. My, you are a pretty one."

Gigi blushed, "Thank you", then answered Ellen, "Papa is getting well. The doctor at the fort saved his leg but he can't walk good now. He is sad and says he no longer can do his traps. He not sure what he will do when doctor let him come home. He so sad." Turning toward the train station, she changed the subject, "I like to see what new has come in on train. It comes this time each day. I see bring many big things, today." Gigi's struggled to keep her words in correct order, but Olivia picked up on the mistakes.

"Yes, I suppose most of them are mine. You see, I'm moving most of my belongings here from Charlottesville and there will be many more items yet to come. It will be a struggle to find places for them at the fort."

"That big one, with odd shape, what is it?" Gigi asked.

"That, my dear, is my piano. It's been in my family for years. You must come to visit and I will play it for you."

"My Papa said that building, over there, the one with the small doors has a pee-yan-o in it. I like sound," said Gigi.

"Well, then your visit must be soon. It will be nice to play for someone that loves music as much as I do."

"I would like that very much. Thank you. I ask Mother when she want to visit Papa to the fort. I can come then."

"Well, when you do, make sure you have time for a cup of tea. We can chat and get to know each other better."

Gigi smiled broadly and nodded. "I talk to Mother."

After Gigi left Olivia turned to Ellen and said, "Tell me about that girl. Have she and her parents lived here long?"

"No, same as Clan. We all captured by the soldiers and brought here; except her father. He's a trapper. He followed us. Commander married him to Anita when he saw Gigi's hair and eyes; same as Gabe."

"Why was she with your clan? Was she a captive? Or was her father trying to rescue her?"

"No. She is Anita's daughter…and Gabe her father."

"I don't understand. Her mother…"

Ellen interrupted, "Anita was captive of my clan from other clan. Her name was Sparrow. When Commander

61

marry her to Gabe, they give her white woman's name, but it also name of her first Clan. Anita Clan."

"Oh, my, Gigi has such a light complexion and the hair… and eyes…she could easily pass as a white girl."

Ignoring the statement Ellen said, "Most of clan shun her for it. We all learning white man's ways, but she going to town's school now, so she learn faster."

Seeing a slight jealousy stirring, Olivia quickly stated, "You are doing very well, young lady, and very close to using proper English now. Corporal Thorton loves you deeply; it is in his eyes when he looks at you. His teaching, of the basics shows daily, and what he lacks in the woman's touch, I will teach you. You have nothing to worry about," assured Olivia, patting her arm. "Now let's see about those patterns."

# Chapter 14

Without Gabe, Will was doing the trapping on his own, bringing the carcasses to the cabins where he, Blue and Anita skinned and prepared the hides, which they stretched on wooden frames. Gigi helped when not in school. When the hides were cured they were stacked on the sled which Angel pulled to town.

They sectioned, salted and wrapped the different meats, separating the venison from the rest. The storeowner bought only the venison, as the townspeople rejected much of the rest; the raccoon, possum, coyote and beaver were preserved for the two families and the fort.

On other days he worked for Smithy, who expanded his list of chores until Will was becoming a blacksmith without knowing it. He began to enjoy the work and found himself looking forward to the days spent there. *Working with Smithy is more like fun and trapping is more like chores. Both are important but one more enjoyable. He even makes it more fun with his stories and singing as he works. The way he sings and hammers to a rhythm, rocking with each beat of his hammer. It's like music. He's is a good, caring and thoughtful human being and a good friend.*

The hours flew by when Will worked at the forge. Even on the hottest days, the heat from it seemed to give him comfort. He enjoyed seeing the red hot iron turn into something useable, whether it was a horseshoe, or a wagon wheel, under Smithy's hammer it formed to his wishes. As Will watched the man work he thought, *I wish I could be half as good as he is; even half as good of a person as he is. Yes, Smithy is a good man.*

He was jarred from his thoughts by a bellow, "Mo far', boy. We's needs a heap mo far'!"

Will smiled as he added more firewood to the forge. When he finished he thought of Becca and decided it was time to head back to the cabin. *I can't have her thinking that I'm happier away from her. I love her so much. I know, I'll pick her up something pretty at the store.*

"I'm going to go now Smithy. Think you can hold down the fort without me? I'm heading home to Becca."

"I's ben doin' it 'lone fo' as long as I's bemember, sonny boy. You's jest conseecrate on dat bootyful wifey of yern. I's be jest fine."

"I'll be back tomorrow." Will called as he was leaving.

"Good Lor' willin'...an' da crick don' rise!" Smithy yelled back as he pumped the bellows, raising the flames higher and making the forge hotter.

As Will entered the store he looked around, trying to find something special. He stopped short and listened intently. When he was sure it was Becca, he snuck up behind her so he could encircle her waist and give her a hug.

He was not expecting what happened next. First her elbow came back and caught him in the pit of his stomach, then that shoulder pushed him backward and she turned with a force that knocked him almost off his feet. He was able to duck as her now straightened arm swung over his head. When they both came to a stop she was standing in a fighting stance and he was crouched on his heels with his arms shielding his head.

"It's me, Becca...it's me....Will!"

Her squinting eyes opened wide as the fire melted from them and her set jaw relaxed, "Will? What you doing? Are you crazy? NEVER sneak on me again. I not know who lay their hands on me!"

Laughing now he said, "I don't have to worry about anyone snatching you away. *They* would be the ones running for dear life!"

Mr. Hamilton, standing on the other side of the counter, had witnessed the whole scene. He burst out laughing, "You have a feisty one here, Mr. Hudson. She was just delivering her latest beaded belts and moccasins." Still chuckling he turned to Becca and added, "And very lovely items they are, Mrs. Hudson, here is your price, per item, that we agreed upon."

Leaving the store they could hear the proprietor still laughing. Becca slipped the coins into her leather pouch as she said, "I also come at this time so I maybe give you ride home. Are you done at Mr. Smithy's?"

Teasing, he crouched as he slid his arm around her waist to lift her to straddle Angel. "Yes Sweetheart. Oh, darn. I was going to buy you something before our skirmish made me forget."

She asked, "What is skirmish?" as he mounted and settled behind her.

He pulled her up tight against him, "It's another word for fight, or battle."

She responded by snuggling back against him, "I not skirmish with you."

He snuggled her neck and whispered, "But if I had been someone else?"

Away from town she repositioned herself to face him, "Yes. If you someone else…Big skirmish."

# Chapter 15

Gigi had heard the sound many times before, but it always seemed to quit as she went in search of it. This time it continued and she followed it to the building with the tall pointed roof. The sound was warm and inviting, like nothing she had heard before.

Before the capture, the clan men played on flutes of reeds with various tones, but this was of many flutes all at once and ignoring her Papa's advice, she let it entice her to enter the building.

A young man was sitting in front of what at first looked like the large roll-top desk behind the Hamilton's counter. But it had white and black long buttons he was pushing with his hands and his feet took turns pumping on things below. The music vibrated through her body and she followed it as if being pulled by a string until she was standing near the man.

Sensing someone in the room, he turned slightly and saw her; standing with head back, eyes closed and body swaying to the rhythm as he played. He didn't want to stop and spoil the moment, afraid she would leave, but wanting so much to speak to her. He held the last note a few seconds, not wanting the moment to end.

When the music faded away she opened her eyes and smiled at him with an angelic expression of complete peace that melted his heart.

Wrapped in emotion, she forgot her lessons of proper English and spoke her heart, "Most beautiful,"

"Thank you. I'm glad you enjoy it," he responded.

"What is that?"

"The song is "How Great Thou Art.""

She came closer and touched the organ, "What is *this*?

Surprised, he answered, "It's called an organ."

"So good. I like this or-gan," she sighed, "I go now."

Rising from the bench he pleaded, "No, don't go. I've seen you around town but never got the chance to introduce myself. I'm the minister here; Abraham Chandler, but my friends call me Abe."

She began to recover her senses and her language lessons, "That sounds like my Papa. His name is Gabe." Patting her chest she added, "I am Gigi. Pleased to meet you. I must go to see him now, at the fort."

He walked with her down the aisle to the door. "Will I see you in church next Sunday?"

She stopped, "Papa talked about church. It might have music like store with the short doors. Where is *church*?"

Confused; he stammered, "Here, this church."

Also confused, she said, "But pee-yan-o sound different. You call it or-gan…and you already see me in *church*."

Searching for some stability in the conversation, he explained, "The piano and the organ are different. And I meant for services; Sunday services."

Giving up, she waved her hand as though to clear the discussion as she turned and walked away, muttering, "I don't know 'services'. I talk to Papa."

Watching her walk away he finally sensed that she had less education than most her age, and wondered about her mental capacity. He called after her, "Alright then, I hope I see you again, Gigi." *And I'll be asking around town about you, because my heart tells me you are a gift from God.*

She made her way through town, and to the fort. Sentries on guard, above the open gates, waved her in.

Many of the soldiers had shared their admiration for her beauty, but kept their desires to themselves. She was friendly with everyone, which made her all the more attractive. As she made her way through the gates and across the grounds, it was hard for the men to concentrate on their duties.

Finally reaching the infirmary she found Gabe sitting beside his cot, "How are you today, Papa?"

The doctor answered, "As far as I'm concerned he's ready to go home to finish healing. There's nothing more I can do for him here." Then turning to Gabe, he added, "As long as you stay off that leg until there's no pain."

"What about the foot rolling? There's more pain in it than my leg. I can't walk without a crutch."

"It would be easier with two crutches. It will give you better balance and it keeps the body straighter, with less strain on one shoulder," suggested the doctor.

Gigi nodded, "I will see he do right. Make another crutch. You ready now, Papa?"

"As ready as I'll ever be, I guess. It will take a long time getting home," he answered.

When they got out to the parade ground Thomas was waiting with the wagon. "I'm heading to the train station to pick up some supplies. Can I give you both a lift?"

"You are a Godsend, my boy!" said Gabe.

"Well, then, let me help you up to the seat."

"It would be easier if I just slid up on the back of the wagon and let my feet dangle…easy on, easy off that way."

"You may have a point, Mr. Adams," said Thomas.

Confused, Gabe said, "Mr. Adams? You haven't called me that since you escorted me to the fort awhile back, and got me married off to the woman I love…name's Gabe."

"When we get past these gates, I can call you Gabe. Inside these gates, protocol says I use your proper name."

Gabe shook his head, "Well, let's keep with protocol, *Corporal Thorton* and get me the heck past those gates!"

Gigi climbed up and took the seat beside Thomas. As they rode the distance to town he asked, "Do you have arrangements to get your father home?"

"Not yet. I will get William to help us. It not take long."

Entering the conversation, Gabe spoke up, "If you can get me to the livery, I can rest there while Gigi fetches Will and the sled."

"I know how to hook Angel to sled. I not need Will," Gigi stated defiantly.

Seeing her ego bruised, he decided to let it go. "Let's just see how things go…in case your mother may need something from town."

Gigi helped Gabe down from the wagon and into the Livery. "Wal' look ol' Red up on his feet 'gain. Doin' purty good too. Sit yerself do'n on dat bale o hay. I's be fetchin' ya…"

"No, Smithy. This is fine. I don't need anything but a place to get off this no good foot of mine."

"Ifn ya don' mine me takin' a looksee, I been ponderin' 'bout me ol' Unc' Tad. Did I tol' ya my Pappy wuz a Smith too? A slave he wuz on a plantashun ner Charlotsville. Da Masta dun put me in wid him when I was near as dis tall." Holding his hand down hear his knee, he continued, "He says I be follerin' in Pappy's place sumday. Whal me

Pappy's brothur had dis here stub ov' a foot and Pappy, he dun fix't him up wid a boot dat dun able' Unc Tad ta walk proper. I's be thinkin' on it sum…fo sho."

Gabe offered his foot to Smithy who measured it with his hands and quietly nodded once in awhile. "Yas, I's t'ink sum mo and sees 'bout it."

"Well, dear friend, there's no hurry. I'm not going anywhere on it. Once I get home, I'll be settled in for awhile. I won't be much use to anyone like this, anyway." Turning to Gigi he said, "Go now, honey, and fetch the sled for your crippled old Papa."

Smithy and Gigi both knew it was not like him to feel sorry for himself or to mope around, but then again, he never had reason to before.

It wasn't until her walk home that she realized that she hadn't asked Papa about the meeting she had with the man in the white building.

# Chapter 16

When Will went out to check the traps, what he found would alter his life forever. A wolf's foot was in one of the snares, just the foot. He found a pool of blood next to it and a trail of blood leading away.

The trail led about a half mile up to the she wolf lying, and nursing her pups. She had little strength left but to roll her eyes up at him and growl softly.

The pups were unaware of their mother's pain and suffering, as they gleaned their last meal from her. Their eyes were barely open as they climbed over each other seeking yet another nipple with more milk to offer.

The strength drained out of Will too, as he stood watching the scene. *Oh, no. What have I done? This brave and loving mother killed herself in order to get back to her babies. She must be without a mate or he would be here to protect her.*

His stomach, then his throat began to spasm before he turned and vomited. It's wasn't the dismemberment nor blood that caused his nausea. It was in knowing for the first time that each of the animals he had any part of killing might have had families depending on them. *Killing in self-defense or for food to feed a family, that's what God put them here for. Not just for their hides or sell their meat.*

He wiped his mouth on his sleeve and turned back to see her release a dying breath. *What is going to happen to these pups? I can't leave them out here to die of starvation or be eaten by predators. But I can't feed them, and I can't walk away. How will I keep them alive?* He argued with himself while he placed each of the four pups inside his shirt and headed back home. His trapping days were over.

# Chapter 17

Anita was content to have her husband home. She had time with him and when she needed time to herself, she went to her garden. She had planted rows of seeds purchased from the store and tended them as a mother tends to her children.

Gabe had hobbled along and helped her erect a fence to keep the larger animals out and a makeshift scarecrow to dissuade the birds, but she still had problems with gophers underneath and rabbits above ground.

She secretly worried about their future. With Gabe and Will no longer trapping, her trade goods were diminished. No more extra meat to sell at the fort or hides to make items to sell at the store. She depended more on the garden for trading her extras, and as a place to escape her worries. There she could go into her own world, whether it was the past or dreams of the future; it was hers to visit.

Gabe's gait went from a hobble to a limp, which was good enough to aid him in gathering all the tools that needed cleaned or sharpened and arranged a place to sit while working. *At least I can do something. Not being able to support my family makes me physically ill. What is a man's worth if he cannot do even the most menial of tasks?*

His ego received another blow when William gathered up the tools and said, "Gabe, don't waste your time on these. I can do them in half the time at the livery. The grinder will sharpen this ax in no time. It would take hours for you, when it will only take minutes for me."

Anita saw Gabe's expression before he let his chin drop and she stepped behind him and motioned to Will to join her outside.

Will excused himself. "I think I'll see if I can help Anita with that wood."

When he joined her she said quietly, "You hurt him bad!"

"How? I don't want him to sit around here all day doing what I can get done in no time," he whispered.

"He has time and need to feel needed."

"Oh, of course. How stupid of me. I never thought about his pride. I was just trying to make his life easier and I've made things worse. If I try to change it now it will seem as if I pity him. What can I do, Anita?"

"Don't do good job; he will fix."

"Yes. That might work. But it will have to not be too obvious or he will catch on."

"He my husband. I know him good. Let him show you how to make sharp better."

Nodding he said, "Yes. Good idea. Now load me up with wood so he won't get suspicious about what we really came out for."

The plan worked. The tools were done well, but not up to Gabe's standards. Dropping them off on his way to his cabin the next evening, Will knew that his mentor would inspect them and set to work on them, either quietly to not offend him, or the teacher in him would demonstrate how to do it correctly. Gabe chose the latter, and instructed Will on how the whetstone could give the edges a smoother, sharper edge.

Will glanced up from the work, over Gabe's shoulder to see Anita smiling and nodding.

# Chapter 18

Becca was ecstatic when she first saw the wolf pups, two males and two females, then saddened when she realized they were too young to be weaned from their mother. After Will told her the story she cuddled them and through her tears she asked, "How will we keep them alive?"

"I don't know, honey. I just knew I couldn't leave them out there…maybe Anita or Gabe? Or maybe the Hamiltons at the store or someone at the fort will have some advice or something that will help," he struggled for ideas.

"Let's go see."

Gigi came forward to hold one of the whining pups and instantly took charge of the situation. She turned to her mother. "Isn't there something we can do for them? You know I've always wanted a puppy, and they are so cute." Turning to Becca she offered, "I'll go with you to the store; maybe they will know something. They are very nice people and we've become close since I've been selling my jewelry there. She even has me watch the store while she has to go upstairs to their house or the stockroom out back. She taught me how to give change to people and how to write their purchases down in the charge-book that she keeps under the counter."

"I'd say wait until tomorrow, but I don't think these little ones can wait with empty tummies, so, hitch up Angel and we'll go see if they can help." said Will.

Dorothy took one of the pups from Gigi, "What have you here? Oh, my, little wolf pups? Aren't they adorable?"

"Yes, but their mother…died and left her poor babies behind. I feel responsible because she got caught in one of my snares and chewed her leg off to get back to them. Our problem now is how do we keep them alive? I owe that much to their mother!" admitted Will.

"First off, they will need milk. I understand from Gigi that you have a goat, so that's no problem, milk is milk. But how to feed it to them is the question," said Mrs. Hamilton. After pondering a minute she offered, "Perhaps if you took the corner of a piece of cloth and twisted it, dipped it in the milk and let them nurse on it?"

"I think I've got it," said Mr. Hamilton, "Just a minute."

He went to a cabinet behind the counter and rummaged around, then came back with an eye dropper. "This is mainly for doctoring eyes to wash them out or apply medicine, but it could easily feed a pup."

Gigi jumped up and hugged him, "Oh, Mr. Hamilton, you are so smart and I just know this will do the trick. Thank you so much. You can subtract the price of this from my jewelry payment."

He smiled and patted her arm, "No, my dear, no payment necessary. I've overheard you tell Dorothy that you've always wanted a puppy, so if this works we'll all be happy. And if any survive, we might even see about getting one for a watchdog around here."

"You will sure get your pick of the litter…after me of course!" laughed Gigi.

The eyedropper was a success and in time, homes were found for each pup. Will and Becca agreed that only one was needed for both homes, so Gigi chose the proud Alpha who dominated his siblings. The Hamiltons took the other male while one of the females went to Smithy and the other to Commander Wadsworth at the fort.

# Chapter 19

Gabe was out back splitting wood when Will approached, "Smithy told me to let you know that the thing he's been working on is ready for a fitting. He wants to see if it will work for you and make sure everything fits right."

"I hope he has something rigged up so that I don't have to hobble around much longer. I'm not sure what he has up his sleeve, but I'm willing to try anything. I feel next to worthless that way I am."

"You never know until you try. I've seen that man work miracles when it comes to correcting a horse's gait or injury, with just knowing how the animal placed his foot. He has even created a shoe that prevents a horse from putting weight on that foot until the injury is healed properly. Strangest thing I ever saw, but it worked."

"I guess animals are alike as far as walking, at least I hope so. I agree that he is an exceptional farrier, and if you learn all you can from him, you'll be just as good. As soon as I get done here, I'll head on over there. It will take a while."

"You go ahead, Gabe, I'll finish up here, and you can take Angel. She's due for some exercise anyhow."

"I think I'll take you up on that. I'm getting to enjoy riding; it's just adjusting the length of the stirrups that takes the time. If I didn't I would have my knees up under my chin like the jockeys in those fancy horse races."

"Yes, I heard about those. The more elite students at the university would go and bet good money on the horse races in Charleston. Quite an event I'm told, but not for my blood. Money is too hard to come by than to go squandering it on whose horse is fastest."

"You and me both, Son. I've never been able to wrap my mind around having more money than I need."

Will smiled to himself when he heard Gabe call him *Son*. It warmed his heart to know that the man felt fondly enough of him to use the endearment, and it took all he had not to give him a warm hug. *He would knock me on my hind side if I tried...but maybe it would be worth it.* He thought about it once more and decided not to chance it.

Gabe handed Will the ax and headed two doors down to get Angel. After saddling her and lengthening the stirrups, he headed out. "Would you mind hanging on to the pup? He has begun to follow if not tied up or inside the house...and could you stick your head in the door and let Anita know where I'm going. I don't want her to worry."

"Sure, no problem. If it's too dark to head home there's always that cot in the back of Smithy's. I don't want to have to come looking for you in the dark again. I'll let Anita know so we won't worry until tomorrow night," teased Will.

"Don't make me get back down off this horse and tend to you. Bad foot or not, I can still..." Looking Will up and down he recanted, "Well, maybe not...but you mind your manners and respect your elders!" Gabe laughed.

Will watched as Gabe waved goodbye and headed toward town, then said a soft prayer, "Lord, I do love that man. I'm blessed beyond measure that you sent him to me when I needed him most, and I'm ever so grateful."

"Who you talking to and where is Husband going?"

Bringing the ax to his chest in defense, Will turned quickly to the voice. "Anita, you about scared me half to death sneaking up on me like that. I could have killed you!"

She brushed it off, "Silly talk. Answer question."

"Smithy has rigged up a thing for him that might enable him to walk better and wants to see if it fits. He needs Gabe there to measure things, I guess. I was going to tell you when I brought your wood in...and that he might not be home tonight if it gets too dark. "

Reaching for the wood she said, "I carry. You take some home." Looking to where she had seen Gabe go, she added, "I no worry, he blessed by his God and my Yowa."

The path from town to their cabins was wide enough for the sled and was beginning to show ruts where it slid along the ground. Angel's tracks made a third groove between the runners. She knew the way and it was no time before they reached the livery.

Sliding down Gabe made sure that his good foot landed first to bear his weight. He led Angel through the corral gate before removing her bridle and saddle, then placed the saddle in the barn and the bridle on a peg nearby. He patted her neck and whispered, "Angel, you truly are a gift from God". All three had honored God with a form of prayer.

"Will tells me you wanted to see me. I guess this old hoss needs a new shoe. Know anything about that?"

Smithy flashed his big smile and came to shake Gabe's hand. "Yas, I gues' I does. Sit yerself ober dere and gibe me yer boot. I b'lives I got sumptin dat'll fix ya right up!"

Gabe did as told and watched as the big man turned his attention to his work. Not wanting to disrupt Smithy's work but not wanting to be rude, Gabe broke the silence, "You know I appreciate you wanting to help me, Smithy, but don't feel bad if things don't work out. I'll have to learn to manage somehow."

The big man had his back to Gabe and nodding his head he turned, "I know's dat. I's be righ' prou' callin' ya my frien', Red, so's ifn dis don' work, we's keep tryin' and we's fin' sumptin. Trys dis on."

Gabe took the boot and checked it out as he turned it around and upside down. "Looks like I could do some serious damage at a hoedown if I were to do some boot stomping dancing." Then he bent down and pulled it on, testing his weight as he rocked back and forth.

"Walk on ober ta da anvil thar. See's hows it does."

Gabe reached for his crutches, but Smithy shook his head. "I's wants ta sees hows ya does wit'out em', I be's right her' if'n you needs sumtin to grabs hol of."

Gabe took a step and was surprised to find that his foot did not roll outward. He glanced at Smithy with a smile and said, "Hey, look at me. I can walk almost normal!"

"Don' go gettin' 'head of yersef...keep walkin' and put your weit on that bad un'. If ya needs a cushun' in side, hav yer missus do dat. Dat be's way beyon' my x-per-tise."

Looking down at the boot Gabe rocked it sideways to see how it was made. "It's not as heavy as it looks. I see the braces running up each side are clamped together under the arch and near the ankle and that must be what gives it the stability."

"Naw, Red, I done made da weight on da inside arch hebier so's to balance da foot ta hol' it in place."

"You are a genius, Smithy."

"Naw, I does it all da tim' fo hosses dat haf da same prob'm. I make's 'em jest a mite hebber on da inside dan da outside. Simp'l as dat."

"Well, I feel like a new man, thanks to you! I can't wait to get back and show Anita and Gigi. I can't go back to trapping, though." Gabe sat back down and looking at his friend he said, "You know, Smithy, when I was trapping alone, or even with Will, I never thought about what would happen if something went wrong out there. But now that I have the girls, I can't think of leaving them without someone to take care of them. And I don't like being out there all alone, anymore. I never knew life could be so good being close to someone."

"I knows hows ya feel, Red. And I's glad dat ya dun foun' som'one dat mak' ya hap'y. Ya deserv's it!"

"Speaking of my girls, I'm excited to get back to them and show off my new boot...and that I can walk like a man again. I don't know how I can ever repay you, Smithy, but you can rest assured that I will find a way!"

"No need, Red, ol' frien'...I's jest hap'y it do da job."

# Chapter 20

As they were relaxing after dinner, and Gabe was watching Gigi play with the pup, he asked, "What are you going to name him?"

"I'm not sure. He's so strong and proud. I want to give him a special name," said Gigi.

"Well, the way he lorded over his siblings, it could be something like 'Zeus'. That is a noble and regal name."

"What is Zeus?"

"Zeus was a Greek god."

"Another god? How many gods are there, Papa?"

"Zeus was a mythical god in ancient times."

Sighing she sat beside him and said, "Those are words I don't know. Tell me about them."

"Well, in ancient times…that means long, long ago…in a country called Greece…on the other side of the ocean… they believed in many different gods that had different duties. 'Zeus' was the god over all the other gods."

"Like a king? Ms. Evans say that they have kings in other countries, but we have presidents. What is the difference?"

Seeing that the discussion would be a lengthy one, he side- stepped and stated, "That's a good question to ask Ms. Evans. She will be happy to see that you are thinking about what she teaches."

"Alright, but is that 'Zeus' as big as our god?"

"No, honey…none of the gods are as big as our God. He is the most powerful of all…and now it's time for you to get to bed. Remember to say your prayers."

Stalling she asked, "Could we name the dog God?"

"I don't think that would please our God. It would make Him feel that we do not honor Him. And how would it sound if you went around calling, "Here God, Here God?""

"Papa, can I go to that church I told you about that I visited awhile back? Maybe I can learn more about our God and find ways to make Him happy. Does God have a wife, or a daughter?"

As she stood in front of him he took her hand and said, "No, He doesn't have a wife or a daughter but he has a son. Which is a whole long story that we will have to discuss at another time. And…you have a good idea. I think it's time we all went to church. I'd like to meet this preacher you spoke of and find out how he performs his service."

"*That's* the word I couldn't remember after I left him to find you. I like the music his machine makes. It's different than the one the building with the short doors makes. He asked if I will go to his Sunday service. I was going to ask you, but I forgot the word. What does 'service' mean?'

Sighing deeply, Gabe looked at her through his eyebrows and said, "Young lady, you are always full of questions this time of night, but they will have to wait for another time. I will answer this last one…Sunday *service* is like your school classes. Each one teaches you something different, reading, writing or arithmetic. Sunday *service* teaches about God. Now…off to bed!"

Picking up the wolf pup she said, "One more thing, Papa. I decided…I'm going to name him, Zeus, like you said."

# Chapter 21

Ellen's determination to learn to read, mostly so she could understand the directions on making white-woman's dresses, spurred her on. The commander's wife, Olivia was there for her, answering questions that Thomas couldn't and the two women spent many afternoons sitting with garments in their laps as they sewed the pieces together. As soon as Ellen was confident in her ability she took the supplies to Anita and Becca.

Becca also took to it right away and they used money from the crafts they made and sold at the Mercantile, to purchase their needed supplies.

Anita spent more of her time in her garden which was growing larger with each packet of seeds brought home. She had help from the rest, but she spent more time there than the others. The vegetables she grew filled both families' cooking pots, as well put money in her pocket from selling them at the store. She shared what she couldn't use and didn't sell with the fort to help feed the clan.

But when she did sew, her fabric choice was the heavier, more durable cottons, cut in the same manner as the hides, so no pattern was needed. A piece of string was all she needed to measure, but she treasured the scissors, metal needles and thread that came in a small sewing basket that Gabe had given her.

The other girls liked the more elaborate style of dresses that were gathered at the yoke and hung to the floor. They could be worn loose for comfort or tied at the waist. They made aprons to protect the dresses when working around the house, but the undergarments and bonnets were the hardest to get used to.

It was during one of these sewing days when they were sitting and chatting that Anita quietly said to Becca, "You have not told your husband that you are with child."

Becca first looked down at her waist, then up at Anita, "How did you know? Am I getting fat?"

Anita shook her head, "No, child. You have a glow about you that all pregnant women have."

As she looked down at her body she asked, "If I have this glow, why hasn't William seen it?"

"Because men are blind. Their minds are off in their work and they see nothing. How long has it been since your last moon cycle?"

"Almost three."

"Then you best be telling him soon or he will wonder why his beautiful wife is spreading at the middle."

"Oh, Anita, am I going to get fat and ugly and he won't want to…want to…"

"Love you? My child, you have nothing to worry about with William. He loves you. But why have you not told him? Do you fear he will not be happy?"

"I'm not sure what he will say or do. We have so little to keep ourselves fed, let alone another mouth to feed. He is working so many places."

"That baby won't be needing anything but your milk for months, and by then Will can find better work, and all things will be fine. Don't worry. But tell him you must!"

Ellen bounced up and chirped, much like her namesake the squirrel, "I know. We can start by making baby clothes. That will 'tell' him without you saying a word…right? Let's start now. We'll see how long it takes for him to catch on… oh, I'm excited. A brand new baby…" Then her face saddened. They all became silent for just a few seconds before she snapped out of it and added with a smile, "I'm happy for you."

Later that day Will came home from working at Smithy's and gave Becca a warm hug, then turned to the wash basin. He took the enamel pan outside to fill it at the stream when she stopped him and offered a pot of heated water.

"My darling wife, this is why I love you so much. You think of me and find ways to make me love you even more, if that is possible."

Their eyes met and held for a couple of seconds, but long enough to express that their love was mutual and would last a lifetime. They both smiled and he nodded, the message was sent and received that tonight there would be a warm and loving union.

After dinner he sat near the fireplace on their hide-covered wicker couch. He stretched his legs and leaned back to rest his head on the pillows strapped head-high. His vision was in line with the fireplace hearth. His eyelids drooped but he fought to keep them open, waiting for Becca to join him.

He saw something unfamiliar and out of place beside the smoky kerosene lantern. He blinked, focused his eyes and then frowned, not sure of what he saw. Getting up he went to satisfy his curiosity and found a tiny pair of moccasins.

Thinking they were her work for the mercantile, he picked them up and turning to her he said, "Becca, these are so cute. They will sell really great at the store, I'm sure. You did a really good job on them."

"I did not make those to sell at the store."

"Then who are they for? Is Anita? Ellen?" Then he saw the smile on her face and he froze. "You! You are going to have a baby? I'm going to be a father?" He rushed to her and scooped her up and twirled her around the room. "Oh, my sweet, sweet wife, WE are going to have a BABY!" He let her feet hit the floor but kept one arm around her as he tenderly brushed a lock of hair from her face with his free hand, "You've made me the happiest, luckiest man on earth!"

# Chapter 22

Anita chose not to join the group that Sunday morning. She claimed a headache and argued with Gabe that he should go ahead with the others to escort Gigi, knowing that it meant a lot to her daughter to satisfy her curiosity about the white-man's 'church'.

Gigi and Becca donned their new gingham dresses with bonnets to match and buttoned up their ankle-high, hard-soled shoes. Both were excited about their new adventure and smiled at each other as they rode the sled to town.

Before crossing the church's threshold, Will and Gabe removed their hats and took their ladies by the arm as they entered and stood inside the door, wondering where to sit.

Their arrival caused a stir in the congregation, who turned to watch the group come in. Seeing the confusion, the young pastor quickly left the pulpit and approached the newcomers. When he saw that one of them was that angelic girl who had visited the church some time ago, he smiled and gave them a warm, "Welcome, welcome, come in, here's a pew that will fit all of you nicely."

Gabe, in the lead, nodded and with his hat in one hand and Gigi's elbow in the other he directed her to sit. The pews were simple backless wooden benches, placed so close that one had to walk sideways.

Seeing a man sitting at the other end, Gabe chose to enter first, followed by Gigi, just as Will directed Becca to sit beside her, keeping the girls between them.

Still standing at the end of the pew and smiling at Gigi, the pastor said, "It's so nice to see new faces join our congregation. Would you care to introduce yourselves?"

The pastor's eyes did not go unnoticed by Gabe who did the honors by standing and stating, "My name is Gabriel Adams, this is my daughter Gigi."

Then Will stood and said, "My name is William Hudson and this is my wife, Rebecca."

A soft applause, with murmurings of, "Welcome" came from the parishioners, while some shot glances to one another after Becca was introduced as Will's wife.

"My name is Pastor Abraham Chandler and each of the congregation will be happy to meet you after the service."

After more nods were exchanged, both men sat back down and the pastor returned to his pulpit.

The service was exciting to the girls, but not so much to the men, who remained respectfully patient. Gabe also saw how often the young pastor looked in Gigi's direction.

Gigi's movement caused Gabe to glance sideways to find her slightly swaying to the organ's music. Her head was tilted back, with eyes closed and a contented smile that gave her the image of a porcelain doll. He had never seen her through the eyes of another man, and now he knew that he would have to guard her more than ever…starting with this Pastor Abraham fellow.

After the service they were leaving the church yard when they heard a voice call softly, "Gigi, it's good to see you again." They turned to see Commander Wadsworth's wife Olivia approaching. "I have the piano all tuned up and ready for that visit you promised. From where I was playing the organ this morning I could see how much you enjoy the music. Mr. Adams, you must be very proud of her. She has learned quickly to help the Hamiltons at the store, and I hear she is doing quite well in school."

"Yes Ma'am I'm very proud of her. She does learn quite quickly everything she wants to know, and I was not aware until today that she is so fond of music."

"I've invited her to the fort for tea and a visit, while I play the piano for her". Then turning to Gigi she asked, "Are you still interested in our visit? If you wish, I would love to teach you to play." Turning back to Gabe she continued, "I've so much time on my hands and it would be a real pleasure to have her company."

"Although I'm very grateful for the offer, I'm afraid we don't have the finances to….,"

"I'll not hear of any finances…the lessons will be free and be as much for me as for Gigi. I have no one to pass on my music and it would be a waste to not allow someone that loves it as much as she, to be deprived of that learning. Besides, I get pretty lonely with so few women-folk around the fort to sit and chat with."

"Is that something you would like, Gigi?" asked Gabe

"Oh, yes. I would love to make the sounds," said Gigi.

"Of course her mother is invited as well, or you as an escort, but I'm assured daily, from Frederick…Commander Wadsworth…that everyone is safe now," claimed Olivia.

"Is tomorrow too soon, Mrs. Wadsworth?" asked Gigi.

Reaching out and patting Gigi's arm, she smiled, "No, of course not. Let's say right after school? We will have your first lesson and finish with a cup of tea. I'm looking forward to seeing you, Gigi."

# Chapter 23

Gabe was getting used to the boot and was pleased that he could walk longer and faster each day. It was not perfect, but made traveling easier. On most of his walks he took Zeus and had trained him to respond to many commands.

The wolf took to the orders as a game and worked hard to please. The praise and playful romps made each learning experience a reward. He quickly learned the elementary commands: *sit, stay, come, lie down, fetch* and *roll over*, but knew others that pleased his humans more. At the command of *find*, they would hide and he would search until he found all that were hiding. If a name was added, *find Gigi*, he knew it was just for her. He could *crawl* on his belly with chin outstretched and close to the ground, *hide* where he hid well enough that the family had a hard time finding him. When he was commanded to *play dead* it was hard to see him breathe. Combining *hide and stay* meant that he had to stay hid until they found him.

The pup was taught that if he wanted something, or his answer to their question was 'yes', he would walk in circles in front of a person, but if the answer was 'no' he would lie down and face them.

Gabe knew that he would have to watch Zeus closely when the time came to leave the property, so he sometimes used the leash Will had made while working at Smithy's.

The pup was growing fast and as he had been separated from his siblings almost since birth, he assumed that these humans were his family and this man was the Alpha; to be obeyed without question. He grew fast with two families feeding him table scraps plus meat from fresh kills he caught himself. His favorite meal was the rabbit, and the love of the chase made it even sweeter. He kept the garden free of all the varmints that threatened Anita's harvest.

He was on the leash during his first trip to the fort, even though Gabe realized that the soldiers would be used to seeing a wolf, since the commander had taken one of the females. Her name was "Sashay" because according to Olivia, it was the wolf's stride. "She just sashays everywhere she goes."

When Zeus saw Sashay, he froze and became fully alert. Ears came up, legs stiffened, and hackles rose slightly. It was his introduction to his own kind and he was not sure what to make of her.

Tension in the room grew as Gabe edged Zeus closer, ready to restrain him if necessary. Everyone watched in anticipation, no one knowing what to expect as Zeus bowed his neck and advanced stiff-legged to where Sashay stood next to Olivia. The female was just as confused, but stood her ground and met him half-way. They sniffed as they circled each other, allowing the information to travel from nose to brain.

They both felt, but did not understand, a vague familiarity to the scent. Something told them that this was something they did not have to fear, something that gave comfort in a strange particular way, something acceptable. When they both felt acceptance, they relaxed and began to rub against each other. She put her ear against his shoulder and pushed her body down the length of his side. He returned by lifting her chin with his nose and rubbed against her chest.

Everyone breathed a sigh of relief, knowing the two had recognized each other as kinship and had nothing to fear.

Zeus' second trip was to the mercantile where the Hamiltons had adopted the other male in the litter. They had waited to name him until something in his nature provided it. They decided on Tory, a name that Charles had remembered from school as an old English name for outlaw. "I saw him snatch a piece of meat off the counter one day, and it all seemed to fit. I'm hoping that he will be as courageous as a guard dog too."

This introduction was a little different. Zeus was familiar with the sight of one of his kind but Tory wasn't. The scene started to play out as before with Sashay, but this time it was Tory who took a defiant stance. He locked eyes with Zeus, stretched his neck and dropped his head down. He spread his legs and bristled. The low growl came from deep within as he pressed his body against Charles' leg.

The wolves advanced slowly, Gabe letting just enough slack in the leash to allow Zeus the needed concentration. Charles also had Tory on a leash for the safety of his customers and also let out just enough to allow freedom of movement. The only sound in the room was that of the low growls of each animal. As the two circled each other, never losing eye contact, there came a change in Tory. It was an odd feeling of recall...a forgotten memory of somewhere, sometime...long ago.

Tory's stance softened and he slid down to one side and rolled over, exposing his chest and stomach with his tail tucked between his legs; the sign of submission to an Alpha male. Zeus stood over him and tapped Troy's chin with his nose, claiming his dominance. Afterward the two examined each other's scents, and then reclaimed their previous positions by their humans.

The people sighed with relief and all got back to normal except for Charles' ego that had received a slight bruising. The human male ego is fragile and he did not like everyone seeing Tory submit.

Zeus' final trip was to the Blacksmith's. Smithy had named his wolf "Orphy". "Whal, she were uh orphan and it jest seem nat'ral fer her name. She be's real sweet and follers me ri't close. She ben a whol' lot o' cumfert to dis ole man, don' sees why I neber had no dog 'fore, but she be a good'un."

Orphy was curled up next to the furnace when Gabe and Zeus entered. She snapped to all fours, and like Tory, took her stance. When Smithy spoke to calm her down the only thing that moved was the ear closest to him. It was her way of letting him know that she heard, but was not convinced.

From the last three meetings, Zeus' confidence was overwhelming, so he steadily advanced upon Orphy until he towered over her. She moved only her eyes, but growled deeper. Without losing eye contact he let out a huff of breath into her nose. She blinked and took in the scent of his breath. They stood there, with him breathing into her nostrils until, as with the others, she felt it…something new, yet old. Something's there…deep down, but not quite sure of what. Then with a warm sense of security, she also melted to the ground and rolled over on her back; acknowledging him as her superior.

At the end of each of these visits Gabe showed the others all of Zeus' tricks, then rewarded him with praise and hugs.

As things went well with each meeting of Zeus and his siblings, the owners decided to have them all meet in one place. All were on leashes, and the mood was still apprehensive, but after their initial introduction to Zeus it was easier for the rest to accept that there were more of their kind and they united as if never separated. They formed a bond much like they would have in the wild.

After that, the wolves greeted each other much like humans, only with sniffs instead of a handshakes and Zeus continued to hold his position as the Alpha male.

# Chapter 24

The garden took most of Anita's time. She was content to nurture it and see the results of her toil in the praises from her family and the money she received from sale of the produce. She took pride in knowing that the vegetables she sent by other members of the family were of the highest quality, but preferred the others deliver them.

When asked why she didn't want to deliver them herself and maybe shop at the mercantile, her answer was always the same, "I happy here. I praise Yowa that he give me nice home, good husband, good daughter, happy life. I no want nothing there. If I need, family bring. Life very good. I safe when wolf here. He comfort to me. And since I learn blow gun so good, I bring in meat to add to pot...if I fast enough to keep away from Zeus! " She laughed.

Gabe had pretty much given up on correcting her English because she was content in knowing enough to make herself understood and that was all she needed. Because she did not want to communicate with the outside world, he felt she had the right to choose and she chose not to. He smiled and said, "And I praise *God* that He has blessed me with you, my dear wife. He is so loving that He wants me to have the love of a good woman and loving daughter. I also think of William as my son and Blu...Becca like a daughter, so their baby will be as a grandchild to me. One big happy family...Yes, God...and Yowa has blessed us!"

Gabe provided Anita with wooden boxes that he created from slats he found at the new sawmill across from Smithy's. After venturing over and browsing around, he saw the thin slats used for roofing shingles and imagined them made into boxes to transport Anita's vegetables. After a little resizing here and there, they worked perfectly. When he saw the approval on her face, he was pleased.

He was also pleased to hear Mr. Hamilton ask if he could make some of the boxes for the store, "It would be a relief to not have to worry about customers bumping shelves and making the jars of canned goods slide off the shelves. If you like, you can take measurements of the shelves and make the boxes accordingly. Just let me know the cost and we can go from there."

And so, Gabe became a box maker, and he was good at it. Each box was cut and built precisely and delivered to the buyer or the train to be carried to destinations far and wide. He and Smithy had even devised a branding iron for the end of the boxes that read, "G. Adams Box Co."

Anita's vegetables arrived at the store and the fort clean and fresh, without blemish, and were highly in demand. His box business began to grow and Gigi's jewelry was selling to all the train travelers. Life was good and each day brought more blessings.

# Chapter 25

"Commander Wadsworth, Sir, there is a company of army soldiers ushering a whole lot of Indians into the fort, and it looks like they are being led by Lt. Nichols. He is barking orders to round up our Indians and get them back in confinement," reported Sgt. Wilson.

"WHAT? In MY fort? Who does that degenerate think he is? Have him report to my office at once."

"No need to send for me; I'm here to present you with my papers signed by the President of the United States. *And* I might add that I am no longer a lieutenant but a full captain and I am personally in charge of rounding up these heathen redskins and marching them to Charleston, Tennessee. The President is repeating Andrew Jackson's Indian Removal Act of gathering the rest of these savages who escaped and hid during the first historic roundup in 1830. This time he wants any and all to be gathered and pushed as far west as possible. He has personally assigned me to gather all those in the southwest and I am happy to accommodate him."

"You have no jurisdiction in my fort!" said Wadsworth.

Removing one glove at a time, Nichols smiled, "Oh, but if you will check those papers you will find out I most certainly *do*, and am very willing to follow through with my orders. You won't be able to stop me this time. I will have my way. The President and his constituents are of the same mind and in choosing me they showed their confidence in my ability to follow orders. And I certainly *will* follow through and while doing so gain more respect from them and my peers."

The commander checked over the papers and sat back in his chair in disgust. "I'm still the commander of this fort and what I say inside these walls will still be obeyed. We will try to accommodate the prisoners you have, but you can take your men and bivouac outside the fort."

"What? My men have ridden a long way with little or no accommodations. They have a right to the luxury of a stay inside the fort and to adequate meals and bedding."

"They will get what is left *after* the prisoners have 'adequate meals and bedding'. These people walked while your men rode. There is a difference in what is humane and what is ruthless, wanton abandonment of human dignity. What on earth are the plans for these people?"

"That's no concern of yours. It is solely at my discretion as to what will happen to them. And I will use every resource available to make sure that every one of them gets to my destination or dies along the way, I care not one way or another."

"My God, man, do you hear yourself? These are human beings, with a slightly different skin tone than you and I; but still God's children. By all that's Holy, are you so devilish that you would treat people worse than animals?"

"They aren't human; even Andrew Jackson stated that they had '...neither the intelligence, the industry, the moral habits nor the desire of improvements'...They are savage beasts that should be annihilated from the face of the earth. The horrors they have inflicted upon settlers and traders...''

"*Only* in retaliation to what has been done to them, but these...this clan...Soaring Eagle's clan, are docile and friendly and helpful. They only want to be left alone to live the way their ancestors lived."

"And how was that? In primitive houses made of animal hides or mud and sticks? They have no one place to call home, or make cities nor even the decency to have a toilet."

"Yet they bathe every morning IF they are allowed, and keep their clothes clean and hair styled in the proper manner. I can't say the same for the likes of your soldiers, which I see are more unkempt than your prisoners."

"All of this is of no consequence. I am taking charge and as soon as I know that I have gathered *all* the Indians we shall precede westward, *as per my orders!*" Nichols slapped his gloves in his empty palm, turned and left the quarters... without expressing civil protocol.

Nichols' men had conversed with the fort soldiers and found out that the Corporal's wife was Indian and two other men had married Indians and they lived off the premises. As soon as he got back to his group he stated, "I'm taking six of you men to round up the ones outside the fort. Men, be ready for hostility, but remember you have the orders from me and the President of the United States, himself."

A soldier stepped up and spoke, "Captain, Sir, I just came from the bar in town and one of the guys says that there are squaws married to two trappers who live on the same piece of land outside the town a ways. He said they have been mixing in with white folk and doing business and the like, just like they were some of us. The merchants in town have been real friendly with them, too."

"Well, we'll just see about that. We know they will never be equal to white folk, so we best get out there and find them before those townspeople warn them. Did you get an idea which way these squaws are now living?"

"Yes, Captain, Sir, that man pointed out the direction to me and I saw a trail that might take us there."

"Six of you saddle up and find that path and bring in any Indians you find. Six more are coming with me to town and we'll see what we can find."

Thomas was standing just inside the room while the conversation unfolded and after Nichols left, he ventured to say, "Sir, the Indian prisoners he has brought are a mixture of Chickasaw, Choctaw, and Creek. And other tribes that are enemies. They may even start to war against each other along that route to Fort Loudoun in Tennessee. And...what does he mean ALL the Indians? He can't mean my wife. She is a citizen now that she's married to a soldier...isn't she? He's *not* taking Ellen. I won't allow it. If it's all the same to you sir, I would like permission to find her. She went to the mercantile with your wife, I believe. Then I'll have to alert Gabe and Will. This man is a lunatic."

"Yes, Corporal, *go*. We don't know how far he will go in order to impress his superiors...and there seems to be no way I can stop him. Sgt. Wilson, send a telegraph to Army Headquarters. Ask them to verify all of this."

Thomas discretely left the fort and hurried to town to find his friends, "Smithy, have you seen Gabe or Will?"

"Naw, cain't says dat I has. Cou'd be dey at da sawmill, or at dere cab'ns," answered the blacksmith.

Thomas moved on to the store and found Rebecca, Ellen and Olivia chatting with the Hamiltons. Gigi was working behind the counter and they were all startled at the sudden appearance of the breathless Thomas. "Soldiers are coming! They are taking all Indians prisoners and marching them to Tennessee. We have to get you girls to the cabins and out of sight."

Nichols entered the blacksmith shop demanding, "Where is the soldier that was seen coming in here? He is going against orders and trying to hide the Indian women we know are in these parts."

"Don' ritely knows whar he be…" started Smithy.
Pushing him aside and against the wall, Nichols demanded, "I hear there is a room in the back. Is he hiding in there?"

That brought Smithy's wolf Orphy to her feet and her growl was deep and meaningful. "Das al'rite Orphy, das al'rite. Com' her' girl."

When Nichols saw the wolf he made the mistake of kicking at her. Before he could draw back his leg, she had him by the ankle and was twisting her head and body in order to tear the foot from his body. "Get it off! Get it off!" he screamed.

Smithy reached down and grabbed Orphy's collar and pulled back gently. Talking calmly, and petting her, he convinced her to let go and that it was alright. 'Ya rily shudn't kick a wolf, Mista. She don' lik' dat."

"I'll kill it, that's what I'll do," Nichols demanded.

"The building is secure, Captain. No one is here,"

"Then we spread out. You, go to the saloon, you, go the lumber yard, you four, follow me," barked Nichols.

At the mercantile, Thomas was still trying to make the girls understand, "Hurry girls, get your purchases and go to the livery. We will see how fast Angel can get us home."

"Not so fast, Corporal," came from behind him. It was Nichols and his men. "If you continue to meddle I will have you arrested and incarcerated for interfering with presidential orders. Step aside. Men, take these two into custody and add them to the rest at the fort," said Nichols.

"You can't do this!" Grabbing Ellen and pushing her behind him Thomas added, "She is my wife, and an American citizen now."

"Au contraire, my dear man, I can do whatever I want with these *squaws*. As long as there is a drop of Indian blood flowing in their veins I have the Presidential Power, and a duty to take them into custody."

One soldier held Rebecca and as another reached for Ellen, Thomas knocked his arm away. Instantly the soldiers encircled the couple, the Hamilton's wolf Tory was on his feet and presenting a low rumbling growl just as a voice bellowed behind them all, "What in blue blazes is going on here?" It was Gabe.

"None of your concern, sir. Back away or be arrested for interfering in military business." Turning to Mr. Hamilton he said, "What kind of town is this that everyone has wolves for pets? Control yours sir, or I will," then back to Gabe he continued, "Step away, I say...oh, wait a minute my sources say that you also have a squaw wife. The red-headed trapper...yes and if memory serves me right, there was a squaw amongst my prisoners years ago that had a red-headed daughter... much the same color as yours...and much like the color of that young lady's over there. Men take her too."

Mrs. Hamilton grabbed Gigi and stepped in front of her and pushing her next to Mr. Hamilton, "NO! This is MY daughter! You have no right to touch my daughter."

"Nice try lady, and I'll admit she doesn't look like a squaw, but with that color of hair...and eyes...."

"She…she…" glancing at Gabe and then her husband she seemed to confess, "She *is* my daughter. Mr. Adams…and I…had an affair…before I was married…and Grace is the result," then she dropped her head as if in shame.

Gigi stared wide-eyed at her father, who gave her just enough of a nod for her to understand. Mr. Hamilton put his arm around Gigi and added, "She told me about it. I accepted Grace as my own and we never thought we would ever run into Mr. Adams this far away from Charlotte… where they knew each other." His wolf, Tory stepped forward and leaned against Mr. Hamilton's leg.

Nichols' eyes shifted from the wolf then narrowed as he studied each of their faces, "I'm not satisfied with that story, but I'll let it go for now. Be assured that I will do some research when I return from completing my duty. It all sounds fishy to me. If I find it untrue she'll join the rest and you will all be arrested for lying to an Army Officer." Turning back to Ellen and Thomas he said, "Now step away. Corporal; you will have a day to visit her in the brig before we take her away."

Gabe stepped beside Thomas and faced Nichols, but was immediately surrounded by the soldiers' bayonet-mounted rifles. "Take them all to the brig. We'll sort them out later."

Olivia had been silent during this ordeal but now spoke up, "Officer, is this necessary? These men are good men and the ladies are my friends. Ellen is the Corporal's wife."

"The Corporal that got me excommunicated from the fort with his interference while I was doing my duty. And if I may suggest…Madam, this is entirely none of your business, so I suggest you keep your busy-body nose out of it. Now step aside or you will join them."

"Well, by all means, sir...it looks as if you will have to arrest me too. I shall not stand by and watch you use your power to do harm. The Army that I know does not hold to their personnel abusing women, of *any* nationality."

"Then by all means, lady, join the group. And we'll see what your husband, if you have one, will have to say when he comes to bail you out."

"Yes. I'll be interested in this outcome myself," she said.

The arrested party was surrounded by soldiers as they made their way to the fort, and the brig.


Zeus startled Anita as she worked in her garden. He was in a challenging stance and bristled from head to toe when she looked up and found soldiers on horseback. Some were watching her while others scanned the area. The leader dismounted and approached her, only to meet a defiant wolf who placed himself between them.

"Better watch that dog, Sarge, he looks like a mean one," warned one of the soldiers.

"Drop what you're doing, Squaw. You're coming with us," the sergeant demanded. Ignoring the wolf's warning snarls, he reached to grab Anita as razor sharp teeth pierced his forearm. The soldier screamed as Zeus wrestled him to the ground. A soldier dismounted and ran to his leader's rescue. Not risking a shot in fear of hitting his sergeant, the private swung the butt of his rifle and caught Zeus alongside his head, rendering him unconscious.

Believing the wolf was dead, the wounded sergeant pushed him off and gave orders to tie Anita's hands. She gave no resistance and walked to the fort, surrounded by soldiers who followed the bleeding sergeant.

# Chapter 26

After ushering his prisoners into the brig, Nichols strutted up to the commander's office. "I had to add a few white people to the arrest, but they had it coming. They either interfered or questioned my authority, and I will not stand for that."

"White people? Who?" asked Wadsworth.

Two of them are squaw men, one of which is your own Corporal Thorton, and the other is that red-headed trapper. And there is an old woman that butted into my business and insisted that she be arrested too, so I was glad to oblige."

"An old woman you say?" asked Wadsworth.

"Yes, all she would give me is her first name, Olivia. Just wait until her husband finds out and has to come and bail her out of jail. I haven't decided on how much the fine will be, but I'll make it steep enough that she won't be trying that again anytime soon," Nichols smirked.

Wadsworth was on his feet, "Olivia? Olivia arrested?"

"Yeah, do you know her? I'll bet her husband will be furious with her."

With a calm but shaking voice, Wadsworth said, "I know for a fact that he is very furious, but not at her. Sgt. Wilson, will you go down and retrieve *my wife* from the brig?"

"Your...*wife*?"

"Yes, you *idiot*! My WIFE!" the commander bellowed.

At the commanders' raised voice his wolf Sashay was on her feet, searching to see what had upset her human.

"Well...uh...she was interfering with..."

"I don't give a rat's ass what she was interfering with, you have over-extended your authority and I am reporting you to the superiors you think so highly of...Now get out!

Get out of my office right now...AND STAY OUT! Sgt. Wilson! Get me some paper and pen, and stay close; I've a telegram for you to send to headquarters right away."

Zeroing in on the source that upset her human, Sashay snarled and took a cautionary step toward her foe.

Nichols, remembering the ankle biting from Smithy's Orphy, and the threatening growl from the Hamilton's Tory, sprang to his feet and streaked across the floor. Leaning forward he reached for the doorknob. Sashay's primal instinct kicked in and she went into attack mode, thinking her prey was escaping. She nailed him in the back of the leg and he went down screaming in pain. "Get that wolf off me! You are all crazy. Wolves everywhere! I'll have them all shot!"

Commander Wadsworth called Sashay off and she came back to him, then followed on his heels as he went to Nichols. Looking down at him he quietly stated, "First off, you will not shoot her. Any fool knows you do not run from a wild animal." Then the commander stepped over him and hurried to the brig with Sashay right behind him.

When he got there he was met by a smiling Olivia. "Oh, my dear, Frederick, don't look so upset. I was perfectly safe with Mr. Adams and Corporal Thorton protecting me. It was all quite exciting. I've never been arrested before."

"Olivia, you are so amazing sometimes. Any other woman would be throwing a hissy fit and screaming to the heavens. You are truly a trooper my dear. All of you, come on out of there. Sergeant, open the doors and let the prisoners have their freedom. As long as I have a say in it."

Gabe, Thomas and Olivia came out and the door was left open for the Indians to go about their business as usual. The prisoners that Nichols had marched in earlier were stunned, not only to see that they were allowed to roam the fort at free will, but also because Thorton spoke to each tribe in their own tongue and emphasized that as long as there was no trouble, they could use the facilities and rest where they were most comfortable.

Gabe found Anita sitting among Soaring Eagle's clan and pulled her to him. "I'm so sorry, my sweet wife. I will see what I can do to clear this whole matter up. Don't worry about Gigi. The Hamilton's stood up to the soldiers and said she was their daughter. Please don't be upset. She will be better off with them for now, until we can be together as a family again. Do you mind…that she is not with you?"

"No, husband. I want best for Gigi. She better off not be Indian. I will tell them 'Gigi dead. Long time back'. I happy for her. I would not be happy if she here."

"I'm going to meet with the commander now. Do you want to come with me or visit with the clan members Nichols brought?" he asked.

"I visit awhile. I no see them for long time."

"Alright, I'll be back a little later. We have to find out where we stand in this whole thing."

When the men met with Commander Wadsworth he was shaking his head and pacing his office with both hands clasped behind his back.

"I've telegraphed Army Headquarters and their reply is not good. I'm sorry to say that there's nothing I can do to stop this insanity. I knew something was happening for months but was not sure what. It is public knowledge that when Andrew Jackson was president he was a strong advocate of eliminating the Indian population. He wants their land for white settlers and the man that followed him is of the same mind."

"Where does that leave Ellen, Anita, Rebecca and Gigi? Can Nichols take white men's wives and children that are half white?"

"Yes, I'm afraid so. If they can trace any blood line of Indian descent, then Nichols is free to remove them." The commander sat heavily in his chair, and staring at the map on his wall he added, "This is a sad day in the history of humanity."

# Chapter 27

"Frederick, there has to be something we can do. The Hamiltons made a bold move when they claimed Gigi, but it was a great idea. Mr. Adams says that his wife Anita goes along with this and is glad for her daughter. She said she would tell them that her daughter died. Bless her soul, how many other mothers could say such a thing? Will you verify it in your record book that the girl died?"

"Olivia, love, you know that you are asking me to do something I can't. That would be bearing false witness and you know the Lord does not approve. I want her as safe as everyone, God knows I like the girl very much, but these are records entrusted to me to be correct and accurate. As much as I am disillusioned by the Army that I've served these past 40 years, I can't dishonor it. It's asking me to abandon my loyalty, my legal obligation and my morality...not to mention my oath to God to always do what is right and just."

"I know. I know, but there has to be something we can do. What is going on is morally wrong." She paced the floor and rubbed her hands until she suddenly stopped and approached his chair. "Frederick, didn't you say there were causalities when that man first brought the clan here? Were there any children on that list?"

Seeing where she was going, he called for his secretary, "Sergeant, bring me the records of those that were taken to the mortuary that day...and from the infirmary also. It seems there might have been...I know there was a pregnant woman that died and that was bad enough, but...."

When the files were delivered he and Olivia went straight to them and started searching.

"Here's one…about 11 months old…" she read.

"No, it has to be around 3 or 4 years old," he sighed.

"Frederick! Here's a child, a *girl* child, that was brought in and died shortly afterward from an infection which brought on pneumonia. The doctors couldn't get it under control and she passed away shortly after arrival. For some reason it doesn't list her age. Could you, legally, morally, loyally, with God's blessing, let others *think* it was Gigi?"

"Well, my dear, I cannot control the minds of others and if they tend to believe that it was her…who am I to argue? I'm pretty sure our Good Lord is willing to let this one go. Otherwise, how would you have thought to look into this and then find it? Yes, Olivia, that child could, very well, have been Gigi!"

"Now the biggest question of them all…What would you say if I took "Grace" and moved back to Charlottesville until you retire and join us? She would only be with me until she can be reunited with her parents. I would feel her to be safer there, away from that awful Captain Nichols' prying mind. He is a detestable excuse for a man."

Wadsworth smiled and took Olivia in his arms. "I'll go you one better, my dear. I am fed up with this Army and want no more of it. I've got a 40-year pension and we have our home, the plantation, and that nest egg we've added to yearly…How would you like it if I retire now, and we all go home together?"

"Oh Frederick, can we? Oh, now we have to talk to Mr. Adams, his wife, and of course Gigi herself. She is the most important one of all. Let's ask her if she would be willing to give up everything and come with us…until she is reunited with her parents, of course."

# Chapter 28

"There *has* to be something to stop this madness! We can't let them take our wives! And Becca, my Dear Lord, is pregnant with our baby! There has to be a law, written somewhere…something showing precedence of past cases, that we can use in a letter to the State, or Federal governments...perhaps the Governor of South Carolina? Or the Bureau of Indian Affairs..." demanded, Will.

"Then do what you have to, but do it fast. I don't want Anita to suffer a march of that magnitude," said Gabe.

"And I don't feel the same about Becca?" snapped Will.

"And me about Ellen?" Thomas joined in.

"Yes, of course, I'm sorry but this has me so riled I can't think straight. They are our wives for Heaven's sake!"

"Thomas, can we use the fort's telegraph? That would be the fastest way to communicate our dilemma," asked Will.

"I have to get permission from Commander Wadsworth, but I'm sure he will go for it. He hates what's happening almost as much as we do. He is a God-fearing man and he sees no Christian act in this. More like Nichols is the Devil reincarnate," grumbled Thomas.

"You talk to him while I go check on Zeus. When I went to the cabins, I found him all bloody and near dead in the garden. That must have been where the soldiers found Anita and he tried to protect her. I brought him to Smithy's on the sled and after getting him cleaned up I found a gash on the top of his head that I sewed up. It's going to leave a scar, but that will be his badge of honor. When he came around he was a bit disoriented, but he's doing much better now. I saw a soldier with a bandaged arm. I'm pretty sure it was from Zeus. When I get back I'm going to see if there is a drop of decency in Nichols. I will volunteer to go with the family and keep them safe," said Gabe.

"I can volunteer as a soldier and go along, too. He can't refuse more help," declared Thomas.

They found him just inside the gate, ready to mount Puma and ride out to the waiting crowd of prisoners.

"We want to volunteer to go with our families, I can hunt and bring in food each day," offered Gabe.

"And I can help assist you as another guard for the trip," suggested Thomas.

Nichols laughed out loud and swung up on the saddle. "Sorry boys, but neither of you is invited to this party. I wouldn't trust either of you as far as from here to where we are heading. No, that is not in the plan and I forbid it." Looking at Thomas he added, "Remember all of this and then think back to the day you came into that old geezer's office and ridiculed me."

"It was not I that caught you interpreting wrong. It was a visiting officer. I was called in afterwards. You can't blame me for what you did…threatening Soaring Eagle in front of someone who also understood Cherokee…was only *your* doing, so don't lay that blame on me."

"It matters not. Neither of you will be allowed to join the march. There will be enough casualties along the way. I don't want Washington asking me why white men were in the group and how they died. You should be relieved that I am saving you from having heathen savages for wives. Get a new wife…a white woman who can raise your status in life and give you beautiful white children. That is what this country is destined for!" He was yelling his last words as he rode through the fort gates.

The new group of Indians was gathered outside the fort, with Nichols' soldiers carelessly pushing them with the horses into a tighter group. This caused friction among rival tribes that from ancestral time had competed with each other for land and food. Edging them ever closer was like lighting a fuse that was getting shorter by the minute.

Captain Nichols rode proudly on the back of Puma, boldly flaunting that he now had Soaring Eagle's personal horse. Circling the large group, he barked orders to his men, "Tighten ranks, men, tighten ranks!"

Some of the Indians were allowed to drag their small travois with their personal belongings, while women carried their belonging or infants strapped to their backs.

When Nichols first delivered the new group to the fort, Soaring Eagle's clan had found neighboring clans and family members, who now huddled together.

Rebecca reunited with her brother, Jumping Fox and his wife Moon Star, and was excited to see they had a three-year-old son. She was doubly excited to hear that they had honored her with one of his names being, 'Blue'. Fox smiled and said, "That is Badger for a strong fierce manly name and Blue because of your warrior spirit; therefore we named him Badger Blue."

Blue told them about the new English names that she, Squirrel and Sparrow now used, then about her pregnancy, which they were delighted to hear, under the circumstances. Then she described the attack that killed many of their clan as well as their mother, and left their father confused.

When asked why Gigi wasn't there, Becca looked around, and seeing there were no soldiers within hearing distance, explained that situation.

Fox shook his head, "I'm not sure I can remember to call you by your new names. Everything is so mixed up. None of us fought back either. None of us deserve this. I know they promise us land and a place to live free, but I don't trust the white man. They are liars and thieves."

"Yes, brother, but *that* one…the one in charge…" pointing to Nichols, "is the worst. He is the one that led the attack that killed our mother. We also heard from Tome-us that he threatened Soaring Eagle with raping us women and castrating our men, while pretending to interpret for Commander Wadsworth. He has no heart…no human emotions. He may carry out those threats once we are away from here." She touched the blowpipe tucked into her belt and added, "When I find a place and time, I will bring justice for our mother."

Looking at the blowpipe, Fox said, "I see you are still the warrior sister that I grew up with. Is it accurate as small as it is? Do you not fear that they will find it and punish you?"

"It is accurate, although it took more practice because of its size, and it is not only me that carries one, but Anita and Ellen too. I taught them and we have learned to bring down small game for the cooking pot. And no, these whites have no idea what it is."

Jumping Fox's eyes narrowed when he fixed them on the man riding Puma. Nodding slowly he said, "You leave that man to me, little sister. It is my right to uphold the family honor and I will see to it that he pays dearly."

Nichols watched the three husbands who came to the group and sought out their wives. He saw the fort soldiers shaking hands with the men in this clan and smirked, *they should all be shot for treason against the government. I wish Jackson was still the president; he would send these soldiers packing. And these squaw men...good heavens, how can they live with themselves, going against what is right and holy in the eyes of the law and all that is sacred? It gives me the creeps to even think of bedding down with one of these savages.*

Gabe held Anita and whispered, "Remember the animal sounds we practiced? When you hear the Owl you will know that I'm close by, the Crow will be for you to come and I will have food for you. When you hear the Dove, it will remind you that I love you and am working on a plan for your escape. The Chickadee call will tell you the plan is ready and for you to come. If just one of you leaves at a time, they won't notice, and we can all be together again. We will go far away."

"Yes, my husband. I will answer your dove call, and I wait for time that we go far from all who do this to us. You pray to your God, and I pray to my Yowa that the great chief in Washington will help."

Will was embracing Becca and telling her of the work he was doing to get this all settled and behind them, "Stay close to Jumping Fox and your family, Gabe and I are planning on following; out of sight of the soldiers."

"But how will you know if word comes that we can be together? Use the big school learning, and search for ways to help us...for the sake of our baby, Will-yum. Promise me...you will stay and fight. I will be fine with most of our old clan together again. We will watch out for one another, but I need to know you are trying to make it so we never have to go through this again. Promise me," begged Becca.

"I can't promise that. I need to know that you are well. I want no harm to come to you or our baby. I will promise to do what I can here, but if it looks like I'm not going to get the answer we want, I will be on the trail to you as fast as lightning flashes across a dark sky. One way or another, Blue girl, my love, we *will* be together and never separated again," Will's voice choked with emotion.

Thomas joined the group. "Ellen, honey, I love you. You must know that I will follow you, I am quitting the army. I can't stay, knowing that the army is responsible for what is happening to you. You belong with me and not out there. I'm waiting for answers now from the telegrams I sent, but who knows what they will say or when they will come."

"No, Tome-us…you must stay here and keep sending more messages to your Army chiefs. They have to know what they are doing is wrong, and that families belong together. You have to tell them, my husband. You *have* to make them understand," demanded Ellen.

Thomas just held her as tight as he could and said, "I love you. Stay strong. I will come after you. Let's not argue."

"Sergeant, have you searched the fort thoroughly? I want no Indian left behind!" demanded Nichols. *I will make them suffer for the humiliation they put me through years ago.*
With his arm in a sling from his encounter with Zeus, the sergeant tried to salute, "Yes, Sir, Captain Nichols, Sir. I searched every inch of it. They're all here. The Indians are now in our charge and ready to go to the next destination."

Standing high in his stirrups, Captain Nichols brandished his sword and raised his arm above his head and waved it forward, as he shouted, "FORWARD, MEN, FORWARD!"

With heads hanging low the prisoners moved slowly, hesitant to leave the fort and the humane treatment that they had received from the soldiers. Their shuffling feet stirred up a cloud of dust as they were forced forward.

Nichols came forward on Puma and smilingly pushed his way between the men and their wives, forcing them into the crowd.

The men were helpless as their wives were hustled even further into the crowd and ushered into the perimeter of mounted army guards. The devastated men turned and faced each other with clenched jaws and fists…and unashamed tears.

# Chapter 29

"Mr. Adams, I'm sure you are wondering why we have called you here. I assure you that it is nothing negative. I'm glad you brought Gigi, for this applies mostly to her."

"Well, I'm all ears," said Gabe

"Me too. I am wondering," chimed in Gigi.

Olivia started the conversation, "Well, this has taken some thought and I'm sure it will for you too, but Commander Wadsworth and I, have discussed the possibility of...taking Gigi to a safer place to live. That is until you and your wife are reunited, of course. The commander has decided to retire, and we are planning on moving back to Charlottesville. It really isn't that far away, you could visit occasionally and we would give her the very best that we can give. We have found in the fort records, of the first attack on the clan that a young Indian child passed away after arriving here and we thought it would be a good way for Gigi to turn into 'Grace' like Mrs. Hamilton conjured up.

"Mr. Adams, we know that you and William will be going after Anita and Rebecca. And I'm sure you will have our own Corporal Thorton right there beside you to get his Ellen back. I understand that William is searching his law books for the legalities, just as Thomas is beseeching the Army about his wife. We wish you the very best in retrieving your wives from that awful man. But until you do, I can't justify Gigi being left here. I'm also sure that the Hamiltons could give her a good home, but we can give her far more. She can go to any school, learn any vocation or none at all. She can continue with her piano, or any instrument...or dance, or anything that she feels drawn to…it can all be hers, if she's willing to join us. Our home is large…some call it a mansion, but it was handed down from my mother's side of the family and has been my home since birth. The plantation grows fields of cotton, corn and wheat. It's truly a lovely place."

"Charlottesville, Virginia, that is a whole state away," murmured Gabe.

"Yes, but you can't take her with you, never knowing what kind of disasters might befall. It's not that far by train. And I have to reiterate, it would only be until you all get back together. We are trying to do what is best for her safety while you are away," Olivia added.

"Well, it's a lot to think…and talk about. And as you said, as soon as Will comes up with a legal solution, or even if not, we *will* be going after our wives. Give Gigi and me until tomorrow and we'll give you an answer. I'm near crazy wanting to go after my wife as soon as possible. We have no idea what is happening out there on the trail."

"Mr. Adams, if you wish to hear my view on the subject, I will tell you that I would be honored to keep your daughter safe from harm and away from the laws that are demanding all people of Indian descent be placed on a reservation. It makes no sense to me, and I'm sure not to my loving God. So if you both agree to this, I will do all in my power to right the injustice this world is now guilty of, if only to one family," stated Commander Wadsworth.

They all stood and the men shook hands, "We'll let you know tomorrow. I know I would prefer Gigi being with you two, but it will be entirely up to her." With that said, he took Gigi's arm and guided her to the door. Olivia reached out and gave Gigi a warm hug, "Until tomorrow, dear."

119

# Chapter 30

The trail was moderately passable with Nichols choosing the available and obvious trails. The walking was something that Becca's clan was not accustomed to since their incarceration at the fort. At first being bunched tightly together made the pace awkward…either someone ahead walked too slowly or someone pushed from behind. But eventually it evolved with the younger ones in the lead, and the elders following, and the procession changed its form from a packed oval to a long thin ribbon.

The first few days found the families reacquainting and time passed quickly. At night those who had dwellings to erect, did so, while others laid out bedding on the ground. The early fall days and nights were still warm enough to be comfortable and food was sufficient.

The guards had it different, with one large tent and a cot for each soldier. Captain Nichols had separate quarters.

Campfires were built and meals were cooked. The Indians formed a line and held out their individual bowls as they passed the pot. If they had no bowl, one was supplied but it had to be cleaned before returning it.

After a week on the trail an officer approached Nichols, "How much further to the next fort, Captain Nichols?"

"Protocol, soldier, protocol!" demanded his superior.

"Yes, Sir, Captain Nichols, sir," answered the sergeant with a brisk click of his heels and sharp salute.

"That's better. At ease, Sergeant. I've been going over this map and according to our guide it looks like we are making only three miles per day. That is unacceptable. At this rate it will take us months to get there."

"Where, Captain?"

"Charleston, Tennessee," answered Nichols.

"Is that our destination…Sir?" asked the sergeant.

"Yes. I've been designated to cover the area from Charlotte, North Carolina to Charleston, Tennessee. That's a lot of miles and a lot of Indians. But if I had my way I would stay with this project clear to Oklahoma Territory. I agree with Jackson and Van Buren that it would be best to drive these redskins completely off the face of the earth. I'm going to be famous for eliminating this infestation and show how much better I am that the others who couldn't even get all them rounded up the first time. I'm more thorough and my success will be recognized and I will be raised in rank and someday become a famous General…or even President! But at this rate, we'll still be traveling through the winter."

"I don't know how we can drive them any faster. Many are old and some have children that have to be carried. Since this first began we've covered a lot of miles and the men are getting tired to the bone. The Indians are becoming irritable and starting to fight amongst themselves, and some are stealing from others. It's hard to control them."

"That's *your* problem, sergeant. That's why you have those stripes on your sleeve. Now earn them. Make a public proclamation that if one of them is caught stealing, he will get his hand chopped off…then *do* it! That should show them we mean business and they will fear us even more."

"But Sir, the infirmary has its hands full just keeping up with the dysentery and injuries derived from the march. They are not set up to do amputations."

"Who says it has to be surgical? Chop it off with a bayonet right in front of everyone. Then stop the blood by searing it with a burning stick from the bonfire. I'm telling you that if you want these heathens to respect your authority, you have to show them you mean business!"

"But that might make them all rise up against us and we are so few…"

"See how stupid they are? They could overtake us at any second and they don't even know it. Makes it even more exciting, doesn't it! Just keep an eye on the leaders mostly; perhaps have your men be designated to certain individuals, but I'm not worried. They are an ignorant lot, sergeant. Hell, they didn't even know what to do with the gold found on their lands…imagine that!"

"Yes, Sir…Imagine that," the sergeant said as he turned to go back to the guard's tent.

"Protocol, Sergeant, Protocol!" snapped Nichols.

"Yes, Sir, Captain Nichols, Sir. May I be excused to tend to my men, Sir?" barked the sergeant.

Smiling and nodding, Nichols stated, "Yes, Sergeant, you may be excused."

As he turned and walked toward the guard's tent the sergeant's expression changed to complete disgust and utter disrespect for his so-called superior. *He's gone totally mad. He's irrational and should be replaced.*

# Chapter 31

"If I can't go with you, then I will go to live with the Commander and Olivia. But Papa, I could help you on the trail. I know I could. I know all the animal calls and I know how to find food in the forest. You know I can. You and Becca taught me many things. I want…"

"It's not always what we want, my sweet, sweet Gigi. It's what is best for all concerned and that means you too. I *know* you are capable of many things, and yes, because I taught you those things. But you have to realize that I will be traveling fast and over rugged terrain, with no roof over my head or food in my belly at times. I remember how I survived being a trapper…a mountain man some call it. You have not had to do those things and I don't want you to ever have to…"

"But Papa, you can't travel as fast as you used to because of your foot. What if a bear attacked you? You won't be able to run and get away."

"And that's another point. If a bear were to attack, what could you possibly do?"

"I have this," she pulled the six-inch blowgun from her pocket. "Becca taught me. I know how to make it and the darts. I have brought food to the pot by killing rabbits."

"Yes, honey, *rabbits*. Compared to a bear? Those darts would only make him angrier and more set on killing than before he was stung with one. Don't get me wrong. I'm very proud of you knowing how to make and use it and how to replace the darts…all of those things, but they are not for defense. They are for hunting small game…maybe even might bring down a small deer if it hits the right spot, but not a bear. Please, Gigi, listen to me. Go with the

Wadworths and stay where I will know you are safe. It will give me less to worry about, I assure you. You and your mother are the loves of my life and I want you both to be safe and secure. So please, for *me*, do this so I can go and help your mother. She needs me now, and I can concentrate on helping her as long as I know you are safe. Who knows if there are others like Nichols that might find out you have Indian blood and drag you away, maybe even to a different place. If you are living with the Wadworths, as a genteel lady, no one will ever know."

"But I'm proud of my Indian blood, Papa. I'm proud to be mother's daughter. The Hamiltons and the Wadworths know and they accept me."

He took her in his arms and cradled her. "I'm proud of you too, sweetheart. And proud of your mother, but there are those that don't understand and they are ignorant. The Hamiltons and Wadworths are good Christian people that have love in their hearts for all God's children. You are learning a hard lesson right now, and I wish I could protect you from all this, but I can't. Please understand…remember how the clan treated you and your mother, because you were half white? That is the same with some white people. They will shun you, too. So once you go, you must never tell…anyone…that you are half Indian. Promise me."

"Ok, Papa. But it's not right."

"I know, baby…but it's so. Now let's pack your things and go talk to the Commander and Olivia. They are waiting for your answer."

Zeus followed close behind Gabe as he took Gigi and her belongings to the fort. The wolf approached Sashay and lay down beside her. Gabe gave Gigi a kiss and told her he would see her tomorrow. Then he turned to the couple, "I still have plans to make with William and Thomas. I don't know if either of them will join me, but decisions have to be made as soon as possible."

"I understand, Mr. Adams, I believe you will find Thomas in his quarters, or hovering over that telegraph machine at his desk. Olivia and Gigi will be on the next train heading east and I will join them as soon as I get my retirement papers and my replacement arrives. Leave Zeus here. I will make sure that he and Sashay join me when I leave…or you return for him."

Gabe quickly wrote down the commands he had taught Zeus and said, "If word comes that the wives will be legally freed from this ordeal, then tell Zeus *this one*" pointing to *find*, "then say my name. When he finds me, and I know he will, then I will know we can return. If there is a problem, attach a message to his collar. I can't thank you enough for this. I will find you in Charlottesville and reunite my family." The men shook hands and Gabe gave Gigi another hug and kiss then cupped Zeus' head in his hands, tussled his ruff, gave him a pat on the back and left.

It was not Thomas but Will at the telegraph. Gabe startled him by blurting out, "I can't wait any longer. I'm going to find Anita. We can wait for answers and never receive one. I can't handle not knowing."

"You think I don't want to be within sight of Becca? She made me promise to get answers! Thomas is sending messages daily to whomever we think might have some power, or someone who could persuade those who do. The answer *may* come by this telegraph," Will snapped.

"Yes, I know. I'm sorry, but I have to go! I'm going out of my mind with worry. Now that Gigi's settled, and the commander has Zeus…besides, the trail might vanish…"

"Oh, please. A group that big will leave a swath so wide you could drive a herd of buffalo through it! And before you go getting crazy on me, I am entirely on your side and I hear what you are saying. We followed our women before when they were prisoners, we can do it again. Can you wait until I get my bedroll packed?"

"You're not leaving me behind," stated a voice behind them. It was Thomas holding a small suitcase. "The commander talked me into just taking a leave-of-absence instead of quitting the army, and I'm ready…"

"Well, first off, get rid of *that* thing," pointing to the luggage. "Roll a change of clothes and your personals into a blanket and tie it off. That, along with your gun and knife…that's all you'll need," said Gabe. "And if you're waiting for me, we're burning daylight."

# Chapter 32

"Ms Evans, have you seen Gigi or her father today? They weren't in church and I fear perhaps something may be amiss."

"No, but I'm sure she will show up tomorrow. She is never late for school and is doing remarkably well. She is a gifted child, that's for sure."

"Yes, I thought as much, myself. I was wondering how she was coming along with her piano lessons. She stops by now and again just to listen to me play the organ. I have enjoyed her visits, even though she says very little. It's a joy to see someone appreciate music the way she does. She seems to feel it more than hear it..." Then mainly to himself he added, "Yes, very gifted," as he slowly turned and headed toward Smithy's Livery.

"Mr. Smithy, have you seen Gigi or Mr. Adams today? They missed church this morning and I got worried."

Smithy smiled and said, "Jess call me *Smithy*, yon man, no *Mr*, hea'. But naw suh, ain't seed hi'e ner hair of 'em dis day." He knew about the arrests and that Gigi had boarded the train with Mrs. Wadsworth, but he also knew to keep his good friends' secrets to himself. Shaking his head he added, "Ya jest nebber no when dey's gonna sho up! But I be's tellin' 'em dat ya lookn' fer 'em nex' time I sees 'em."

"Thank you Mr..uh...Smithy...I'd appreciate it,"

His next stop was the trading post, "Mrs. Hamilton, have you seen Mr. Adams or his daughter lately? I missed them in church this morning and wonder if they are alright."

"Not since last week. Didn't you hear about the ruckus those soldiers put us through? They came storming in here and arrested Mr. Adams, Mr. and Mrs. Thorton, Mr. and

Mrs. Hudson and Mrs. Wadsworth, then marched all of them to the fort under guard."

"What on earth for?"

"The officer had 'Presidential Papers' to arrest anyone with Indian blood. They are all to be removed further west, across the Mississippi River! Can you imagine that?"

"That's utter nonsense, and why Mrs. Wadsworth and the men? They are white people."

"Because they were protesting the arrest and it got them arrested too. That officer even threatened to kill Tory! I was able to protect Gigi, or he would have taken her too."

"Gigi? Why Gigi? Was she protesting the arrest too?"

Charles came out from the backroom quickly and took Dory by the elbow, "Dory, I need you in the back room."

"But I'm talking to…" she argued.

He stated sternly, "I *need* you in the backroom *now*, Dory. There's a problem with some supplies. If you will excuse us Pastor, we have a problem that needs Dory's attention."

"Oh, of course, thank you. But do you know where Gigi is now…and the rest? I'd like to help, if I can…"

"If we find out more we'll let you know," Charles said as he pulled Dory to the back room and closed the door.

"*Charles*, what on earth is wrong with you? Really, you were rather rude to the pastor."

Lowering his voice to a whisper, he said, "Dory, didn't you understand his question? He doesn't *know* about Gigi."

She looked up at him in disbelief, "All this time and he hasn't known? But I'm sure he can be trusted, he's a man of the cloth."

"It is best that *no one* ever finds out about Gigi. I know you care for her…as do I…so you must keep quiet about her

128

mother. Gigi would be sent away to a reservation just like the others. We shouldn't even tell people that she has gone to live with the Wadworths now."

"I don't know why she couldn't have stayed here with us. She loves it here and loves helping out in the store."

"Gabe was trying to protect us too, because of what that officer said about coming back and investigating further, and if he found out we were lying he would arrest us too. It's better this way. We all know that she will be safe with them, away from here and those who might know."

"Do you know if they have left yet? I see the Wadsworth's belongings on the train dock almost daily, but I haven't seen them board the train. I would like to bundle up a few things for Gigi to take with her to remember us by. Maybe some beads for her jewelry making," said Dory.

"Dory, honey, think about it. She won't be making Indian beaded jewelry anymore. How would she explain it to the elite society that the Wadsworths belong to? She is going to have to live totally as a white person in order to survive. I'm sure she will get the best of everything from now on. That's what you want...isn't it?"

"Yes, dear, I do...I really do."

Charles' actions were suspicious, so Chandler waited until they had closed the door before he moved quickly to hear what he could from the other side. He was only able to make out a few words, s*ent away, investigation, arrest, live with the Wadsworths....* Just then a customer walked in and he had to scurry away from the door and quickly leave the store. As he left he thought, *what is so secretive about Gigi? At least I know now that she was sent away to live with the Wadsworths...why? I will get to the bottom of this.*

# Chapter 33

Rebecca was being called both 'Becca' and 'Blue' depending on which clan she was speaking with. The ones not knowing her new English name, did not understand why she would change it and the ones from the fort were used to it. The guards didn't get personally involved, with any of the prisoners, so it was "YOU there...keep up," or "Squaw, fetch me some water!"

Anita was doing well to keep up; with nothing much to say, but Ellen was miserable and would not stop muttering under her breath. Becca tried to keep an eye on her father lest a guard might yell at him and worsen his anxiety.

Jumping Fox and Moon Star, with the baby, stayed close and they all tried to help each other.

Becca tried to comfort those she felt in need, with a smile or help with their load when she saw them lagging. She had pulled up the front of her dress, by reaching backward and grabbing the back hem and pulling it forward between her legs and tucking it into the front of her belt. This gave her a style of pants with a front pocket for gathering food items she found along the way, such as mushrooms or berries.

"Blue, you have to slow down and take it easy. Do not burden yourself with everyone who is unable to keep up. You have to think of the baby. You'll lose it if you don't," warned Moon Star. "I want little Badger to have a cousin and playmate later."

"I can't help it. They are pushing us too hard. They have to understand. The elders, and the young...they can't keep up this pace. We've already lost some and it should not be so," said Becca.

"I know, sister, but there's nothing you can do to change things," said Jumping Fox. "It's hard enough keeping up with our father…oh, no…he's gone again!"

As the search began to find Swift Arrow, a piercing whistle filled the air and started a ruckus ahead. "Get back with the rest, you old fool! Go now! You have to stay with the group," yelled a guard.

"It's Father, I know it is!" exclaimed, Fox.

"Wait here…I'll find out what's happening," said Becca.

Reaching the whistler she found her father surrounded by soldiers, "What's going on here? What has he done that you would treat him like this?" She demanded of a guard.

"He was trying to escape. I found him hiding over in the bushes," blurted the guard.

"He wasn't trying to escape! He just wandered off. He's sick in the head and that shrill whistle makes it worse…."

"Just keep him inside the perimeter or else!" He shouted.

Becca took her father by the arm and led him back to the rest of the family. "We've got to think of something. They may shoot him next time."

Swift Arrow leaned in and whispered to Jumping Fox, "I have to go."

"No father, you can't go. You have to stay," said Fox.

"No, I have to go."

"Where father? Where do you have to go?"

"You know…GO…I have to go," pointing to his crotch.

"OH, oh, Ok. I will talk to the guard and explain. Father, go with Fox and we'll see what I can do."

After explaining that her father was only trying to find privacy to relieve himself, the guard looked down his nose and nodded. "After this, you control that old man before he gets himself killed. We don't have time to be chasing all over these hills for runaways. We have orders to 'just shoot them'," explained the guard.

"Thank you for understanding. I'll figure something out so it won't happen again," said Becca.

When the two returned to the family, Fox found a rope in their belongings and tied one end around his father's belt and the other around his own wrist, with a ten foot slack,

"Now I have to make sure he doesn't get all tangled around someone. Maybe we can take turns?" he asked.

"Of course, we all will," answered Moon Star.

Anita caught up to Fox and held out her hand, "I take."

Fox nodded and undid the rope from his wrist and handed it to her, "Thank you, Squirrel."

Ellen whined, "I've got enough to do with both my parents. They are always lagging behind and I have to help with their travois…"

"That's alright, we understand. We each have our own responsibilities, and it doesn't look like it's going to get any easier in the days ahead," said Becca

"Stop all that jabbering! Save your breath for walking, you're all going to need it crossing those mountains!" ordered a guard as he pointed ahead.

They all looked up and saw a span of white-covered mountains looming in the distance.

# Chapter 34

The men had kept up a steady pace and were closing the gap between them and the clan. They each had thoughts they didn't want to share;

Gabe was feeling his age and his foot was now shooting stabbing pains with every step, but he refused to let the younger men know. *I am not going to slow us down. We have not only to catch up, but find our loved ones somewhere in that group and then make a plan of escape.*

Will was fighting for air and his lungs were on fire. His legs were beginning to feel like rubber and he found himself not in complete control of each step. *I can't let them know that I'm not in the physical condition that I was when I was younger. The blacksmith shop has made my upper body stronger, but I haven't had to run like this before. Trapping had no running involved, but a lot of backbreaking labor with wet and cold days. Now I do more sweating beside that furnace than I ever knew possible.*

Thomas felt physically ill from his lower stomach to his throat; fighting nausea and dizziness was taking most of his strength. *I've never run this far, this fast, for so long in my life. But I can't be the one to hold us back from reaching our wives. I'm afraid I'm either going to faint or vomit and I'm not sure which will come first.*

Their dilemma was solved when they heard a shrill whistle. They stopped in unison and stood as quietly as their lungs would permit. Each slowly lowered his body to the ground, and looking at each other they knew, and smiled. Gabe whispered between deep breaths, "We aren't as young as we used to be."

The other two could only nod between gasps.

After regaining their breaths they quietly moved off the larger path and advanced through the thicker woods, alongside the caravan.

Dusk was falling and Captain Nichols called a halt for the day. Each Indian tribe or clan made a personal campsite, according to their customs and settled down for the night.

When Gabe decided he could give his first call, he gave the family's rendition of their owl signal, and waited. Receiving no answer, the men moved further along and gave another, and waited, but still nothing. After the third call he heard a faint answer. They moved still further along and he gave another…the answer told him, *That's Anita! She's close by and knows I'm here. It's time to plan on getting them out of there.*

Will was watching Gabe closely and knew the minute he realized the answer was from Anita…his smile told it all.

Gabe motioned for the men to follow and they moved further away from the procession, away from wandering guards.

*Now that she knows we are here, we can set our snares and bring them food. I will signal Anita then. She will know to come to the sound and we will give her the animal. It will be up to her to explain how she got it, but I'm sure they have devised a plan that will keep them safe.*

# Chapter 35

Once the train started moving Gigi fell into the rhythm of its rocking motion and found she could balance herself quite well and after exchanging whispers and a nod from the conductor, Olivia felt she could let her ward explore, so she settled herself comfortably and relaxed.

Gigi was in awe of everything, beginning with each of the cars having different functions. One had two rows of two connected chairs bolted to the floor, all facing the same way, separated with a walkway between them. Another had small tables with one side bolted to the wall of the car and heavy movable chairs around them. Another car had built-in-beds, one above the other running lengthwise of the train, with curtains for privacy. Other cars were connected to the sleeping car, but the conductor said they were for 'baggage', and she recalled seeing some of the Wadsworth's furniture and their trunks being loaded into it.

When Gigi's curiosity was satisfied, she returned to Olivia and took the empty seat beside her. Olivia had left the window seat free so the girl could enjoy the view of the countryside as they passed through it.

"Well, Grace, my dear, what do you think of the trip so far?" asked Olivia.

"Oh, Mrs. Wadsworth, ever thing, so fun."

Lowering her voice, Olivia said, "Since we are away from the fort and all who knew us there, we should decide on a new name you can call me."

"But Papa say I should always mind my manners."

"Yes, but we don't have to be so formal now. You must get used to being called, 'Grace'…for your own protection. I think it would be a good idea if we pretend that you are my niece. So you can call me 'Aunt Olivia', or 'Aunty' for short. We must always be on guard that someone can still arrest you, if they find out about your Indian blood."

"What is niece?"

"That would be a child born to one of the commander's or my, siblings."

"What is sibling?"

"A sibling is a sister or brother."

"We make up story? We pretend and have fun?"

Keeping her voice low, Olivia answered, "Grace, Yes, we will pretend, but not for fun. We must make others *believe* what we pretend. It is very serious and must be believable."

"Yes, so…why I am at fort when you find me?"

Pausing between thoughts, Olivia said, "Maybe…you could have been sent there…after both your parents died…a child of a sibling of the Commander who lived deep in the Appalachian Mountains…that could explain your lack of schooling."

Getting into the spirit of the story, Grace responded, "Pretend they die of big bear who came to eat them."

Not wanting to quell the girl's enthusiasm, Olivia nodded, "That could happen, but maybe something less dramatic. Maybe…let's say…they got sick. A fever, like the one your father had when he broke his leg. The doctor said he almost died…right?"

Nodding Grace agreed, "Mama said, too."

"Well, then let's say they got a fever and died and a friend of theirs knew about Frederick…Mr. Wadsworth… being the only relative. And since he was living at the fort, they sent you there. We will say that you were too young to remember and can't answer any more questions."

"What we say when Papa comes for me? People see our hair and eyes..."

Olivia sighed, "Oh yes, there is that. Well, then, how about this...your Papa is your make-believe father's brother...your uncle, and the brothers had the same color hair and eyes, and you were sent to him but he couldn't keep you because he was a trapper and mountain man. OH, and he had an Indian woman who took care of you. That just might work. Let's go with that...just until he shows up and you can get back together."

With that settled, 'Grace' turned back to the window to see more wonders unfold as the train sped across the crop fields of cotton, tobacco and indigo with workers that reminded her of Smithy.

Beginning her new life of 'pretend' she asked, "Aunt Olivia, do all those people own those farms?"

"The farms are called plantations, and those people are working for the owners."

"You mean like Will works for Smithy...and me for the Hamiltons? Do they get paid much?"

"Not much. Some just work for their room and board."

"What is that?"

"It means for a place to live and food to eat."

"Miss Evans was teaching about slaves...are they?"

"No, Grace, She should have taught you that slavery ended in 1863 when President Abraham Lincoln signed the Emancipation Proclamation that set all slaves free."

"What is that emansuh..."

"It is a law, of sorts, that says that all slaves were to be set free and that no one can own slaves ever again."

"You told Papa that you have a plan-ta-shun. Did you have slaves?"

"My father and grandfather before him did, but the slaves were cared for in a Christian manner and never mistreated. Some even asked my father if they could stay after being freed, but after the war there was little money left to pay them, so they chose to work for room and board. Others contracted to share-crop parts of the plantation."

"What is share crop?"

"That is when a worker lives on a piece of land as if it were his own, then gives part of what he earned, from the sale of his crops to the property owner." Whitmore now, has sharecroppers that are descendants of slaves.

"What is Whit more?"

"Actually it's called Whitmore Plantation, named after my family. Whitmore is my mother's parents' name and her maiden name and why I inherited it after she died."

"What is in-hair-it-ted?"

Olivia slowly closed her eyes; *I've forgotten how full of questions a child can be. Grace may not be considered a child by her age, but she is in her schooling.* Taking a deep breath and letting it out slowly she answered, "That is when a person dies and wants certain items to go to certain people, so he writes it down."

Olivia's expression was much like that of Papa's when he was tired of questions and wanted peace and quiet, so Grace turned back to the window and watched in wonder as scene after scene scrolled by.

# Chapter 36

Zeus was confused about his humans. *Why did they leave me in a place with walls so I could not follow? Although these humans are nice, and the presence of Sashay is somewhat calming, I have to find my humans. The one called Gabe gave the command to 'stay' and I've done so, but this has been far too long.*

He rose from his place beside Sashay and began to pace the Commander's quarters. Sashay stirred when he nudged her, *Sashay, I have to go. I have to find my humans. They may need me. They have never been this long without me and they may be in trouble. Do you want to come with me?*

Sashay bumped his chin with her nose, *Zeus, my man human is here and if I leave he may need me. I'm sure that Tory and Orphy will feel the same. We have our families that need us.*

Zeus gave a hard 'huff' and stared at her.

She stared back, *Don't give me that look, You would do the same if it were one of us asking. Would you leave your humans to go off...who knows where...and leave them alone? No! So don't get 'huffy' with me. When you get back we can get Tory and Orphy and go for a fun run.*

Thoroughly disgusted, Zeus turned and walked to the door. *At least they will let me out of this room to do my personals, so maybe he will open the door and I can find some way to escape.*

More than a week had passed since the forced march began, and Commander Wadsworth was in his office hoping for his retirement papers, when an answer to his query about white men's Indian wives arrived.

The document said, in part, the only way for a person with Indian blood to avoid the transfer westward was if they, ".... abandon their own cultures and traditions and adopt Christianity and other Anglo-American ways, such as western habits of dress and farming..." Since he felt this was already the situation for his friends, Wadsworth decided it was time to send Zeus after Gabe.

"Zeus! Here, boy."

*What can the man want?* as he obeyed the command.

"I have a job for you, boy. *Sit!*"

Sgt. Wilson had typed the quoted message and placed it inside an oilskin pouch. When Wadsworth tied it around Zeus' neck, he said, "You must take this to Gabe."

Hearing his human's name, Zeus' ears perked up and he was instantly alert. Wadsworth beckoned Zeus to follow and as they left, Sashay stood and followed them. The three walked to the area where the procession had gathered outside the fort, before the march began.

Wadsworth stooped down and took Zeus' head in his hands; looking him square in the eyes he said in a serious tone, "Zeus, this is very important. You must get this message to Gabe," then he commanded, *"Find Gabe!"*

Zeus immediately pulled away and looked around. Then putting his nose to the ground he raced around the area, *So many smells...is that him? No. Where? I can't quite tell... Over here? Maybe...No. Maybe over there...No. I think... maybe...YES! I've got him! Now to find where he's hiding.*

Looking up, he saw the man and Sashay watching. She showed excitement and shouted, *You found him! I see it on your face. Good job! This is exciting. Do you still want me to come with you? My human has many others to watch him; he will be safe.*

Zeus hesitated, *Changed your mind pretty quick…it's up to you but you'd better decide now because I'm leaving.*

She looked up at her human who was watching them both. He smiled and said, "You want to go too, don't you girl." She pranced around and wagged her tail. "Then go. When you get back we can join Olivia and Grace at your new home. Yes, Go, Sashay!" He waved his hand away from his chest.

The two wolves ran beside each other, following Gabe's scent, which led them first to the livery. Orphy was the first to alert Smithy that they had company. She tried to greet them in the usual manner, but Zeus had no time for it and set to searching for Gabe.

Smithy was surprised at seeing the two without their owners, and asked, "Wha' cha doin' out here's all by yerself's?" He watched as Zeus traced Gabe's scent around the room, and noticed the pouch around his neck. "Wha' cha got dere, Zeus? Lemmie see." Reading and replacing the message, he said, "So, ya on yer way to fetch Gabe wid dis here mes'age. Whal, he aint' here no mo. He dun took off affer his missus."

As the two wolves were leaving, Orphy started to follow. "Orphy. Ya gots ta sta' here wid me. Ya cain't go high steppin out all ober the contry. Sumbody mite think ya a pack o'wild ones an shoot ya."

Hearing her name she turned back to Smithy, then turned again to watch her siblings leaving. She whined and looked back over her shoulder at him. Smithy sighed deep and shook his head, "Whal, if'n it me'ns dat much, ya mite as well go, but ya hurry back. I likes hav'n ya round." He pointed to the departing couple and she responded with a wag of her tail and a leap forward to catch up with them.

*Wait for me guys! My human said I could come along. Are we going to get Tory too?*

*It looks like we're headed that way, if he wants to join us it would be a fun outing,* said Sashay.

*We are going wherever the scent takes us. If it is that way, so be it, but I'm telling you...this is not a fun outing! This is an important mission and I must find my human as fast as possible. None of you had better slow me down,* Zeus stated sternly.

*Oh my, aren't we just full of ourselves, Mr. High and Mighty himself! Well, we'll try real hard to keep up, won't we Orphy!* teased Sashay.

*I'm serious Sashay! Don't make fun of a responsibility that the commander trusts with me. YOU should be the one to obey his wishes; he is your master,* snapped Zeus.

*Whoa, hold it right there, big brother. There is NO ONE that is this girl's master...unless I choose him to be. Huh-uh, no way...not going to happen,* scoffed Sashay.

Orphy joined in, *Would you two just knock it off. There's Tory, out sunbathing on the platform near the mercantile.*

Softly she said to the others, *Boy, look at him, he is putting on some weight.* Louder she said, *Hi, Tory. Want to come with us? We're going on a secret mission to save the world. Zeus has to get some message to one of his humans and we are off to find him. Come on! It will be fun.*

Tory answered, *Is it very far? I have to be home for dinner. I'm pretty sure a new hunk of beef came in today and I want to be there when the man cuts it up. He throws the scraps to me…mmm, so good…* licking his muzzle.

Zeus slowly shook his head and muttered to himself, *Oh, heavenly bone yard, please…*

*Come on, Tory, you look like you can use a little exercise. Get up and come with us*, beckoned Orphy.

Looking back toward the store and then at them, he hesitated. *If you promise to be back by dinner time…*

Zeus interrupted him, *Tory, I'm not making promises to anyone. I have to go find my human Gabe, and I don't know how far I will have to go to find him. Stay here or join us, but make up your mind because we're wasting time.*

Orphy started dancing around and jumping with her two front feet off the ground…*Come On! We will all be together. Adventures await, we could all come back heroes.*

*More like hungry heroes…*Tory said softly.

Dropping his shaking head, Zeus turned to leave, *I'm going. If any of you want to come, you had better keep up.*

With that he put his nose back to the ground and circled until he found the scent again. Then without looking back he was off at a steady trot.

# Chapter 37

Will's snare caught a fat possum that had to be clubbed to death. The men returned with it to the edge of the clan and after spotting their families, Gabe gave the owl's hoot. When Anita responded, he knelt with it in the brush nearby.

She gave a signal to one of the guards that she needed to do private business and he nodded and moved on. When she approached the sound and found him, her eyes lit up and a broad smile filled her face. Gabe shook his head and brought a finger to his lips. Understanding his moves, she checked over her shoulder again then rushed into his arms.

Silently they embraced and exchanged several kisses, before he handed her the opossum and the bloody limb he had used to kill it. He knew that she would make up a good story if any of the soldiers asked.

He whispered that all three husbands were following and would take turns seeing their wives. She nodded, and with a feeling of elation, she grabbed the carcass and headed back to the clan.

She told the family what had just happened and when they made camp that night they made sure that they were close to the perimeter and brush nearby.

With little to no food on the trail, word spread quickly how Anita had clubbed a 'possum and had prepared it for that night's supper.

When the word got to Captain Nichols, his eyes left the reporting soldier and moved toward the Indians. "A 'possum you say? Fresh kill. I shall have to see about this."

With a bodyguard close by, he marched to where the meat was cooking over Anita's campfire.

"I'm told you clubbed a 'possum while you were out there in the brush relieving yourself."

Anita pretended that she didn't understand by frowning and shrugging her shoulders.

"You're married to that red-headed trapper so you know what I'm saying. He would have taught you at least basic English by now, unless you are too stupid to learn."

Anita dropped her eyes in order to mask the disgust she felt for the man and turned her attention to the cooking pot.

"Guard, take that pot to my tent. It will be nice to have a hot meal and a full belly tonight."

"But sir, she was the one who…."

"If she's so good at bringing meat to the pot then she can do it again. But *this* pot is for me. When I am full, you men can share the rest. Good food cannot be wasted on these… these *animals*."

The husbands, hidden in the brush nearby, saw and heard it all. Gabe had to place a hard hand on both of them to keep from exposing their whereabouts.

The Indians nearby watched in hunger as the pot was taken away and the promise of a hot meal vanished with it.

The men backed away, mainly in fear of losing their tempers and attacking the man that was inflicting such pain and humiliation on their loved ones. When they felt they were far enough away, they still spoke in whispers, and shared wishful threats and plans to make Nichols suffer far more than even he could imagine.

"What are we going to do now, Gabe?" asked Will.

"We will just have to up our plan to get them out and run. If they are forced to continue much longer we could lose them for sure," he answered.

145

# Chapter 38

Grace could not believe that everywhere she turned there were new and exciting sights. She was unprepared to see the grand horse-drawn carriage that awaited her and Olivia to take them to the Whitmore Plantation.

The large white carriage held two scarlet padded seats that faced each other. A platform for their luggage was on the back, where a black man stood after loading it all. The top of the carriage could fold down for fresh air, or be raised if it rained and four white horses pulled it. An old black man in funny clothes and a tall square hat held the reins to all four horses. He sat stiff and proud; his only movement was a nod to Olivia when she gave him permission to proceed.

One road led to another until they turned onto a narrow lane, lined with flowering dogwood trees. This road took them in a swooping curve up to the front of the largest house Grace had ever seen. She thought, *even the hotel in Fort Wells is not near as big,* then said, "Oli…*Aunt* Olivia, What is this place?"

Smiling, Olivia proudly announced, "This, my dear, is Whitmore House, and all of what we've been driving through, almost since we left the train depot, is Whitmore Plantation: your new home!"

Grace squealed with delight and rushed to the door, only to come face to face with a large black woman with a long blue calico dress and long snow-white apron. She wore a matching bandana around her head that tied in the back and a broad smile that showed a row of bright white teeth. "Welcome Missus' Wadsworth. So good to have you home again."

"Thank you, Tilda… It's good to be home. I see that you are keeping up with your English. I'm very proud of you for that. I want to introduce you to Grace, a child that was brought to the fort from the Appalachian Mountains. It seems her parents died of some sort of fever and left this poor orphan to a backward mountain man and an Indian woman to raise. Since they neglected her education and eventually abandoned her, Mr. Wadsworth and I felt it our Christian duty to accept her and give her all the advantages she would not have received otherwise."

Reaching out, Tilda drew Grace's head tightly to her bosom. Rocking her gently she said, "Well, you poor thing. You don't go fretting about nothing. The Good Lord has brought you to two God-fearing people that will make sure you get the best of everything."

Olivia said, "Thank you, Tilda. It's been a long trip and we would very much like a hot bath and a good meal before retiring. Can you have the large guest room in the west wing prepared as Grace's own? We both are very tired."

"Of course, where are my manners, having you stand here jabbering while you need to get off your feet? Relax in the parlor and I'll fetch some hot tea and something to nibble on while we prepare your baths and ready your rooms."

"That will be marvelous, Tilda, and much appreciated," sighed Olivia.

When they were left alone Grace asked quietly, "Why did you say all that all at once, Aunt Olivia?"

"Because my dear, if you tell Tilda, she will tell everyone else and we won't have to go through it all again. Now, Welcome to Whitmore House, Grace dear."

# Chapter 39

Since reuniting with her immediate family, away from Will, Becca sometimes slipped back into using the native tongue. She answered readily to Blue and called the others by their clan names.

She now searched for and gathered anything edible along the path as they walked, determined to keep the family fed and thier spirits up; *Hunger is stealing their desire to keep going. Each day I see clan members stumble and fall, only to be helped back to their feet by anyone close by. Babies are crying and children barely old enough to understand are walking with expressionless faces, clinging to their parents' garments, seeking any form of security. Our braves' prides are broken because of their inability to provide for and protect their families.*

"Sparrow, I found some mushrooms, and these dandelion greens that will give us some nutrition." Then speaking to the family, she encouraged, "Look for acorns, pine seeds, berries...anything. We can mix them together and either eat them dry or boil them to help fill our bellies."

Anita placed Becca's collection into a pouch tied to her belt, "It is good that you keep up our morale. You have a fighting spirit, like your brother calls you 'warrior sister.'"

Becca patted her arm and moved back to the edge of the perimeter in search of more food. Her mind was focused only on her immediate family's needs, causing her to be unmindful that she was being watched intently by someone farther up the line.

With the family's needs uppermost in her mind, she had abandoned the thought of personal safety. Spotting an oak tree up ahead she took Ellen by the hand and tugged her toward it, "Come, Squirrel, help me gather acorns. Let's make it a game to see how many we gather for dinner."

Ellen hung back, letting Becca pull her at arm's length toward the large tree. "The last time we gathered nuts together we were almost eaten by that big puma."

"Don't be silly. There surely isn't any around here with all the noise of people walking or riding horses close by."

"Unless it's trying to decide which one of us to eat."

"Now you are beginning to act like your name again...a scared little squirrel. It will do us good to have something to do that will take our mind off ourselves."

Giving in, Ellen walked with her friend side-by-side and when they reached the tree, she examined all the branches quite thoroughly before gathering the fallen acorns.

Suddenly there came a familiar chirping, constant and determined. Looking up, Becca saw a little blue bird just above her head as if suspended on an invisible wire. Its actions brought back a flood of memories, *It's the little blue bird that led me out of the wilderness when I was lost, and through the cave Will and I found! It always seemed to come when I've needed help or was in danger, but what could possibly bring it now? There's no puma here, or waterfall to tumble over...*Then she heard Ellen gasp in horror, "Snow Wolf!"

Becca turned in time to hear, "Hello Blue," before a fist smashed against her temple, spinning her to the ground.

Standing tall and proud, Snow Wolf straddled the unconscious Becca. Pointing at Ellen he ordered, "You are still my wife, but don't worry, I want no part of you. You just stand there and watch me take what is rightfully mine! Blue is all I've ever wanted."

"You can't! She's married… to Will… and pregnant!"

"She won't be for long. After I'm satisfied, I will cut that seed from her belly, and then carve her face so she isn't desirable to any man…if she lives."

Thinking that she could convince him to stop, she threatened, "Stop! If you touch her, her husband will kill you. He's close by and when he hears of this, there will be no place for you to hide. And he won't be alone. Gabe is with him."

"That's good to hear. I won't have to hunt for him. I welcome the day that I can use the same knife on him that I will on her…and their half-breed seed!"

As he began to disrobe, Ellen gave a blood curdling scream, causing Snow Wolf to lunge at her to shut her up.

The blue bird flew between them and attacked his face. Its talons dug into his cheeks as it pecked at his eyes. Snow Wolf raised his hands in defense to ward off the bird just as Jumping Fox and a guard burst upon the scene.

The bird barely had time to dart away as Fox leaped at Snow Wolf and they began to tumble and wrestle around Becca. The blade of Snow Wolf's knife glimmered in the sun rays as they fought.  As his pants slid down to his knees, the Indian searched for them with one hand, while brandishing his knife with the other, ignoring Ellen now. He turned his back on her while trying to keep eye contact with his opponent.

Ellen didn't think before she lunged ahead and pushed with all her might, sending him sprawling. Fox grabbed the opportunity and straddling his opponent, he grabbed the knife-wielding wrist with both hands, turning it inward and down toward Snow Wolf's throat. Slowly the blade inched closer to Snow Wolf's throbbing neck, as the two men locked eyes in their to-the-death struggle.

An ear-piercing whistle jarred Fox from his kill mentality. He wrenched the knife from Snow Wolf's fist and crouched over him. Breathing deeply and trying to control his anger, he looked up at the whistle blower.

By now Indians and guards alike had gathered as Captain Nichols showed up demanding, "Guard! Report! What is all this ruckus?"

"It seems to me that this scout was trying to shut this squaw up so he could have his way with the other one."

"Protocol! Guard, Protocol!" Nichols shouted.

"Sir, Captain Nichols, Sir… It seems to me…"

"Oh, never mind! I don't see what all the fuss is about anyway. They are all stinking savages that fight amongst themselves like a pack of hungry animals after a fresh kill!"

"This one," pointing to Snow Wolf, "Sir, he isn't a regular. I've never seen him before. Not sure where he came from."

Ellen stepped forward and blurted out, "He used to be my husband, but I divorced him. He really didn't want me. He wanted Becca but she didn't want him. He tried to kill me once and she saved me. He was here to rape and kill her, which would have killed her baby."

Nichols stared long and hard at Snow Wolf. "Bring him to my tent. I'll deal with him accordingly. The rest of you, heathens, get back with the others! Guard, confiscate that knife! And drag that woman back to the trail. She shouldn't have been out here in the first place."

Ellen cried out, "We were gathering food." Looking down at the acorns now scattered all over the ground, "The acorns…"

"*Acorns*? You eat *acorns*?" Turning in the saddle toward the soldier, he added, "See? I told you, sergeant! They are nothing but animals! Do you know that pigs like acorns too? Yes, that about sums it up, filthy stinking animals," he muttered as he rode back to his tent.

The soldier watched him ride off, then turned Snow Wolf over to another guard, "You heard the man…take this one to the captain's tent so he can deal with him."

After the two were out of hearing the soldier turned back to the clan. "You can gather all those back up, but its best you get back and stay quiet for awhile. There's no telling what the Captain will come up with next. And I'll send our medic over to see if he can help with the woman."

Fox nodded, and then carried the unconscious Becca to their campsite where Moon Star said, "We must tell Will."

Laying Becca down gently, Fox shook his head, "No, He would not be able to stay away and then he would also be a prisoner. He must concentrate on the plan for our escape."

After examining Becca, Anita said, "She is lucky. Even with the heavy fall on her stomach, her injuries will only be bruises, a swollen jaw and black eye. The baby is still snug and safe. Where is Snow Wolf now?"

"No one's seen him since he went to the Captain's tent. But we have to warn the husbands. I'm sorry, but I blurted out that they are close by, and Snow Wolf may be going after Will. He said as much."

Satisfied that Becca was safe, the little blue bird went unnoticed as he quietly flew away.

# Chapter 40

Gabe nudged Will and Thomas awake and whispered, "Something's up."

"What?' Thomas whispered back.

"Probably the hair on his arms and neck", answered Will.

They moved in close, back to back, and continued to talk in hushed tones, "You know me too well, partner. Watch for movement; listen for sounds; smell the air."

As they stood frozen in silence, waiting in anticipation, they first heard a bush rustle... then dry leaves crunch... Ever so slowly, in unison, each man cocked his head for better hearing. Gabe leaned forward as Thomas and Will turned an ear toward the sounds.

Gabe knew that if it was too dark to see the enemy, then it was too dark to be seen, so he placed his rifle between his legs and reached behind him with both hands. Tugging on the men's clothes, he signaled for all of them to ease down to a crouch. When they came to rest on their heels, a huffing sound came from in front of Gabe. He had no time to react before the wolf was upon him. The full weight of it hit Gabe's chest, sending all three men flat to the ground.

Gabe could feel the hot breath of the animal as it closed the gap between its fangs and his face. He grabbed the scruff of its neck to hold it at arm's length, but before he could, he got a long wet tongue across his face.

"Zeus!" He whispered hoarsely, "It's alright boys, it's only Zeus!" Just then three more wolves followed their Alpha's lead and joined in. The men had to fight off all the thumps of the tails and the wet kisses.

# Chapter 41

The soldier's tent was more crowded than usual, with men wanting to get some answers and have their say. As their seargent returned from the captain's tent they all gathered in close. He spoke in a hoarse whisper. "I think he's asleep now, but we better keep our voices down. No telling what he'd do if he finds out we're doing this."

Voices fought to be heard from all sides:

"I think he's gone crazy."

"I *know* he has."

"The other day he took food that some of the Indians had gathered and prepared for their families."

"But what can we do?"

"He has presidential jurisdiction to do what he wants."

"So he says. But they don't know what is really going on here. I don't think any of them would approve his actions."

"I'm not sure. I've heard that there are quite a few politicians that want all Indians exterminated."

"Well, I never heard of any prisoners, North or South that was treated as bad as this during the Civil War."

"That's 'cause most of them was white, you dodo head."

"Well, still. They shouldn't be treated so inhumane as they are. I talked to the soldiers at that Fort Wells where we picked up that last bunch. Those Cherokee, and most of the others, never fought us whites. Not unless they was being attacked, anyways."

"All this time on the trail, with little clothing or belongings and no food, and some have even had to bury a loved one along the way...and I hear none complain."

"What can we do about it Sarge? I'm ready to quit and hightail it out of here, just to save my conscience, and my good standing with the Lord."

"I heard in the last march like this, back in the late 30's thousands of them died on the trail. And nobody cared."

"That's what the Captain wants. He wants most of them to die. He thinks that will put him in good standing with some of those big hats in Washington."

"The Captain once told me that they should kill off all the women so there wouldn't be any more 'heathens walking the earth. Kill the seed, get rid of the weed,' he said."

"Some of those boys at that fort also said they had become friends with most of them and they were right helpful and didn't cause no trouble."

"What's going to happen to them once they get to where we're going?"

"I heard they are pushed onto land that has little vegetation or any hopes of it. They even took away their guns so they can't hunt for food."

"I'm sick and tired of the whole mess. His last episode of letting that no-count Indian go, the one that attacked them two women today…what in tarnation was he thinkin'?"

"I was the one that took him to the captain. Nichols done told him that he was free to go and wished him luck in finishing what he started! Can you believe that?"

The sergeant raised his hands for attention. "Keep it down guys…I'm sick of it too. Can any of you think of anything that we *can* do?"

"What would happen to us if some of them, somehow, someway…escaped?"

"Would we be court marshaled? Or tried for treason?"

"Wait, sick you say? That's it! We couldn't be accused of anything, if…one-by-one we all contact some sort of illness," stated a medic. "With less and less guards, the Indians' chances of escape would increase. But how are we going to tell them?"

"What are we all going to get sick from?"

"We're going to have to make it look good. We could all act like we ate something that made us real sick."

"Maybe let him see us run for the bushes, unbuckling our britches."

"Or run and make sounds like we're throwing up!"

"But he eats pert near the same as us, so how's that going to work?"

The camp cook said, "I could add a little bit of laxative to his dinner. Not much, mind you. Just enough to convince him that everyone else got sicker than he did."

"Alright, guys. Now the hard part is telling the Indians that they can go…only a few at a time. Let them plan their own escape and it will look even better for us."

"I'll take on the task," said the sergeant. "I know a few of them speak English and they will spread the word. Now we must make a pact that no one…ever…tells what happened here tonight…or else we all go down together."

He received all positive answers, either by whispers of agreement, nods of heads or salutes.

# Chapter 42

"What did he say, little sister?" asked Jumping Fox

"You are never going to believe me. It doesn't make any sense and I don't know if we can trust him or not. He said the soldiers got together and decided to let us escape, if we only do it a few at a time. He says they are going to fool the Captain into thinking they are all so sick they have to leave their positions along the perimeter and can't watch us close. They are giving us permission to leave!"

"What if other soldiers come for us again?"

"I asked him that. He said it was only his men and that he could not control what the government may do next. We must do what we can to keep from getting caught again."

"Blue, do you realize what this means? I must get word to Soaring Eagle. We must spread the word to the Cherokee. What the others do is their business; we must take care of our own. I will talk to Moonstar and see what she wants. I wish for our family to stay together, the clan rules can't apply any longer."

"I agree, my brother. I need to get word to the husbands. Anita can signal Gabe with her animal sounds and we can discuss our plans when we are all together. Hurry, we have no time to waste. No telling how long these soldiers can pretend to be sick."

"We must continue on the trail as if nothing has changed, but rearrange our packs for carrying only. We must leave behind the travois."

Anita made the call of the chickadee, signaling Gabe to "Come". Hearing no answer, she waited. Each half hour she called until she heard his answer, very close, then seeing no guard, she slipped off into the bushes.

Gabe swooped her up and hugged her tight, whispering, "My little Sparrow, I'm the one who is supposed to call you. I didn't know what to think, so I waited until I could see that you're alright. What is wrong?"

She quickly filled him in on the news and explained that the clan wanted to discuss what to do but was unsure how to go about it without a regular clan gathering.

Gabe shook his head, "Baby, all I want is for us to be together and get the heck out of here. We can go get Gigi and be a family again. She is living with the Commander and his wife in Virginia." Hearing a slight rustle behind him he added, "Oh, look who's here." After Gabe gave his chickadee call, out from the bushes came Zeus! "I told him to 'Hide' and he remembered to stay until called. I'm glad he didn't answer *your* chickadee call, we'd have the whole army on top of us!" he laughed.

Anita hugged the wolf and then turned back to Gabe, "You tell other husbands the news. We all meet tonight when most of soldiers go to their tents."

"Alright, my love, we will be a happy family again and I want that more than anything. I'll bring the men tonight. When you're ready, give the call. We will be waiting."

Gabe gave the command for Zeus to *come,* and made sure the rest of the wolves followed suit, then went for the men.

.

Later that day as the men prepared to reunite with their wives, the wolves lay close to each other.

Zeus spoke to the pack. *"When my human tells me to do something, you need to follow my lead. It makes him happy to see how much I understand, and his commands might save lives…theirs and ours."*

Sashay cocked her head and said, *"Commands? Uh, he can politely tell, or ask, but this girl is not taking commands from anyone! When mine want me to do something they better use a very polite tone in their voice, or I act like I don't understand them. But I know what you mean about making them happy. When I do what they say, they praise me and snuggle me, but it's never anything dramatic like this life-threatening thing...annddd I have to want to first."*

*"My woman human scratches behind my ears and it feels sooo good...but the man gives me bits of meat when I please him, and that reminds me...I'm hungry, and we are a long way from home. I thought you promised we'd be home by supper time,"* came from Tory.

Orphy crept forward and said, *"Speaking of scratching... It feels like things are crawling all over me...and I don't like it out here one bit! I want to be back where I don't have to be looking over my shoulder at every sound...and can you see those spooky shining things in the trees?"*

Zeus closed his eyes in search of patience, *"Those are probably bird's eyes...most likely owls. They hunt at night. Or they could have even been stars you see through the branches. Good Heavens, Orphy, haven't you been out after dark?"*

*"No, why should I?"* she snapped.

*"Well, I don't know about your human, but mine doesn't like cleaning up after my stinky stuff. That's one of the first lessons they taught me,"* answered Sashay.

*"Oh, that. Yeah, I go outside for that, but just out near the horses. Their area gets cleaned every day and I don't*

*have to worry about those spooky shining things when I'm behind the fort walls. What do those things eat?"*

*"All this talk about food is making my stomach growl,"* muttered Tory as he rose to his elbows, with a moan.

Sashay sighed, *"Oh, give it a rest. You're not going to starve, and you could stand to lose a few pounds."*

*"Standing I can deal with, it's all that running that's made me hungry,"* Tory countered.

Zeus shook his head, *"Alright, knock it off, you two. Tory, you will get fed when the humans get through with what they are doing. It is our job to obey their commands."*

Sashay lowered her chin to her paws, *"Humph...Obey their commands... my big, fat, royal....."*

*"Sashay!" Zeus scolded.*

The clan met as best they could that night with runners in between relaying the messages. Soaring Eagle declined to go, saying, "I gave my solemn word when I surrendered to this man who now leads us, perhaps not verbally, but by not fighting back. I am too old now to keep running. I will go to where they have chosen and see what good I can do there. Any who choose to go, may Yowa protect you."

Most of those who chose to stay with him were the older generation that seemed to have finally given up and could see no other way. Those who chose to leave quietly made their private plans, as was the case when the husbands and wives reunited that night outside the perimeter.

In the darkness Will did not notice Becca's injuries, until she flinched when he took her face into his hands to give her a long, loving kiss. He stepped back and looked at her closer. She dropped her head to her chest so he led her into an area of more moonlight where he could see.

"What happened?" he demanded in a whisper.

"It's nothing. I'm fine."

He tilted her face up and asked again, "Becca?"

Behind them Ellen answered, "It was Snow Wolf."

He and Gabe came to attention, "SNOW WOLF? He was here? What happened?" demanded Will.

"Where is he now?" asked Gabe.

"I'm sorry but when I tried to save Becca, I blurted out that you were here. He said he will kill you as soon as he is finished with Becca…and your baby," cried Squirrel.

"No…is the baby…" stopping, he took a breath to calm down. "You don't have to answer that. I know if anything had happened to our baby you would not be so happy right now. But Snow Wolf's time on earth is numbered. I will put an end to him, once and for all."

"He knows we're here…and we know he's here, so that means there will have to be an end to this," said Gabe.

Becca said, "Do not spoil our time talking about him."

Will agreed and began to smile, as one with a secret, "Becca, have you girls thought of a plan? If not, Gabe has a great idea. It will be another long walk, but a destination worth getting to…and only you and I have seen it."

Becca's eyes and mouth shot open wide. She ignored the pain as a large smile spread across her face. Her arms opened wide and she jumped into his arms, "The Valley!"

# Chapter 43

"Grace, my dear, are you happy?" asked Olivia.

Twirling around in her new tailor-made clothes, with hat and shoes to match, she answered, "Oh, Aunt Olivia, I'm happier than I've ever been. I love it here...with you and Uncle Frederic. Everything is so wonderful...and glorious and ohhhh I don't know, just fantastic!"

Olivia and Frederick laughed at her enthusiasm. "I see you are doing well with your vocabulary, as well as your dance lessons," he said.

"And don't forget the piano! You know, dear, her tutors say that she has learned in leaps and bounds and is almost up with her grade level now, and there is very little left to get her up to the standards set by some of the highest schools in Virginia," bragged Olivia.

"And, she is without a doubt, the most beautiful girl in all of Virginia, too," he added.

Clutching her wide-brimmed hat in both hands, and at arm's length in front of her, Grace twirled again, smiling and humming the latest tune, knowing that it pleased them to see her happy.

Her past had quickly become a vague memory and she no longer thought of the mother and "Papa" she once had. They came as dark shadows in night dreams that the rays of the morning sun dissolved.

She quickly brushed the thoughts away and smiled at her two adamant admirers.

"Since we are all here together, there's something I want to discuss. It's about when your father comes for you. What are your plans?" asked the commander.

Grace froze in her dancing and stared, first at him then Olivia, searching their faces. Her expression changed to disbelief as she asked, "You...you don't want me anymore? Do you wish for him to come and get me?"

He hurried to explain, "No, no, my dear, absolutely not. That is what we fear most. We want you to stay with us... forever. What would you say if we adopted you as our daughter? Olivia and I have discussed it and we are leaving it entirely up to you. We have no idea of what is going on out there in the wilderness and it would make us sick to think that you would have to endure it. So many hardships that you won't have to go through if you stay with us. I know this is sudden and you can take all the time you need to think it over, just know that we both have grown more than fond of you...we love you dearly."

Grace fell to her knees with her face in her hands and wept. The commander and Olivia both jumped from their chairs and dashed to her side, "I'm so sorry dear, I didn't mean to hurt you with all of that. You can forget what I said. We'll just leave things the way they are and...."

"No, you don't understand. I dread the day Papa will come and take me back to that awful place. I love you both so much. You have shown me a whole new world. He and the others are content with what they feel is a normal life, even though Papa never grew up there, he feels that it is his refuge from the world. I don't want to escape the world, I want to embrace it and enjoy all that it can provide."

I'll have my attorney draw up the papers and leave the date blank. When your father comes after you, ask him to sign them, giving up custody and parenthood....Then you will be our daughter forever," said Uncle Frederic.

"But, what if he doesn't come?"

"Then after a year we can go to the court with papers that will say that we consider him dead and you have no legal parents. Once they are signed by a judge, if he shows up later the papers will show that you are legally ours. You will be our daughter."

"I would love that. Can we do the papers now? Do you know how long it's been since I came to live with you? Does that time count in the year? Oh, we must hurry and do it as soon as possible." Looking up at them through her tears she added, "Please don't think bad of me. I love my Papa and my mother, but I just can't go back to that dreadful, awful life."

"We understand completely dear, that is why Olivia and I are trying so hard to give you everything you deserve. You have been deprived of many things; it would break our hearts for you to have to tolerate that life style again."

The couple lifted her back to her feet and they all hugged each other. Then Olivia gently wiped away Grace's tears.

# Chapter 44

The plan was set in motion by the camp cook. Captain Nichols was unsure of his body's urge to seek tall brush until it continued hour after hour. The jostling of riding horseback intensified his symptoms, which encouraged him to walk. He chose to stay close to the perimeter and an easy route to the nearest privacy.

He noticed other soldiers having to make the same quick exits from their saddles and head for privacy, so he called a halt for the day and retiring to his tent, called for the camp doctor. "What is this that is going around? Did some squaw slip us poison toad stools instead of mushrooms…?"

"No sir…. The cook…"

"Protocol! Damn it! Protocol! Won't you idiots ever learn?" Nichols screeched, then reached for his lower stomach and groaned.

Swallowing his anger the doctor began again, "No, sir, Captain Nichols, sir. The cook keeps a close eye on the cooking pots at all times and there has never been an Indian near them or the supplies. Many of the soldiers are also ill and cannot hold their posts."

"I'm not worried about these stinking redskins running away. Hell, they don't have the sense that God gave a goose. They are like sheep being led to the slaughter. They don't even know any better. But something sure has gotten to our systems. Where was the last water drawn from to fill our canteens and cooking pots? Was it thoroughly checked? Those creeks and lakes can be infested with all sorts of germs. Spread the word. My orders to the men are to camp here until I feel well enough to go on."

Others were making plans too, that were set in motion, with an invitation to escape that held no discrimination as to tribe or clan; all were welcome to follow or stay. The leaders consisted of Becca and Will, Anita and Gabe, Ellen and Thomas, as well as Becca's father, Swift Arrow, and Ellen's brother Lame Elk.

Ellen and Moonstar had to say goodbye to their parents, as the elders chose to go on and convinced their daughters that going forward was best for them.

After a brief meeting, the plans were shared in the quiet of the night. The first was to have the eighty-plus followers separate and space themselves along the trail, so their escape would go unnoticed. All were to follow the call of the night owl to meet with the leaders.

Gabe's initial plan for the smaller group's escape had to be altered to accommodate the larger number; to leave as little trail as possible, lest Capt. Nichol gave chase.

After saying goodbye to those who chose to stay and with the bright moon to lighten their path, they hoisted what belongings they could carry and slipped away.

Becca translated Gabe's instructions, "About twenty people will walk ahead, forming a point, keeping close enough to see each other, yet wide enough apart to not leave a broad trail of trampled foliage. Some will follow single file behind the leaders at point, on the two outer edges; hopefully the trails will be taken as deer paths."

Will suggested that some of the planners should take point while others brought up the rear, to insure that everyone kept the pace and no one fell behind. Blue had already agreed and took her place behind the middle line, "I'll keep father tied to me. That way he can't wander off."

Among those joining the group, was a lone figure that remained out of sight. As he clung to the shadows he waited for just the right moment to take his revenge. Unknown to him, another shadow lurked, far on the other side of the group, with a similar determination.

The wolves watched the humans with interest. *Why do they talk in whispers?* asked Orphy.

*I don't know, but I'm sure something is serious. Look at their faces and how they act. Like they are unsettled about something,* answered Zeus. *My human gave me the sign to be quiet, but has his attention on other things. I'm not sure what is going on.*

*Do you think any of them have food? More are showing up and gathering together. I think I'll take a walk around and see if I can sniff out something to eat,* said Tory.

*Oh, Tory! You and your stomach! But you know, it has been awhile since our last meal. Zeus, do you think we can go on a real hunt? I think it would be so much fun. And we can hone our skills,* said Sashay.

*What do you know about hunting, Sashay? The last thing you hunted for was a warm blanket,* chided Tory.

*I'll have you know I've hunted and killed rats around the fort. Some were getting into the humans' stored goods and others were hanging around the horses' food. I know how to kill...but I'm not yet so hungry that I will eat them. They are really disgusting,* offered Sashay.

*RATS? Eww, I've seen them around the livery, but I just chase them off. I'm not going to sink my teeth into one even if it is to kill it,* gagged Orphy.

*They are all around the train depot and the store, but I just watch them. They don't bother me so I don't bother them. I started to once, but they are pretty fast, too fast for me. So I just lie back down and watch them,* said Tory.

*Sashay, I too feel the urge sometimes to find out if I could bring my human food. He feeds me and asks nothing in return, except to play once in awhile. He likes to throw a round thing and have me get it and take it back to him. He likes that a lot. I would like to show my appreciation to him and his family. The girl that was with us, went somewhere, I'm not sure where,* said Zeus.

*I know. She went with my woman human. They got on the train by the store with all sorts of boxes and things. They hugged my male human and he was real sad after they left. Remember Zeus? Remember how he sat in his chair and talked to us real quiet like? And then he hugged us both? Don't you remember Zeus?* asked Sashay.

*Yes, I remember. You went and put your chin on his knee and he put his head down on yours and his eyes leaked.* Clearing his throat he said, *Maybe Tory's right. We should look around for something to eat.*

Just then Gabe motioned to Zeus to "come" and the wolf responded immediately. The others followed and found themselves surrounded by these humans that seemed to be in a hurry to go somewhere.

Becca motioned for Zeus to stay near her and Gabe gave him a nod and pointed to her. Confused he turned and went to walk near the woman human. Not having any human of their own there, the others followed him.

# Chapter 45

"Where is that squaw that speaks English, the one with the retarded father? I've looked up and down this pack for her and the other two squaws who walk with her...and... the buck with a wife and kid...are missing too. These redskins seem to have thinned out, or they are straggling along so slow that some are lagging far behind. It's your job to keep them moving at a decent pace. We have to make up time we lost. What is going on, Sergeant, I demand to know!" Nichols was screaming from atop of Puma, who was showing displeasure at the loud voice by side stepping and swinging his head.

"Straighten up, you stupid horse!" yelled Nichols as he brought his quirt down on the horse's right shoulder. Puma had never felt pain before and in total confusion responded by jerking away from it, causing the rider to grab the saddle horn in order to stay in the saddle.

Red-faced, he screamed, "Search the area! Do your jobs or you will all face a court martial! Find those heathens!"

During their search, one of the soldiers rode up and spoke quietly to the Sergeant. "Sarge I found what might be their trail. What do you want to do? It's your call."

Hoping the clan had time to get far enough ahead, he answered, "I guess we'll go along with the crazy fool. Maybe he'll think he's going the wrong way and quit chasing them."

Approaching his superior the sergeant dismounted and said, "One of my men...."

PROTOCOL! DAMN IT! WHEN WILL YOU IDIOTS EVER LEARN TO USE PROTOCOL?" the Captain screeched as he slammed his quirt against his own leg. The pain was so intense that he shrieked aloud before controlling himself and added, "SEE? See what you made me do! It's all your fault! You made me do that! I'll put you on report, I will!" Then as he watched the sergeant take a deep breath and stand at attention, he added, "WELL? REPORT!"

"Sir, Captain Nichols, Sir, One of my men thinks that he may have found a trail that the Indians might have made."

Also taking a deep breath, Captain Nichols raised his chin and looked down his nose at the sergeant. Quietly now he stated, "Then why are you standing here? Why are you not out there bringing the savages back? Do I have to do everything myself around here?" Not waiting for an answer he added, "Yes, yes I guess I do. I will lead my men to recapture those animals."

The sergeant immediately turned to leave, afraid that his facial reactions might divulge his disdain for this man.

"PROTOCOL, SERGEANT!" the captain doubled over, stomping his feet, swinging his fists in the air, "YOU HAVE NOT BEEN DISMISSED PROPERLY!" Not waiting for the ceremonial protocol that he just insisted, Nichols began barking out who was to stay and who was to follow him. Brandishing his sword over his head, he swung it around in a circle as he kicked Puma's withers and shouted, "Follow me men!"

The mounted soldiers looked at each other, then back to the captain's back, already at a full gallop but not yet knowing in which direction the soldier had found the path. Exchanging smiles and light chuckles, they all gave a "whoop", and slapping their legs with their hats, they followed the galloping stallion.

It didn't take long before Nichols realized his mistake and reined to a halt. After calling for the soldier who had reported seeing the trail, he found to his great relief he had luckily chosen the right direction and could save face before his men. Assuring himself that he was blessed by the gods, he continued showing his authority by leading at a fast pace with saber still swinging and chopping at branches and bushes that got in his way.

The escaping clan did not succeed in ridding themselves of this sinister Captain.

Becca heard the bird's twitter overhead and looked up to see the blue bird. He was acting frantic and hovering in an upright position with wings flogging the air around him.

She had come to realize the reason for his appearances and began to panic. Looking around she saw the mounted soldiers just seconds before she heard the thunder of their horses' hooves. The leader stood in his stirrups, leaning forward, swinging his sword overhead and yelling, "HOW DARE YOU RUN AWAY FROM ME, YOU STINKING REDSKINS!"

He was riding hard before he pulled heavily on the reins, almost running over Becca. She had little time to react before he leaned from his saddle, swiping his sword inches above her head. Swift Arrow pushed her down and stood between them. As she looked up she saw the Captain's blade pierce through her father's body and protrude out his back. As Swift Arrow crumpled to his knees, the captain jerked the blade back out from the slumping body. He swung it over his head and down toward her again.

Zeus attacked out of pure instinct, which prompted the other three wolves to join him. With all four wolves

171

lunging toward the rider, Puma reared up in total panic, throwing Nichols off balance and into a downward plunge.

Still screaming obscenities, his hand released the sword to break his fall. The blade landed upright and his body had no alternative than to become impaled to its hilt.

Shock overtook everyone who witnessed the scene. In an instant the area went from total chaos to complete silence, except for the wolves tearing at the dead Captain's clothes as he lay with his blade still protruding through his body.

Will rushed to Becca. Finding her shaken, frightened but unharmed, he turned his attention to the wolves and waded into the bedlam.

Pulling Zeus off the captain inadvertently turned the wolf's attention to himself. With the smell of fresh blood filling their nostrils and the adrenalin flowing through their bodies, primal instinct had taken over and the wolves were feeling the rush of a mixture of excitement, fear, and bold kill-nature.

Zeus faced his new challenge with front legs spread, and a deep threatening growl. Hearing the growl the other three stopped their attack and assumed his stance. They waited for their Alpha's next move, ready for any decision he would make.

By this time Gabe had made his way back to the scene and was stunned at what he saw. Zeus was challenging Will! The silence was heavy as the man and wolf faced off, both in confusion at what was happening.

Becca moved to reach Swift Arrow, causing Zeus to turn slightly at the movement and growl deeper. Everyone froze.

Only Zeus' eyes moved, but when they connected with Gabe's, there was a flicker of memories that brought scenes of warmth and love.

Seconds went by. Gabe walked slowly and spoke very softly, "Zeus. It's me, boy. What's the matter? All this got you upset? Us too. Let's all simmer down a bit and let things cool," speaking as much to the people as he was to the animal. As he talked, he slowly made his way between the wolf and Will, then ever so slowly he reached out and motioned for Zeus to 'come', causing the wolf to waver between his loyalty to this man, and to the strange feeling *to kill* that coursed through his veins. The other three wolves still held their stance, waiting for his decision.

When Gabe knelt all the way down to Zeus' level and left himself vulnerable, the action reached deep into the heart of the wolf. His hackles slowly relaxed, the growl softened to a whine and he came slowly to Gabe's open arms.

The other three followed his lead and ceased their attack but slowly, with heads lowered, retreated to reunite. They remained unsettled, and paced around as they watched and waited.

# Chapter 46

The soldiers and the clan united in digging a grave and giving Swift Arrow a final resting place there in the mountains. After witnessing the Cherokee ritual for Swift Arrow, and burying Nichols, the sergeant came to the clan, "If some of you want to come back to camp, we will return your weapons so you can hunt and at least protect yourselves and families, but go ahead with your plans. We will notify the army of Captain Nichol's demise and make sure that his passing was by no means caused by any actions of the captives. He was a very sick man, and now rests in peace, if God can forgive him."

Gabe approached the Sergeant, "Thank you, and your men, for all the compassion you've shown and your help in allowing this group to start over somewhere. We hope to find that the note attached to my wolf is true, that Indian women can stay if married to a white man with a stable income. Corporal Thorton should have no problem, Will and I will find proper work that the government deems 'stable' and we can live our lives quietly and without fear. If it is not asking too much, could you allow Chief Soaring Eagle to have his horse back?"

"Of course, I'll see to it. I've been told by the soldiers from the fort about the bond the two have and it was such a shame that the captain would confiscate the horse when it could be so much comfort to the chief. Please know that we will continue taking the others on to the destination the army has prepared for them, but they will be treated humanely and with compassion. We will share foods and any comforts we have with them. I believe that the march will be much easier on all of us now. As there is no more threat to your group, perhaps it would be easier on you to find your way back to the trail to take you home. It's well worn by now. Oh, and one more thing. I think it goes without saying, but…we'd appreciate it if the story of your 'escape' does not include the help of us soldiers."

"What are you talking about, Sergeant? We out smarted you all the way," Gabe said with a wink and a smile.

They shook hands that showed a mutual respect and trust.

When Gabe got back to Anita, she informed him that Becca's witnessing her father's death, had started her labor. "It too soon. Need one more month. Not good."

"What can we do? Should we make a shelter for her? Should we tell the others to go on? How long will it take?" the questions came busting out of Gabe.

"Others say they stay. Everyone settled. Becca is near the creek. We do nothing. Woman's body does the work. We call on Yowa to make easy." Anita said as she dug a fire pit to prepare for the birth. "Maybe you find wood for fire. Maybe find fresh meat for pot?"

"So, in other words, you are shooing me away and out from under your feet," he said with a smile. "Well, I'll find Will and see what we can do."

After explaining to Will, they went to other clansmen with the idea of a hunt, then formed a quick hunting party and set out to find some fresh meat.

The women searched the woods and creek area for edible vegetation. Others began making cooking fires and setting out what little articles they had for a comfortable night.

With less threat of capture, chatter and laughter could be heard by the new clan as they gathered around their individual campfires.

# Chapter 47

*I'm not sure what that feeling was that came over me, but when we attacked that human I never felt so excited before...and I liked it! Humans must get it too, like the one on the horse. That feeling...I felt it clear through my body and it was so intense, I think I can even kill a rat now!* said Orphy.

*You feel it too? Wow, I never had anything come over me as strong as that was. I wanted to dominate the world... and felt like I could! I'm still trying to calm down inside, it was better than any raw bone my humans ever gave me,* added Tory

*I don't know what it was, but I'm going to make sure that I feel it again. If Zeus doesn't go with us we will go on a hunt without him. I loved it! And I'm ready right now to find the trail of something...anything to get back that feeling. I'm just wondering how Zeus is able to adjust so quickly back to his human's orders. Is he truly our Alpha?* asked Sashay.

Turning, ever-so-slowly, Zeus made solid eye contact with her, and then slowly approached until his chest bumped against her, he huffed, *You want to challenge me now? What is going on today? I attacked that human because he was about to harm one of those who helped raise all of us. Don't you feel you owe them something?*

Sashay dropped her head and stepped off to one side in submission to his authority while the other two dropped to a shoulder and offered their belly to him. Sashay would not let it go, *You mean to tell us that you felt nothing when you attacked that man? Nothing different than you ever felt before?*

He continued his stiff stance, but yielding to the question, he admitted, *Yes. Yes I did and it was strange...and yet normal too. And we will feel it again. We will go on a hunt before we get back to your humans...but I will be the one to decide when, where and what to hunt. Is that perfectly clear?* He looked long and hard at Sashay, *Sashay? Is that clear?*

A deep sigh escaped as she dropped her head and turned away, *Yes, it is 'perfectly clear', Zeus almighty.*

*Sashay, why do you give me so much grief?*

*Because I don't understand an Alpha male that will cower to a human. They are not our gods, yet you act like that big one is. You answer to his beck-and-call as if you were a puppy still squatting to pee. Show a little backbone, stand up to him and show your rank,* she snapped.

He glanced at the other two and knew his position was in jeopardy. He demanded, with more authority than he felt, *I AM the Alpha male and you may be the Alpha female, but you still rank under me, and you will do what I say.*

She knew his patience was running thin and that she could possibly push him too far; his ego would not allow her much more leniency, but she too had pride that would not be dominated. When she turned away she muttered, *Yeah, whatever.*

Zeus also knew her, and that it was time the confrontation was dropped, while she was in the mood to consent.

The cry of an infant gave him reason to take his leave and keep his pride. He went to investigate and found the humans gathering around the woman they saved. She was lying on the ground with a bundle in her arms, but she was

177

smiling and the other humans were too. The men were back from their hunt and one of his male humans was excited.

"It's a boy!" yelled William.

"Congratulations there, son, and with a fine strong pair of lungs too! And look at how handsome he is; it's a good thing that he has a good looking mama!" Gabe chided as he pounded Will on the back. "I wish I had some cigars to pass around. I feel like a proud grandpa."

Filled with emotion, Will quietly answered, "You know, you are the closest thing to being a grandpa that he will ever have, now that Blue and I are both orphans. You are my family and have been for many years."

Both men's eyes grew moist as they hugged each other, but they regained control when Anita shooed them away and took the baby to the creek to wash him and replace the blanket with a clean and dry one.

As she dipped the baby in the creek, in the Cherokee custom, his body tensed, and his hands became fists, but he did not cry out. Anita crooned to him, "So you had to enter the world on your own terms, little brave, a whole month early, but you show no signs of lacking anything. On the contrary, you are already showing your Cherokee pride of not showing pain and discomfort. That is good, my little one, for you shall need it growing up in this white man's world." She cupped her hand with water and poured it over his scalp and watched as his eye lids tightened, then opened to look her full in the face. His little chin quivered and he brought his knees up as he gripped the air before him...but his eyes never wavered, "Yes, you will be strong and give your parents many reasons to be proud."

# Chapter 48

When Puma's reins were handed to Soaring Eagle, he looked into the eyes of the sergeant and gave a slight nod. Although no words were needed, the soldier broke the silence with, "I'm sorry that he was taken from you. As far as I'm concerned it won't happen again."

The chief waited his chance and that evening he took Puma off the trail and upstream from the clan. There he faced the stallion and stood with foreheads touching, "I'm sorry, dear friend that bad things happened to you. They are happening to many of Yowa's children." He then pulled hunks of moss from a nearby oak, dipped it into the water and began to rub the horse down.

Puma stood in the knee-deep water, accepting the loving gesture. As the man bent to add more water to the moss, he reached around and playfully nibbled at his hair. "Oh, so you want to play?" asked the chief.

The horse vigorously nodded his head, not understanding the words but the loving tone of them.

Soaring Eagle moved to embrace the horse's neck while still rubbing down one shoulder. Puma lowered his head and pulled the man close. The man and the horse stood quietly for a few minutes exchanging their mutual love.

The sky looked ominous as the new clan reclaimed the trail that led back toward Ft. Wells, and many were concerned that the downpour the clouds threatened, would come before they could find adequate shelter.

The wind grew quickly from a slight breeze to a roar, so much so that Thomas had to lean forward to hear and be heard. He yelled close to Will's ear, "I don't remember

seeing any form of cover as we passed this way before."
Another gust of wind made him grab for his hat as he
continued, "We have to find some protection for the
women and children. I think this is going to be a bad one!
Do you have any suggestions?"

The wind was trying to whip their clothes from their
bodies as Gabe came running up, with the wolves behind
him, "Have the men scout quickly for some place we can
get undercover until this blows over!"

Will pointed off to his right, "Our only hope is that thick
stand of pines!"

Gabe shouted back, "I'll spread the word and set the
people in that direction! I think we're in for more than just
wind and rain!"

He was right. The clan was spread out and on the run for
the trees as the rain started. It quickly became hail and as
the clan ran hunched over, they covered their bodies with
what they carried.

Becca shielded the baby with her own body, clutching
him to her chest while the cradleboard on her back took the
brunt of the pellets. Will ran beside her, covering them with
a blanket to shield from the hammering of the hailstones.

The wind carried away people's cries of fear as it tore
through the trees, carrying loose bark and foliage in its
wake. Older tree snags were uprooted and crashed down
upon anything, or anyone that had found refuge under it.

It was not the best shelter, but the massive pine branches
gave some protection to those who had sought it. Members
of the clan watched from beneath the branches as the
ground turned white, then ankle deep with the massive
hailstones.

As the storm lashed out in fury, the people were held hostage, forced to crouch low behind the massive tree trunks that diverted the debris that was sent airborne.

Will continued to shield his family, by covering them with his body and the blanket. As they crouched he held two corners of the blanket while Becca held the other two as tight as possible around them, forming the best shelter they could for their newborn. They could hear the crash of trees falling all around and prayed to their individual god that the tree they were under would hold. Minutes seemed like hours before the storm lifted and all was quiet. When the clan emerged from the trees they waded through the hailstones and looked up at a bright blue sky, then to one another with unspoken questions of what they had just witnessed.

"This must be a sign from Yowa, but I'm not sure good or bad," Anita whispered to Gabe.

"Yes, dear, either Yowa or God, and like you, I wonder. On the good side, when the stones are gathered and melted, we will have fresh clean water."

Becca looked at William and asked, "Do you think that our son's name should be part of what just happened?"

Will thought, "Wind? Thunder? Rain? Hail? I know… how about 'Running for cover'?" He laughed, but stopped after seeing Becca's expression; she was not amused.

When she had time to think she had to relent a little and approached Will with, "What about "Storm Runner?"

"Hmmm, Storm Runner Hudson…wouldn't that apply to us instead of him?"

"Yes, you are right. We think more on it."

# Chapter 49

"Gabe, do you think we should head directly to the valley, or back to Ft. Wells first?" asked Will.

"We're going to have to get our bearings about where the valley is. After the soldiers attacked and took them hostage, we were fixed more on getting our women back than mapping the area," answered Gabe.

Thomas added, "As for me, I have to go to the fort and find out if there has been any solid proof that our women can be excused from any future replacements. I hope you will keep Ellen with you until I find out for sure. I wasn't with the group that arrested the clan, so I have no idea of what you are talking about. And I have to report to Commander Wadsworth on my leave of absence. The news will determine whether I remain in the Army or join you at this valley you all talk about."

Gabe agreed, "We understand, Thomas, and of course we need to know too. All our lives depend on that news." Turning to Will he added, "We will be close to Ft. Wells tomorrow, so I think you should discuss this with Becca."

Thomas interrupted, "I'm not sure she will be much help. When she came to the fort she was in a mental state and Ellen was taking care of her. She said Becca had been that way since she saw her mother killed in the attack."

"Maybe it would be better if we get our wives together and have *them* discuss it," offered Gabe.

Piecing together what the men could remember, as they followed the soldiers and the clan, and their own recollections, it was Anita and Ellen who remembered most. Becca's trauma left her without input, so they all calculated that if they continued straight to the cabins,

182

using the obvious trail, it would make it easier to backtrack from there to the valley.

"The undergrowth will have covered the trail used back then, so we will have to rely on larger landmarks and instincts. Perhaps something might trigger memories of that time and place and help us along the way," offered Gabe.

"And after all...we *are* trappers and most people call us 'Mountain Men' so we should know what we're doing... right?" laughed Will.

"No doubt we will find it. It's just a matter of time and the will of God. Prayers would be a good idea about now. Have you put any thought as to what will happen if we are able to live among the whites?" asked Gabe.

"Then it will be up to the individual as to who lives where. The valley looked big enough to sustain life for the entire clan," said Will

"I'm going to talk to Anita...I want to go get Gigi in Charlottesville and if I can't come up with the train fare, it will take me about a month on foot, and even longer with her to get back. As best my geography memory recalls, it would be close to 400 miles. Mrs. Wadsworth said by train I could get there in a couple of days. If we still have any of our tools at the cabins, I could sell them for the train ticket there plus Gigi's and my way back. A lot of time saved."

Will nodded, "I understand. We can go to Ft. Wells, the clan can camp out by our cabins so no one will know they are anywhere near the area, and we'll take it from there. Knowing Anita, she will make good use of her time while waiting for you and Gigi...probably mothering this new clan."

Gabe laughed, "That she will. She seems happier knowing she is heading far away from the white society."

Will was walking away; as he turned he waved and answered, "And who can blame her?"

As they neared Ft. Wells the wolves got anxious to be home to their humans. Trotting along shoulder to shoulder, they shared their excitement about getting there. *Mine are going to be so happy to see me. They will probably rub my coat and talk in that funny voice they use only for me. And I hope they have a big fat bone waiting, I'm not used to going so long between meals.* said Tory.

*Speaking of bones...my feet are bone tired from all this walking and running. It will be nice to get off them and be close to that hot fire again. My human always talks to me...and gives me hugs...and scratches behind my ears...mmm it feels sooo good,* sighed Orphy.

*Yes, it has been tiring, but I want to know when we are going on that hunt. Zeus, you promised! I think we could go out at night and no one would even know we were gone...and then be back before they woke up. That day, with that man, such a feeling of...power...came over me, like together we could....*

Zeus answered her, *Sashay, you might as well say it. I know you want to go out and kill something. I know because I've been fighting the same feelings since that day, but for what? We get fed, and are all well taken care of. We don't have to hunt.*

*Is everything in life about have to? What about wanting to? Besides, it feels like it is something we are supposed to do,* she argued.

*Well, either way, we are all going home. We will talk about this later, after we get back and settled in. For now, stop your lusting for a kill, and think about what the fort butcher has out in that shed for you.*

Tory drooled, *Oh, yeah, Sashay...you have a lot more bones at the fort than I do at the store. If I come up there, will they throw a few my way?*

Sashay snapped, *Tory, for howling out loud, can't you think of anything other than your stomach?* Then mellowing she added, *Yes, I'll be happy to get rid of a few. I'm tired of burying them.*

*It seems like you guys get your fill. My human doesn't have much food at the livery, but I get enough so I don't complain. He shows me a lot of love and that makes me happy,* said Orphy.

*Do you go hungry sometimes? You just come to the store and I'll sneak you a bone or scrap of meat when I can,* offered Tory.

*That's the nicest thing I've heard you say on this whole trip, Tory. You actually thought of someone other than your stomach,* chided Sashay.

*I think of others! It's just that we've been on the go so much and I've missed so many of my meals...*

Stopping suddenly, causing the others to collide with one another, Zeus turned, *Pleeasse... you guys knock it off! Sashay, stop complaining about Tory's complaining; I'm sick of your complaints.*

*I wasn't...* whined Orphy.

Closing his eyes and shaking his head, he added quietly, *I know Orphy. I know you weren't. I was talking to the other two.*

# Chapter 50

Just before reaching Ft. Wells Thomas approached Gabe, "I think I should go alone. I am expected back from my leave of absence and if they see you they will know that the clan is close by."

"You have a point. I'll keep Zeus here and you take the rest of the wolves with you." So the party split with the new clan skirting the town and heading to the cabins. Thomas made his way to the fort as Orphy and Tory separated and ran for their homes.

Upon returning to his quarters and donning his uniform, Thomas knocked on the Commander's door. Sergeant Wilson answered and then stepped back and stated, "Corporal Thorton, would like a word, Sir."

Thomas entered the Commander's office, and was taken aback to see someone else behind the desk. Worried about protocol he snapped to attention. "Sir, Commander er..uh.., Sir...Corporal Thomas reporting back from leave, Sir."

With a slight wave of the hand, the man behind the desk said, "At ease, Corporal. I choose to not use all the falderal of most officers. I understand my predecessor felt the same. But by all means, get to the point."

"Sorry sir; I thought I'd find Commander Wadsworth."

"And I'm sorry to disappoint you, Corporal, but Wadsworth should be settled comfortably in his home in Charlottesville by now. I am his replacement, Commander Matthew Simmons. Now, how may I be of assistance?"

"It's a long story sir," began Thomas.

"I have a lot of time on my hands." Turning he said, "Sergeant Wilson, bring up a chair for the Corporal."

After reporting what had happened to the Commander, Thomas sat back and waited for a reply.

Simmons rummaged through his desk and pulled out an envelope addressed to "Corporal Thorton" which Thomas recognized as Commander Wadsworth's handwriting. After tossing it across to Thomas, he turned back to Wilson and stated, "Get me the file that states what the requirements are for Indians to remain in the territory." Then to the corporal he continued, "Where is your wife now?"

Becoming fidgety, Thomas answered, "I'd rather not say, Sir. If things here go sour, I will have to resign my position and join her and continue to keep her safe."

"I like your honesty, Corporal, and commend your desire to protect your wife...quite admirable. But if the orders state they are to be turned over to the army, and you don't, it would be an act of treason..."

"I'm aware of that Sir, but if I've resigned from the Army, I will just be a regular citizen protecting my wife... is that not so?"

Sighing deeply, the two briefly locked eyes before Wilson stepped forward with a file in hand, "Here is the file, Sir."

"Oh, thank you, Sergeant. Now we'll see if all of this is worth worrying about."

After taking a few minutes to read the document, he turned to Thomas and said, "It reads here, that 'the only way for an Indian to remain, and avoid removal, is to accept the federal offer of 640 acres or more (according to the size of the family) of land in exchange for leaving the tribe and becoming a state citizen subject to state law and federal law.' So it seems that not only can she stay, but she will also be given acreage to do so. Is that something you think she would be willing to do? Leave her tribe and become a citizen of South Carolina?"

"Commander Wadsworth sent that to us in a note, but the officer in charge of the removal laughed and tore it up. He expressed he had presidential orders to round up all natives, with no exception. So, who or what am I to believe?"

"As for those *presidential orders*, that I am not aware of, and without knowledge of the document, I will consider it moot. Do you plan on settling near Ft. Wells? If so I will sign a document that waives any 'removal' of your wife."

"Sir, may I be so bold as to ask the same for two of my wife's friends? They too are married to white men who live nearby. They were all adjusting quite well to society before they were taken prisoners."

"As far as I'm concerned, if they will abide by the terms of this proclamation, they will also receive the same document signed by me and protected by my authority."

Jumping up and reaching for his superior's hand, Thomas blurted out, "You can't possibly know how this will affect our lives, Commander. Thank you, Thank you! Since we were all married in this office, with Sergeant Wilson as a witness, he also has documents that prove our marriages."

Standing and smiling broadly, the commander accepted Thomas' hand and shook it vigorously, "You can rest assured that if you bring them here, I will personally swear them in and start the procedure to accrue those acres that this proclamation declares."

After leaving the new commander's office and heading back to town, Thomas opened the letter and read, "Dear Corporal Thorton, will you please pass on this letter to Mr.

Adams. It is to inform him that I was denied the privilege of taking Sashay with me on the train because she was considered a risk to other passengers. Even though I assured them she was not, they clung to their company policy. Please keep her with Zeus and give her a good home. She was a loving pet to Olivia and me."

# Chapter 51

The Whitmore Plantation had spacious lawns around the mansion. In the back there was a massive White Oak that had stood for generations and shaded the whole area.

One morning during breakfast, Grace turned on her newly found 'southern charm' and coyly approached Uncle Frederic with a desire to have a swing, "One large enough to hold the volume of my dress and layers of petticoats."

He was happy to oblige but Olivia was hesitant. "It would not be ladylike to swing high and expose your under garments, dear."

"Oh no, Aunt Olivia I have no desire to swing high. I just want to feel the breeze it makes on a hot summer's day. The shade of that magnificent tree is so delicious and the swing would just add to that."

"Well, in that case, my dear. Uncle Frederick will see to it that Jebediah erects one right away."

Thinking that loneliness had created the desire for the swing, Olivia ventured, "Do you miss not having friends?"

"I have you, and Uncle Frederick."

"I mean people your own age."

Thinking back to her past life, she stated, "I never thought about it. I was not happy with others my age. They made fun of me, and treated me poorly."

"I'm sorry that you had to endure that treatment."

"I've all but forgotten most of it. I'm happy now."

Later when they were alone, Olivia turned to Frederick and suggested, "You know my dear, we could plan a party to introduce her to her peers. In that way she may overcome her unfortunate past and create new friendships."

She continued, "Perhaps, because of her lack of proper education, we sheltered her too much. It's time for her to meet the rest of the world…and the rest of the world to meet her."

"How about finding a girl her age to help her along with that, to prepare her for the event?" he asked.

Olivia was ecstatic, "What a great idea! I can ask some of my friends, who have daughters her age, if they would like to come to tea. Maybe a small tea party will help her to form friendships! Oh yes, this will be her first test to see how she handles herself with her peers. There were none her age at the Ft. Wells School."

"I was speaking more like a handmaid for her. Someone she could become close friends with. You know our friend's daughters have turned out to be young snobs. I've watched them be very rude to their servants and even to each other at times. Besides Olivia, to me, Grace has no peers, just like you, my beautiful Buttercup." he said as he pulled her into his arms.

"Now, Freddy, you know a lady demands respect from the staff, and if those girls were rude, it was probably just to keep the servants in their place. They were probably being disrespectful in some way and had to be corrected."

"But there are ways of correcting servants, usually in private; without embarrassment to the person. I don't want our Grace to turn out like that."

"I'll teach her to treat them with respect and kindness."

Knowing he was treading on thin ice he added, "Yes, dear." And then rang the bell to summon Tilda.

A few weeks later, Grace was enjoying the newly built swing, when Tilda came to the back yard to announce the arrival of guests.

Grace left the swing and ran to the back door, only to have Tilda stop her and explain that "a lady never greets her guests all flushed and sweaty. You must go to your mirror and freshen up before greeting them."

"More powder, Tilda? How much of that stuff do I have to pat all over face? I look like a ghost already."

"Yes, Miss Grace, enough to eliminate the shine of perspiration, my dear."

"I like my face shiny. That way people know that it is clean. This way, they don't know what I look like under all of the powder," Grace whined.

"Your Aunt Olivia wants you to learn the proper ways of the young ladies your age, and this is one of the rules. Now go…powder your nose, your guests are waiting!"

When she entered the parlor she found four girls her age, all in fine, fashionable dresses and in an array of colors. Her eyes were immediately drawn to a scarlet satin that a blonde girl was wearing. *Aunt Olivia says I shouldn't wear red because it will clash with my hair, but it is so pretty.* Continuing with her observation she scanned the rest to find slightly similar dress styles but adorned with different laces or ruffles. Some had long sleeves and high necks while others were short sleeved, yet the arms were covered with elbow-length gloves.

Some carried decorative hand fans that they opened and closed with a flick of their wrists, and fanned themselves with chins held high.

Tilda and another servant arrived with two trays, one filled with tiny sandwiches and the other with a pitcher of lemonade and five glasses that held a slice of lemon wedge on each rim.

Olivia followed them into the room and while one servant poured lemonade, and the other offered sandwiches to the guests, she began her introductions, "Thank you all for coming to meet my sweet niece, Grace. She came to us while my husband was Commander at Ft. Wells in South Carolina. After her parents' demise it was found that her mother was Mr. Wadsworth's sister and he was her only relative. She was brought to us as an orphan and we decided it was our Christian duty to adopt her. I would appreciate each of you introducing yourselves, as I introduce to you…Miss Grace Wadsworth!"

The girls all stood, side by side, and each stepped forward as she gave her name along with a little curtsey.

With each girl's curtsey, Grace remembered to bow just her head, in acceptance.

"My name is Hannah Bowers"

"I'm Suzette Rhodes"

"Marylee Pruitt"

"And I am Rose Ann Stuart".

Upon getting a nod from Olivia, Grace raised her chin and smiled, "It is a pleasure to meet each of you and thank you for coming. I hope to make you all lifelong friends." Then seeing Olivia's smile, she knew she had quoted her lines correctly.

# Chapter 52

Gabe and Anita led the clan as they traveled between the town and the cabins and neared the path the horse and sled had made. Something made him signal the group by raising his hand high and using the shrill whistle of the kite bird for silence. He sensed someone was outside the perimeter and motioned for everyone to hunker down.

As they all squatted, hardly breathing, a lone man with a wolf came out of the tree line. It was Thomas with Sashay.

Signaling that all was well, Gabe told Anita to continue as he waited for Thomas, "How on earth did you find us?"

"I just told Sashay, 'Find Zeus' and she brought me here. I have news from the fort."

Thomas quickly recounted the new commander's promise and handed Gabe the letter from Commander Wadsworth.

"Do you trust this new commander? What if it is another trick to recapture our wives? Would you do me a favor? After you meet with Ellen, hold off in mentioning this to anyone, just yet. I'll call for a meeting after everyone is settled around the cabins. I don't want the clan thinking that we are abandoning them before we even get them to the new valley. I feel like Moses, responsible for the safety of the multitude that God put in his charge."

"I have to tell Ellen. She has been through so much and needs reassurance that things could be better."

"I understand, Thomas, but I hope you see my point. They must all feel the same hope for their future. When we get to the cabins we can all discuss the issue and those that want to continue on to the valley can, and the others can go back to the fort and take their chances."

"Alright, I'll only confide in Ellen," said Thomas.

After reading the letter he said, "So, Sashay is mine now too?" Looking at the two wolves traveling side by side he added, "Well, I'm glad that the two won't be separated. They get along well and will make good company for one another. Besides it will be twice the security for the family. Or maybe Will and Becca will take her and we can all be one big happy family...that is after I go and bring Gigi home. I'm getting pretty antsy about going to get her."

"Have you acquired the train fare yet?"Asked Thomas

"No, but I'm fixing to see about that very thing."

"I wish I had the funds to give you, but with my Leave of Absence I have no pay; at least for another month."

"Thanks, but don't worry about it. I'll find a way. I want to get to the cabins and see what was left behind that might be worth selling in town, then get these people to that valley and settled in. If there's nothing to sell I'm setting off on foot to go after Gigi."

"Gabe, walking all that way is all well and good for a man that has no foot problems, but for you it would be almost impossible, besides Gigi probably won't want that trek back here. That's a long way for anyone, let alone a man in your condition and a young lady."

Gabe nodded, "No doubt she can out-walk me now, with this darn foot. But this is something that I have to do...it's been a mighty long time since I got a 'Papa Hug' from that girl!"

Jumping Fox, Moon Star, and their son Badger Blue had been keeping close to Becca since their father's death and knew that she was not herself. She had become despondent since then and had shown signs of sliding back into her 'quiet place' where she no longer resided in the present world. She methodically fed and changed the baby, at times getting help from one of the women when necessary. But suddenly she became excited as she recognized the path to the cabins. Turning to Will, she looked into his whiskery face and said, "Home!"

Will smiled, knowing that she was now fully connected with reality, and gave a sigh of relief. Pulling her close, he ignored her family and gave her a hungry kiss, trying hard to control the passion he had held back since her father's death. She leaned into him and whispered, "Tonight, after we have long bath in warm water tub?"

He and Smithy had made the tub from slats of wood caulked with resin and bound with iron rings, and now he recalled the sight of her standing beside it, nude and wringing her raven black hair. The chain of memory pulled forth his first vision of her body glistening in the sunlight as she stepped from the creek that day, in the new valley…

She gave him a light shake that jarred the image from his mind and brought him back to her smiling face, "You going to stand here all day or are we going to show Fox and Moon Star our beautiful home?"

He laughed and grabbed her hand. With the baby strapped on her back they hurriedly led the way.

The families found their cabins much as they left them, except for a few cobwebs and mouse droppings. The women immediately reached for brooms, and the men went in search of fire wood.

Gabe couldn't let himself think of Thomas' news and did not want to believe or could not trust it to be true. He thought, "*Why now, Lord? What if I tell them and they all get recaptured and all of this is for nothing? But who am I to make the decision for them? Should I wait until we get to the valley? But then there would be that much more walking for the clan if they decide to return and take their chances. If it's true we can all live in peace and not have to struggle with losing the modern comforts we've all become used to. Should I go after Gigi now? What if I lose Anita again? This Valley Plan is a good one, one that answers the question of freedom. Now I'm not sure if I have the right to hold the news from them. If I keep quiet, Thomas will tell them anyway. He believes this new commander. But...I'm just not sure."* Gabe was torn in both directions but decided to stick to the original plan, in case those that heard Thomas' news still wanted to continue to the valley.

He sought out Thomas and spoke quietly, "It's up to you now. I can't be a part of turning these people over to the army that they just escaped from. I understand your wanting to believe, but I've been disappointed by 'officials' most of my life and...I just can't do it. You decide, it's your news, when or if you tell everyone."

This left Thomas in a quandary. He began to have second thoughts. *Can I trust that new commander? I didn't see the statements on that document that he read from. What if he was making it all up? What if I'm taking Ellen back to be captured again and start the march all over for her? She would hate me and even doubt that I love her...she may even think I betrayed her. But am I to do the thinking for other people that might want what the document offers...if it's true? Who wouldn't? The offer is a good one. But what if the offer is good only to entice everyone into coming to the fort to be sworn in? Oh Lord, I don't know what to do, give me a sign, something that will show me the right way.*

"A penny for your thoughts, my dear husband. You look so sober and your brow has so many deep furrows one could plant seeds," said Ellen.

"Oh, hi honey. I'm hassling with a very hard decision and I'm not sure what to do."

"Do you trust me to help you with it?"

"I'm thinking you are the one I *need* to talk to about it."

"I'm listening."

Ellen stood quietly and listened to the news, "Oh, my dear husband. This is a hard choice to make. I'm afraid I have to agree with Gabe. I can't go on another march. I saw hunger and cold, old ones falling and those that tried to help them get whipped. There were soldiers that befriended us, but I saw others who wanted us all dead. We did not know who to trust until some of them gave our braves back their weapons and allowed us to leave, promising that the clan members who stayed would be treated fairly. Even after Nichols' attack, we were constantly looking over our shoulders, in fear that another rider, swinging his sword over his head and screaming like a crazy person would come bearing down on us. I can't make the decision for you, but I for one am not convinced; and I'm not sure how to trust anyone."

Thomas decided to sleep on it and see if the Lord would guide him further. He thought that one of the answers was the message from Ellen, not to trust, but the nagging feeling that he *could* trust was wearing strongly on his conscience.

After explaining to Ellen the next morning that it was something that he felt he had to do, and that it seemed like the only right thing *to* do, he made the decision to tell the clan and let each person decide for himself.

She nodded, "I understand. It is true. They *should* know and choose for themselves. Then we will be relieved that we have left it up to them. I'll stand with you."

Quietly the clan answered the call of the Chickadee and gathered around the two. Ellen translated Thomas' message as he told them of the new commander's promise and how each person should follow his own conscience and decide whether he could trust this stranger or take his chances in the new valley. He drew a line in the dirt and said, "Those of you who wish to go on to the valley cross the line…if you wish to return to the fort stay where you are."

It was as if they were all tied together as they quietly advanced forward and crossed the line.

Ellen spoke for Thomas as she cheerfully stated, "That settles it. We will all go on to the valley!"

The next morning, the cabin owners began to decide on what they could take and what they could live without. Surely Angel would carry the brunt of the load, but once in town the sled would have to be left behind because its tracks would be too hard to erase. They decided to load it up with what they knew they could part with and hopefully sell in town. What they thought would be needed in the new valley was set aside.

The men hated to give up any of their tools, so Will decided to start with the traps and snares. Gabe immediately questioned, "What if we need one, for a bear or cougar that could be in that area?"

"And they could have babies waiting, for them to come home to feed them," countered Will.

"Well, I'm not going to forfeit the lives of my women over their offspring. And you should think of your new son too; as well as Becca, if she has him out and alone."

"I understand where you're coming from Gabe, but you didn't see the tragedy unfold about that mother wolf getting back to her cubs."

"You think in all the years of my trapping that I didn't come across situations like that? I saw their mate lying close by them until I came on the scene and only leaving because of fear of me. And then my having to club the trapped one to death knowing that mate was probably watching from a hidden thicket. It's a hard life that has its downfalls, but it provided a living for some of us who preferred to stay away from society."

"If you take a few...for protection...I'll agree to it. But don't ask me to set any more...I just can't."

The women were having problems inside. Anita knew she could only take the most necessary items and chose their clothing, bedding, pots, metal dishes, a few utensils, sewing items, seeds, salt, and a small medicine box. At the last minute she added a beaded necklace that Gigi had made for her.

Becca wanted it all. She felt she couldn't leave her furniture, the bed Will made with the straw-filled mattress, the chair and couch, the kitchen table and chairs...and the little baby crib...he had made them all at Smithy's. The porcelain bowls and dishes, as well as her butter churn and wash tub would all have to be left behind. Will found her slumped down onto the floor in tears. "Will, how can I leave all of this? You made them for me and our baby and I can't leave them. There are many memories in each one."

"We can replace them, Becca, and the new ones will give us even more memories. We will be giving our son a safe place to grow with no soldiers coming to take him away."

Gathering herself together she said, "Are we doing the right thing? What if the new chief of the fort is telling the truth and we can all live in peace? What if we didn't have to leave all of this behind?"

"And what if it's a trick? What if you are put back on that trail and marched again over the same ground? We have to think about what is best for our son."

"I know, I know, we must." Changing the subject she stated, "I've thought more about his name. I want one of his names to be like my father, Swift Arrow."

"Would you mind if one of his names was after *my* father, as well?" Will asked.

"Of course not, he should have a white-man's name first. What is it, your father's name?"

"That's a problem. *I* was named after *him*, William. So I was thinking...We can name him William, but use the last four letters of it and call him Liam. He'll carry the tradition of the William Hudsons, but with separate middle names. "

"Liam Swift Hudson...hmmm that sounds good. Sounds like an important white man's name."

Will smiled, "And I've even thought about our second son's name..."

Laughing, Becca patted his chest and said, "Now, how are you so sure it will be another boy? It is way too soon to be talking about it. We must think about the valley now."

# Chapter 53

Tilda knocked lightly on Grace's door, "Your Uncle and Aunt wish to have a word with you in the parlor."

Grace turned, "Do you know what for? Have I done something wrong?"

"I can't say, missy. They just told me to fetch you."

When Grace complied she was met with an enthusiastic, "We have decided that today is your birthday and we are going to throw you a party!"

"What is that?" she asked.

Olivia chose to answer. "It is a celebration for one person to be honored. You will be the center of attention. We have no way of knowing when your birthday is, so we have decided that it is today."

Grace became excited. "Does that mean I will get gifts and meet new friends?"

"Well, we would have to decide if they are worthy of your attention. We don't want you seen with less than the best. Society judges you on your choice of companionship and you must be seen with only the elite, of the elite. You are growing into a refined lady and you do not want to smudge your image. After all, you *are* a Wadsworth. But we are getting off the subject here a little. Since this is your 'official' birthday, we want to give you a personal companion, a 'handmaid' so to speak. Tilda, would you bring her in, please?"

Tilda opened the door and a black teenage girl stepped in. "This is Sadie. She has been on the plantation all her life and will now share your quarters," said Olivia

Grace was stunned. "My quarters? In my room? I don't understand. Why?"

"Well, dear, most of the young women you've met all have handmaids. They are a companion…a friend …"

"I don't need a handmaid…and am I so pathetic that you have to *hire* me a friend?"

"No, no my dear. She will help you dress and fill your bath and comb your hair, keep your clothes clean; she will be your helper in all things you don't want to do."

Grace grew silent and looking the girl over, she thought; *maybe it wouldn't be so bad. She could make my bed and clean my room.* "Well, I suppose we could see how it goes, but I will *not* share my room. There must be another one, perhaps within my calling distance, where she can stay."

"Tilda, is there a space we can clear on that wing that would be suitable for Sadie? A space of her own?"

"Yes, Ms. Olivia… There is a storage room just next door to Missy Grace's room. We can fix that up for Sadie. She would be able to hear if Missy Grace calls out."

"Then that's what we'll do. Would you see to that? Make Sadie comfortable, then the girls can get acquainted."

When Tilda and Sadie left the parlor, Frederick retrieved a packet of papers from the desk nearby and said, "Now it's my turn. My present to you is this." He handed the packet to Grace but couldn't wait for her to open it. "They are the adoption papers. We'll keep them in this desk drawer. Our attorney has a copy that is ready for the judge to sign as soon as the year is up. I've notified the authorities and the documents state that, so far, your parents cannot be found, which will make it an easy adoption."

"What if Papa or Mother come to get me? Can they stop me becoming your legal daughter?"

"If they come you can ask them to sign the papers here…on this line. If they choose not to, we will have our lawyer make them prove they are your parents. Do they have a birth certificate?" said Olivia

"No, but Papa's hair…and eyes…they are the same."

"We would have to go back to the story of him being your uncle and you having an Indian woman as your nanny and what your lifestyle was before you came to us. The courts will choose in our favor. You have nothing to fear my dear…you *will* be our daughter soon."

Changing the solemn mood, Uncle Frederick said, "Now let's make plans for that party!"

# Chapter 54

Gabe spoke to Anita as they sorted through the last of their belongings. What could they part with and what could they carry to the valley? He took her in his arms and held her close, "I'm sorry we have to part with all the things we've worked so hard to get. These things have made our house a home. The sawmill offered to buy back all my box-making supplies and Smithy will buy and try to sell the rest, so we might have a little left over when I get back.

I will leave the sled at Smithy's then go to the station and buy my ticket. Will said he will bring the sled back and load it up with his and Becca's things. The Hamiltons have offered both of us a good price and plan on reselling what they don't need. We are so blessed to have friends that help us and keep our secrets. So this is our last night until I return. I'm glad that the clan is here for your protection. It might be a week before I get back with Gigi, but we will be a family again and I'm looking forward to that."

Tilting her chin up and looking into her eyes he added, "I know one thing…that bed is the last thing I'm loading on the sled because it's going to get good use tonight."

Anita's eyes crinkled as she smiled and patted his arm. "Yes, my Husband. I glad to see Gigi too, it been too long. And I welcome the last night on our bed."

The next morning Gabe pulled Anita into his arms and gave her a lingering kiss. "That's going to have to hold me until I get back. I love you, my little Sparrow."

"I love you too, Husband. You hurry back. I already am missing you."

# Chapter 55

"Grace dear, there's someone to see you."

"Who is it, Aunt Olivia?"

"That would spoil the surprise."

Expecting to see one of her schoolmates, she patted her hair in the mirror and turned to see her aunt's anxious expression.

Standing, she looked past Olivia and saw the guest. This man was well groomed, clean shaven and was smiling broadly. He wore older but clean clothes, and held a fur hat. As she studied his features her eyes settled on the color of his hair; red mixed with grey and...suddenly she recognized him. Her hand rose to her chest as she took a step backward. All those dark shadows in her night dreams and vague memories came slamming back as reality; all those that she tried so hard to suppress and leave behind.

Grace quickly looked around to see if anyone else had seen him, "Papa!" she whispered.

She had never seen him clean shaven before and she could barely recognize this man that had once been her whole world. Only her eyes moved as they darted over and around him in search of what she feared to see most...her mother. She felt embarrassed and displeased.

Gabe became confused, expecting her to run into his arms, but seeing her react just the opposite; he stiffened and held back, "Gigi?"

Olivia, seeing the exchange, decided to give them privacy and said, "Well, I'll leave you two some time to catch up. Grace, see your guest to the parlor, dear. I'll have Tilda bring in some tea."

Grace led Gabe into the parlor, but kept a slight distance between them, then arranged herself in an armchair, leaving him no choice but to sit in one facing her.

Still confused, he watched her every move. Silently she rearranged her dress and picked invisible threads from it, all the while avoiding eye contact.

When he could wait no longer he asked, "Gigi, what's wrong? Aren't you glad to see me?"

"Well, uh, yes, of course…but…my name is Grace, and could you please keep that in mind? It would be a little confusing to the staff if any of them should hear you."

Frowning, he obliged by answering, "Yes, Grace dear." just as Tilda came in with the tea.

"Set it there, Tilda, and after you pour you can leave. Mr. Adams is my uncle, here to discuss matters stemming from my childhood in the backwoods of the Appalachians, before my parents died and left me an orphan. I was lucky that Aunt Olivia and Uncle Frederick took me in."

Gabe sat back in his chair and waited for the servant to leave. Taking a deep breath and exhaling it slowly, he ventured, "Is that the story? Well, it sounds plausible, but that's all behind us now. I've come to take you home."

Grace began shaking visibly, "Please keep your voice low. And where is 'home' exactly? That dirty little cabin in the woods? Where we scraped animal hides that stunk to high heaven and mother crawled around in her garden, picking weeds and bugs off of her precious vegetables? Where you tried so hard to hide me from the white people? 'To protect me', you said. Well, Papa, the only *people* that ever accepted me, *are* those white people."

Ignoring her new name, he questioned, "Gigi! What about Becca and Ellen and...your mother? She has always loved you and protected you...."

Through gritted teeth she answered, "Yes, Papa, what about them? Mother never protected me. She never stood up to those who pushed me and pulled my hair and rubbed dirt into it *to change its color*...and the other two? They too, were some of those who mocked me, or ignored me. Or didn't you know that? I put it behind me then, for mother's sake, but I remember it all."

"Your mother had no place to go. The clan provided...."

Grace stood and paced the floor, wringing her hands, and keeping her voice low she blurted, "The *clan* provided us with starvation, humiliation, and heartache," she turned to face him and continued, "After you came, I felt what it was like to have a full stomach...*for the first time*, accepted... *for the first time*, loved and protected...*for the first time*. And all those white people at Fort Wells, *they* accepted me. Papa, look at the color of our skin. We are white, like all the people here. *This* is my life now and I will *not* go back and live that other way again. Aunt Olivia and Uncle Frederick will keep me. They want to give me a better life, and I want it too. If they didn't I would have run away and found a new life somewhere as far away from..."

Gabe stood and went to her. Taking her elbows in his hands he looked deep into her eyes. With his voice barely above a whisper, he asked, "Far away from *what*, Gigi? From what you owe one-half of your existence? Say it, Gigi...*Indian*. The last time we spoke at the fort you said you were proud of your mother *and* your Indian blood..."

Pulling away, she put space between them, "Yes, before I found out how right you are. Remember it was YOU who told me to never speak of it. Never let anyone know, lest I be shunned as I was in the clan. Well, white people don't shun me, Papa. I have many friends now that all treat me as their equal. YOU are the one that wanted me to learn the white man's way and now that I have, you want me to leave it all behind and go back?"

"We're not going back to the cabins. We're going to that valley that Becca and Will found; the one…"

"Oh, yes. That precious, 'bowl shaped virgin valley that stretches for miles and has a crystal clear stream running through it with all the wild animals and food in abundance.' I've heard it all a hundred times from your precious Becca. If you want a daughter so bad, then by all means, take her. She's always been thrown in my face. 'Becca can hunt like a man.' 'Becca has a great spirit' 'Becca is so courageous' Well, here, I don't have to compete with the likes of her. And furthermore, *I don't want to*. I don't want to hunt like a man or skin and stretch another hide. I like things just the way they are, and I'm staying right here."

Gabe couldn't believe what she was saying, or how she was acting, "Gigi, girl, what has gotten into you? Why are you acting this way? And what do you mean you're staying here? What about your mother? What should I tell her?"

Raising her arm, she gave a shooing motion with her hand, "Whatever you wish. You are good with words and I know you love her, so you will find the right ones that she will accept." Facing him again she added, "If you still want what is best for me, let me be adopted by the Wadsworths."

She went to a desk drawer and pulled out the packet of papers. Offering them to him she added, "These are adoption papers for you to sign so that I can be happy."

"What are you talking about? Sign papers for you to become *their* daughter? No, Gigi, You can't mean this." He brushed them aside and reaching out took her arm, "How can I? You are my daughter, my own flesh and blood. Your mother and I...are your family. I have precious memories of our times together..."

Grace took a step back and pulled free, pleading, "Then keep the memories, Papa. Revisit them whenever you wish, but please, for my sake..." She offered the papers again.

"You need more time to think this over!"

"No, Papa. I've had enough time to know what I want and I want this life more than anything."

A long moment of silence draped the room as they stood there, she trying hard to prohibit eye contact as he tried just as hard to engage it. As it became apparent to Gabe that he could not change her mind, he felt an overwhelming surge of sadness penetrate his soul as he understood it was useless to plead any longer or prolong his stay.

He first dropped his arms to his sides, then reached for and took the packet. He crossed the room to the desk and slowly placed his signature on the dotted line.

In deep sorrow, Gabe turned back. He tilted his head slightly to one side, and pleaded, "Can you give me at least one last hug before I go? I've dreamed of holding you in my arms again for so long, and now they feel...so empty."

Holding her body ridged, Grace slowly went to him and entered his outstretched arms. Her last words to him were, "Thank you, Papa."

He fought back tears and choked audibly as he fully engulfed her in his embrace. "Remember always that I loved you when I first saw you, I love you now, and I will love you always." He gave her a quick kiss on the cheek, then turned and granted her wish by quickly walking away.

Neither of them were aware of someone lurking nearby that had heard and saw it all before slipping silently away.

# Chapter 56

Will rose before daybreak and saddled up Angel to get to work at Smithy's. Before leaving Becca and Liam in bed he leaned over and whispered, "I love you, Becca Blue". Turning, she smiled and gave him an inviting kiss. "Don't start that, or I'll never get to work." They laughed softly as he slowly backed away, eyes locked in a lingering moment.

Zeus raised his head and Will told him to "stay". The wolf whined and went to the door and scratched. "Ok. I'll let you out, but I don't want you following me. You stay home and protect the family." Turning back to Becca, he added, "Be sure to let him back in before long."

Becca nodded and waited a few minutes before going to the door and looking for Zeus. Not seeing him, she thought, *I'm not waiting all morning for you to decide which tree is just the right one.* Then after checking on Liam she blew out the lantern and slipped back into bed.

She dreamed of happy times they would have in the new valley until the loud twittering of a blue bird penetrated the scene and became louder and louder until she awoke to Liam's muffled cry. It wasn't his normal wake-up cry; this was different and definitely wrong.

Throwing back the cover and sitting up, she first realized that the lantern was relit and as she stood, came face to face with Snow Wolf! He was holding Liam by the back of his neck, with his body dangling and a gag partially in his mouth. Smiling, Snow Wolf said, "You want *this* to live? Then you will do exactly what I say. You will not alarm the other clan members camped all around....oh yes, I know. I've been watching this place for a long time. I've waited and waited knowing that my time would come and after I saw that *squaw man* leave, I can finally take what is mine."

"Give me the baby", she pleaded.

Swinging him slightly by the neck, Snow Wolf shook his head. "How long do you think it will be before he is dead? I could wring his neck or bash his skull against these walls. Or I will let him live…a little longer. It's up to you."

"I'll do whatever you want, just don't hurt him anymore. Give him to me," she continued to plead.

"No, Blue. You are under *my* rules now. Put this around your neck. We are going to get Sparrow and leave with or without this white man's spawn."

"Sparrow? What…"

"I said put this strap around your neck! If any of the clan comes here I will kill him instantly. You will find out what and when I want you to."

She took the rawhide strap from his outstretched hand and saw that it was a leash much like what the men use for the wolves when taking them to town. She looked around quickly for Zeus and realized that she had forgotten to bring him back in before going back to bed.

"If you're looking for the wolf pup, he waited a few minutes before he and the other one followed that white man. They're not around to help you now."

Liam began to squirm. Becca reached for him but Snow Wolf pulled back the arm holding the child and shoved her backwards. "I said put it on!"

She hurriedly placed the strap over her head as he tightened it around her throat. Never taking his eyes from Becca, he placed Liam in the cradle of his free arm, relieving some of the child's pain and softening his cry.

"That make it better? Mess with me; I go back to the neck. Now, come bitch dog, and we shall join the others."

"Give me my baby! He's hungry and probably needs changed. I will feed him and he will be quiet. What do you want with Sparrow?"

Ignoring her plea, he said, "I don't. You will see."

Anita awoke with a hand over her mouth and a knife at her throat. "Move, try to scream, and I slit your throat!"

It was too dark to see who the intruder was. As he edged his hand away from her mouth she felt the blade against her throat pierce her skin to the point of releasing a trickle of blood that ran down to her pillow. She remained still as his hand left her mouth and slid a loop over her head and tightened it around her neck. His tug told her to stand and she complied, knowing it was not the time to resist.

When she was on her feet she reached up to the cut and could feel that it was small and the blood now running down between her breasts would be minimal. *Nothing to worry about. Just take time and do what he says. Later there may be a chance to fight.*

The moonlight coming through the east window produced eerie shadows and only gave her the outline of her intruder, but she knew. She knew his voice; as well as his smell.

He stood her by his side, facing the door, tightening the noose to insure she would not defy his orders. When he heard her gasp for air, he loosened it and said, "We wait."

When Becca and Snow Wolf entered, she saw that Anita was also leashed…and beside her stood, Angry Frog!

"How? Who? What is going on?" Becca cried out.

214

Snow Wolf laughed, "Angry Frog and I found each other at a white man's saloon and realized we were on the same quest. You both are meant to be ours so we decided to go after you. When we heard you were captured and being taken by the Army soldiers, we followed to rescue you. Much to our anger we watched as the soldiers gave you back to the white men. We waited…again, and knew there would come a time when we would have you. Now you are coming with us, far away from everyone. It will be as it was meant to be years ago. *We* will be your husbands."

All the while Liam fought for air and cried as he was shifted from one arm to the other with Becca still pleading, "You have us now. So give me the baby and I'll do what you want. Just give him to me."

Angry Frog tugged slightly on Anita's leash and said, "You hear? This time you will obey or we kill that baby and hang you in a tree…*after* we have had our reward."

The women looked at each other, knowing that there was no way to stop what was happening and that possibly, if they pretended to give in, they might have a chance to escape and survive. Anita loved Liam too, and they both knew that as long as their captors had the upper hand they would have to be very convincing.

"If you give me the baby, I will let him suckle and that will keep him silent as we make our way past the rest of the clan. I just need a few things, his back-board and clothing. Changes of clothes for both of us…." Looking at Anita, she tried to get the message across to leave a clue for their husbands to follow.

"You won't need any clothes," interrupted Snow Wolf.

"You want us to look nice…like before? Maybe even like a wedding ceremony?" asked Anita.

Angry Frog yanked on the leash, jerking her head backward, "Yes, you leave white man's dress here. Only take clan clothes. It *will* be as before!"

Snow Wolf looked at Becca's skimpy nightgown, but envisioned her in the white ceremonial dress, and he too nodded. "You wear that now, but bring only clan clothes. We have our own ceremony when we are settled."

Anita turned to gather her things with Angry Frog closely watching. She had very few white woman's clothes, so it was easy packing. At the last moment she snatched the necklace Gigi made for her. Angry Frog grabbed her wrist, demanding she show him what she clutched. "It is a gift from my daughter. You want me to look pretty, don't you?" He gave a sharp nod and released her hand.

Snow Wolf pulled Becca back to her cabin and watched as she laid out her calico dress on the bed and retrieved her clan clothes that had been packed away. She began to untie the bundle before he stopped her. "No. Change later. Put this spawn to suckle."

To each of the women's distress, they had passed all the clan camps and were deep into the woods by daybreak.

216

# Chapter 57

Gabe left the train station and walked over to Smithy's, still feeling Gigi's rejection in the pit of his stomach.

Will was cleaning his work station and readying to leave for home. Zeus saw Gabe first and ran, lunging forward to greet his human. His paws landed high on Gabe's chest, catching him off guard, and finding nothing solid to grasp, the man fell backward with the wolf straddling him and planting wet tongue kisses all over his face.

Will ran to the rescue, and grabbing Gabe's outstretched hand, pulled him to his feet. Zeus was not to be denied, and squirmed around Gabe's legs, wanting desperately to show how much he was missed.

Gabe's expression was not that of a happy-to-be-back-home man. Will asked, "What's wrong, Gabe? You are not happy to see Zeus?"

Gabe reached down and scratched Zeus behind the ears and answered, "It's not that, Will. It's Gigi."

Looking over Gabe's shoulder, he searched. "Oh, yes. Where is our girl?"

"She has been engulfed in the white-man's world and no longer wants anything to do with any of us. She has gone completely the opposite of what she was when she left. She has no love for us and expressed her desire to be adopted by the Wadsworths and wants no one is to know about her past in any way."

Will was stunned, "You can't mean that. Not Gigi."

"She is no longer Gigi. She is Grace Wadsworth now. Or will be as soon as a judge signs the adoption papers."

"You didn't sign the documents, did you?"

Through tear-filled eyes Gabe choked, "It's what she wanted and what she asked me for. She said it was the only way I could make her happy, which said to me that she wants nothing more to do with us ever again."

"She can't mean that. Gabe, in time she'll come around and come back. She's just caught up in the glory of all that the world has to offer and she will change her mind."

"You weren't there, Will. She is different. She was like all the young southern belles; dressed in a fine gown, hand fan and all. She had her hair up in curls, blush on her cheeks, lipstick…it was not our Gigi. She was cold and distant and wouldn't let me touch her…until I was ready to leave. I had to beg her for a hug goodbye and even then she was stiff and uncaring. I don't know how to tell Anita."

"Well, you better start thinking hard because I'm saddling up Angel and we're headed that way. We were all waiting for you and Gigi to get back so we could move on to the valley. I guess we have nothing more to wait for. I've dropped off all the things from the cabins that we aren't taking and Smithy can use or sell."

"Where is he? I wanted to say goodbye before leaving. He's been a great friend and helped us in so many ways."

Will unhitched the sled and they both mounted Angel. Along the way Will tried to ease the tension by answering, "Smithy went home early and told me to lock up. It's funny because he has no locks on the doors. Just the bar to hold them shut. I guess that's what he calls a lock."

"Fort Wells is a good place to live. Everyone can trust each other and there's no need for locks…a good place to raise a family…"

"It's alright, Gabe. She'll change her mind."

"Well, if she does, she won't know where to find us."

"As soon as we are settled and we come back for things the valley doesn't supply, we'll let our trusted friends know to keep her until our next trip. They already know that we will be popping in when they least expect us, and they're happy with that."

"Speaking of trust, what's up with Zeus and Sashay here with you? I thought they were supposed to stick close to home when you and I were away."

"He wanted out when I was getting ready to go to work and I told Becca to let him back in after he marked his territory, for the thousandth time. I told him to stay like you showed me, but I guess he didn't mind, and wherever Zeus goes, Sashay is close behind. Nothing to fear though, with the clan scattered all over creation out there. No animal is going to get by them."

As they were heading home, Jumping Fox came running up the path. In his broken English he said, "I come for you. Something's wrong. No find Blue or Sparrow. They not come out of house this morning and no one see them all day. Things not right in houses. You must come, now."

"I'm not sure Angel will allow three of us…"

"Don't worry about me. I keep up. We must hurry."

With no more explanation, Will kicked Angel in the flanks and they shot off so fast that Gabe just had time to grab Will around the waist and hang on. Surprisingly, Jumping Fox was able to stay close behind.

Upon arriving at the first cabin, Gabe swung his bad leg over Angel's rump and jumped to the ground running. He pushed open the door to an empty home.

Will kept riding Angel up to his door where he pulled hard on the reins. She was not quite stopped when he left the saddle and went running through his doorway. He saw the dress across the bed, his mother's trunk lid left open and Becca's clan clothes gone, Liam's crib empty and his cradleboard gone.

He ran back out, only to come face to face with a panting Gabe. "She's gone," they said in unison with Gabe adding, "There are drops of blood on the pillow; not enough to say that it is a serious injury, but…"

They stepped back into Will's cabin and searched for any clue that would tell them where the girls had gone. "All of Becca's dresses, petticoats, shoes…they're all here, except her clan clothes, and most of Liam's things are gone."

"Anita never liked the calicos but I see that all of her clothes are missing too."

Hearing a low whine beside them, they looked to see Zeus sniffing the area. "That's it! Zeus will find them! We know they didn't go to town or we would have met them along the way. If they have been gone all day, then we have no time to lose. Something *is* wrong. Get your trapping clothes on, Will. We will have to travel light."

Changing his clothes and adding his knife belt, Will turned to his friend and said, "If you're waiting for me, we're wasting time!"

Jumping Fox came to them and said, "I find track of Blue, Sparrow, two men…clan."

The men froze. Locking eyes, they suddenly knew what had happened and whom their loved ones were with. "Show us where!" demanded Gabe.

Taking Zeus to the spot where Jumping Fox had found the prints, Gabe took hold of the wolf's ruff and looking into his eyes he said, "Find them."

Zeus put his nose to the ground and was off on the chase, thinking it a game, but wondering who left the other smells. He didn't like them; *they are too musty, vile smelling. Not like my humans, but...still human.*

Sashay was right beside him, excited about the new adventure and happy to see her Alpha taking charge. As they ran she said, *You know you are very good at this. Will it take as long as the last trip?*

Zeus stopped, sniffed around, and took off running again. *It will take longer with you bumping into me! Move over and let me concentrate on my human's command.*

*There you go with that 'command' again. I can't abide by taking commands from anyone, much less a human.*

*Sashay, shut up or go home. I have a family responsibility that I want to accomplish as quickly as possible and you are not helping.*

*Oh, alright. I'll see this to the end and we'll just see what you receive for your hard work. Mmm Hmmm. We'll see...*

*I said shut up!*

Sashay accepted this as a suggestion rather than a command and decided to do as he wished.

Will signaled to Gabe, and between gasps for air he said, "You know...in our panic we forgot...all about Angel. She sure would come in handy...right about now. Even though I'm anxious... to find my family...I'm not used...to this running. I can't catch...my breath."

Gabe nodded and slowed to a halt. Whistling for the panting Zeus, to come back and lie down, they waited until they could all breathe easier. "Yes, she would! My foot is on fire, and they have so many hours ahead of us…"

"I know, but with Zeus' nose, we won't lose their trail, no matter how hard they try to hide it. They won't be expecting a wolf to know the things you've taught him."

"You're right, Will. We can take it a bit slower. If our suspicions are right, they are now in the hands of Snow Wolf and Angry Frog. No other clansman would have reason to kidnap them. If those two are still of a mind, as they seem to always have held, that they are going to make our wives, *their* wives, I feel they won't hurt them…or at least not kill them."

"But what about Liam? You know Snow Wolf will hate anything about Becca having a white man's baby. He will kill him for sure."

"Give Becca some credit. Liam is still alive or Zeus would have found his body…or hers, because she would lay down her life for that child. She will do everything in her power to make sure that he lives. You know, Will, Liam is like a grandson to me. And it seems we are always chasing after those girls! I'll be glad to get them back, get to the new valley and stay hidden there, forever!"

Feeling a little more at ease, Will stated, "You got that right, 'Gramps', so tell Zeus to start the chase again…but maybe just a wee bit slower this round."

"Easy on that 'Gramps', Son, there's still a few good days in these old bones…I hope." Then looking at the wolf he said, 'Ok, Zeus, Find them.'"

# Chapter 58

The first night the captors camped near a brook. The men took Blue and Sparrow to separate trees and threw the leash ends over high branches and tightened them until the women's feet barely touched the ground. Snow Wolf kept Liam close, leaving Blue vulnerable to his wishes, unable to still her baby's cries, and began to build a fire.

"Don't you think a fire and his cries could lead the white men here?" asked Angry Frog.

"I welcome the meeting with the squaw man. You should too. We can kill them now and be done with it." Pointing to the women he added, "Then they will truly be our wives."

Angry Frog knew that Snow Wolf had too much pride and thought too highly of his fighting expertise, and asked, "Then why was our plan to sneak in and take them while their men were gone? Don't get so puffed up with yourself that you forget that they, too, have fought battles and still live to tell."

"I did not see you as a coward, Angry Frog."

"Because I am not. I welcome the challenge with this Gabe fellow," he answered.

"Yes, as long as he is now old and crippled. I did not hear of you challenging him when he came to the clan camp to take Sparrow back," mocked Snow Wolf.

"Best keep respect in your tongue. At that time there were too many clansmen around that would take his side and probably interfere... here there are none."

"Then what is the problem? If we both welcome the fight, we might as well camp here and wait for them. After we kill them we will have no more problems with the women."

"We don't know yet how many are coming. They may have Jumping Fox and many others."

"Then we go and find a place to secure the women, and wait to see the size of the search party," said Snow Wolf.

"You can have the fire, but quiet that kid."

Wanting to show Blue his power, Snow Wolf jumped to his feet and challenged angrily, "Who are you to be giving orders? Remember I brought you into this plan…"

"Don't try to impress Blue with your misguided ego. You are not the leader here, so don't get so full of yourself that you challenge a superior," demanded Angry Frog.

"Superior?! What makes you think…"

"Because I am! You never understood your place in both clans and that is why they no longer want you. So, like I said before, keep a decent tongue in your head and we will see this through together. Otherwise I will take Sparrow and leave you to find your own way through these woods."

Knowing that he needed Angry Frog's knowledge of the woods more than Angry Frog needed him, Snow Wolf decided to do as told, but couldn't let it go without having the last word. "I'll let it go now, but this is far from over."

Angry Frog turned and smiled, thinking, *He just can't let it go. It's not worth any more words tonight. But soon I will leave him and his worthless ego to rot out here. Tonight I have Sparrow to myself, our first night together. She may fight me now, and I like a little fight in my women, but she will come around and soon she will come crawling to me with her wants.*

After tending to the fire Snow Wolf approached Blue, still secured to the tree. The child was still crying and Blue's face was wet with tears.

Trying desperately to find any decency in him, she said, "Snow Wolf, I told you, I will do what you want as long as you give me my son. Let me tend to him. He is hungry and probably needs his garments changed. You want me to come to you willingly, don't you? Then you have to meet me halfway. Be understanding and I will do as you say."

He thought about it and could see that she was weakening and might come around altogether, "Only if you don't try to get away. You can't run far or fast enough and when I catch you again, I won't be so good to you." With that he untied her from the tree and let her slump down to Liam.

She gathered the crying child in her arms and held him closely to her breast, rocking him back and forth. Then she untied the night gown's neckline and exposed her breast. He hungrily took the offering and began to suckle.

Snow Wolf watched intently, knowing that it was time that he, too, could experience the pleasure. He watched as she made a dug-out bed and gently placed Liam in it.

Snow Wolf could see that she was exhausted and ready for his advances, but taking no chances he repeated, "Do as I say and I let the boy live."

The little blue bird that followed along now twittered incessantly among the branches above Blue. He flew down and made a lunge at Snow Wolf, who absentmindedly swatted at him, nearly connecting with the little fellow. The bird had no option but to seek a higher branch and was powerless to uphold his post as her protector and dropped his head in shame.

With the threat on Liam's life and denying mentally what was happening, Blue quietly laid back and put up no fight.

Angry Frog pulled Anita away from the others. She knew a search party was coming, but they would not be soon enough to stop his plans for her.

As he slowly took his time with his advances, she began to struggle but found that it only excited him further. After spewing curses and name calling, she found his knife back at her throat, forcing her to silently give in to his lust.

For two more days this scenario continued. Blue and Anita began to lose hope of being rescued

# Chapter 59

Each morning found both parties on the move, one running, the other chasing.

The running party was still many hours ahead and moving as rapidly as they could force their captives.

The women's silent compliance each night was foolishly thought of as willingly given. This softened their captors' mind-set and lightened the previous harsh treatment, even to the point of the men allowing the women to help each other with their burdens and Liam.

Both women knew that Zeus would be leading the pursuit and bring the search party, so each day they purposely slowed down; not enough to be suspicious, but hopefully enough to give the search party more time to catch up.

Becca now carried Liam and would pretend to stumble or carefully fall and take time to get back on her feet, while Anita would grab her chest and pretend to be exhausted. They would take turns being out of breath or having a need to stop to shift Liam's cradleboard or the clothes bundles until Angry Frog took Anita's load to carry.

Blue and Anita exchanged concerned glances as they approached a river with the men bent on crossing it. Blue sidled up to Anita and whispered, "If we cross the river, Zeus will lose our scent. What are we going to do?"

"Act fearful of the water…stall as long as you can."

Blue spoke up, "Snow Wolf, I can't cross the river. You remember when I almost drowned, when you came to save me? I've had a fear of the water ever since. Plus, we have Liam and all our clothes. Isn't there another way?"

"It isn't deep. You can wade across it," he said.

Blue began to wail, "No. I can't. I can't go in the water. It will wash me over the falls again. I'll drown for sure."

"Then I will carry you," he said gently.

"Stop this! There's no falls!" yelled Angry Frog.

Blue pulled back, and grabbing Liam she shook her head vigorously, "No, I can't go near the water. I'm afraid. Snow Wolf, please, you know I almost died that day. You saw me. I can't, I just can't."

Angry Frog advanced toward her, "You *will* cross it or you will *die* here!"

Snow Wolf stepped between them and pushed Angry Frog away. "Don't you come near her; she has a right to fear the water. She barely escaped death that day. And she is no concern of yours."

"She is a concern to our plan. She is just pretending. Can't you see that? Are you so taken in by her that you do not see that she is playing you for a pitiful fool?"

"Don't start with me, Angry Frog. You, who are carrying Sparrow's load, you have no room to talk about being played a pitiful fool," countered Snow Wolf.

Angry Frog turned on him then and swung hard with his left fist. It connected with Snow Wolf's jaw and sent him backwards and off his feet.

Jumping back up, Snow Wolf bent forward and rushed at his opponent headlong. Angry Frog side-stepped and gave Snow Wolf a push in his forward direction, sending him crashing to the ground again.

This time Snow Wolf's anger overcame his judgment and he went at Angry Frog full bore. With arms flailing and screaming obscenities, he was blinded by rage, an easy target for the older more learned fighter. As the younger man lunged forward the older one took his time and aimed precisely…with fists doubled as one he swung with a mighty blow, connecting with Snow Wolf's temple, and knocking him unconscious.

Angry Frog turned to Blue, "When he wakes up, you can follow us, or you can gather up that kid and make a run for it now, I don't care. You mean nothing to me."

"What about Sparrow?"

"Sparrow is mine now. She belongs with me. You tell the crippled old trapper to leave us be."

The women locked eyes and they spoke volumes.

Sparrow's eyes said, *"Go, now. Tell Gabe to come. My heart is his. I only stay with Angry Frog to live until Gabe comes for me."* Out loud she said, "Run, take Liam. You don't know how much longer Snow Wolf will be unconscious. Leave your clothes bundle and go, NOW!"

Blue responded by throwing off the leash and springing forward, clutching Liam to her chest and ran. As she ran she tried to remember the path they had just traveled. Where she could, she stepped on rocks to hide her tracks, or soft grass that would bounce back quickly. When she was out of breath she found large trees or boulders to hide behind until she could run again.

As time went by Liam started to fuss. In panic she spotted a large, old tree that would hide her as she sat to nurse him. What she found was that it had a large hollow opening on the opposite side. The hollow was thick with cobwebs so she tore off a nearby small branch and cleared them. She slipped inside and down to the ground. After being fed and changed, Liam fell back to sleep. She placed him back in the cradleboard and tightened the laces to lessen the bounce as she ran.

Stepping out of the tree, she searched the area to make sure it was safe to continue her run. She took the time to look around and get her bearings. *Is this the right way? Where is the tall tamarack with a broken branch?... like what Gigi taught us when we were lost coming back from town that day...I noticed it when we passed by before, but I don't see it now.*

A loud twitter from above sent Blue quickly back inside the hollow tree. She recognized her spirit guide's trill and respected his warnings.

She stood, remaining silent and listened for any sound that would tell her who or what it was...and how close.

Liam's started to stir. Panic began to rise as she realized he might make a sound and divulge their hiding place. She jiggled him as quietly and gently as possible, then as she saw that he was waking, she placed her little finger in his mouth. He clamped down on it and began to suck.

A long man-shaped shadow emerged beside her hiding place, forcing her to ease as far back into the log as possible. Breathing slowly through her mouth, she hoped that the loud beating of her heart could not be heard.

Feeling a tickle on her arm she looked down to see a large hairy-legged spider slowly crawling upward. Her left arm held Liam in his cradleboard; her right little finger was keeping him quiet. She removed her finger and tried to shake the spider off, but Liam's face first frowned then contorted, threatening a full blown squall. She quickly replaced her finger in his mouth and blew quietly at the spider. It stopped for a second before continuing its climb.

Once more the blue bird's twitter broke the silence. She saw the bird's shadow nearly collide with the larger one, causing it to duck and turn away.

Remaining quiet, she felt the spider climb to her shoulder. With each blow it would stop, then continue, up over her shoulder, turn and go down and inside her nightgown. Just then she felt another on her leg, following the same path of the first. She tried to shake her leg, but felt off-balanced, so was forced to stand still.

It seemed like hours before she felt it was safe enough to come out. When she did, she set Liam in his cradleboard against the tree and hurriedly tore off her clothes, swatting at anything that tickled. Not seeing where the spiders fell, she used her gown to scrape across her back and down to her feet, and then began to shake out her hair, only to find a tangled mass. She realized then that she had not cared about cleanliness or her appearance since the capture.

So intent on ridding her body of the spiders and with Liam's cries, she didn't hear the blue bird's second warning. Still bent over shaking her hair, she saw the shadow return. As she slowly straightened she was again, face-to-face with the smiling Snow Wolf!

# Chapter 60

The chasing party was gaining rapidly but realized that Zeus and Sashay were hard to keep up with and had to be constantly called back before losing them all together.

Zeus couldn't understand that if Gabe wanted him to "Find Them", that he should be allowed to do it.

Sashay was becoming bored with the game and asked, *Why does he keep calling you back, then sending you out again? Does he, or does he not, want you to find them? Maybe you should just go back home and let him find them for himself.*

Zeus put his chin on his paws and looking at Gabe he said, *Maybe this is a new twist to the game. I like to make him happy and I've got the time. If you are bored, go home.*

Sashay shook her head, *I'd rather see this through so I can find out what you truly see in this human that makes you want to please him all the time. Besides, it's a long way back there and I don't want to go by myself.*

Zeus raised his head and looked her squarely in the eyes, *Weren't you happy with your humans? Didn't you want to please them? Did they mistreat you or what? You seem to be very cold-hearted about who was putting food in your bowl. Don't you feel now that you owe these humans for all they have done for you?*

Trying to make him see her side, she answered, *Oh, I suppose so. But Zeus...you are the Alpha Male and you shouldn't take commands from anyone, much less humans. Four-legged animals are much more trustworthy than two-legged ones...*

Zeus snapped to all fours, this time giving Sashay a cold hard stare, *Again, what have humans ever done to you that you mistrust them? Mine have always treated me like family and I love them. I'm sorry for you that you don't know that kind of love, but don't question my Alpha Male way of dealing with it. It's time for you to go back, Sashay. You are only irritating me and I need to focus.* He turned and walked away from her and went to Gabe's side where he lay back down.

Sighing heavily, Sashay knew she should have kept her mouth shut. She thought, *I'm always getting on his bad side when it comes to these humans. As mad as he is, I'd better steer clear of him for awhile and head back home before he tears into me…but I'm NOT going to apologize. I'll just act like it was my idea to go anyway.* She stood and strutted stiff legged, past him. Knowing the way home was long, she took a deep breath and let it out in a long sigh. *Me and my big mouth. I can't stay after all that, but I've never gone anywhere by myself. Apologize? Uh, No.* Looking back down the path she thought, *Oh, come on Sashay you wuus, get some courage and show him what an Alpha Female can do. WAIT… yes, that's it! I will go ahead; no one will call me back. I will follow the scents we've been following and catch up with these people Zeus is so bent on finding for his human. I CAN do this.* With that she skirted the camp and found the trail and was off to win Zeus' favor.

No one saw her leave as they again gave Zeus the command and all went forward on their hunt.

Will and Gabe knew they were gaining on the running party because of the tracks they found along the way. Upturned stones were still damp, showing the sun had not had time to dry them. Bent twigs had not yet begun to straighten back toward the sun, and the footprints' edges in the loose earth crumbled when touched.

Gabe looked at Will and said, "I'm thinking our girls are leaving us a pretty good path to follow. Even without Zeus we might have been able to find them."

"Yes, but there may come a time that the men will notice and put a stop to it. What will they do to them then?"

"Don't let your mind go to the negative side, Will. We will get them back soon. Just keep praying to God."

"And to their Yowa…I'll grab at straws when I'm sinking in quicksand."

"I totally agree, Son."

# Chapter 61

Snow wolf stood there smiling through his bloody lips...holding the noose. "I didn't think you were so willing, my love, but since you are already undressed....."

As he advanced the bird descended in full force. Snow Wolf's hand caught the bird in flight and sent it crashing to the ground. Snow Wolf advanced, intent on stomping it to death, Becca called out, "No, don't! I'm sure it has a nest nearby and was only defending it."

"Then why didn't it attack you? I've fought it before and in other places. This will make an end to it."

Once again the captive, and in survival mode, she played on his ego, "I'm sure they were separate birds. And maybe it's your manliness. Your size...you might pose more of a threat to its nest."

Knowing he had the upper hand again, he looked at her and handed her the leash. Helplessly she took it and placed it back around her neck.

He turned away from the bird and pointed to the ground.

She shook her head, "Liam needs me. He is hungry and needs changed."

He removed a knife from his belt and cocked his head.

She lowered herself to the ground and submitted.

After he was finished he said, "Get up. I want to catch up with Angry Frog. I have a score to settle with him. He will not treat me that way and get away with it. It was a lucky blow that I did not see coming. When I woke up no one was there. I didn't know if he had you, or what he planned on doing with you, or if he let you run away. When I saw your bundle of clothes, I knew. And that you would try to run back to that squaw man. I will give you credit, you

235

were pretty good about leaving no track, but you forget my expert tracking abilities and I was always only steps behind you. What you didn't realize is...you were running the wrong way. You have almost made a complete circle. I could have stayed where I was and you would have run right up to me. So now...we go back to the river and you WILL cross it, and you will carry your bundle and that... *seed* all by yourself. I have no reason to be nice any longer. And once we get to the other side, we will take time to camp and you will bathe and make yourself presentable for me. You stink and your hair is a mess. You will make yourself back to the Blue I fell in love with years ago."

Becca hung her head and redressed. She gathered the still crying Liam and followed Snow Wolf as he continually jerked on the leash.

She found it true. They were very close to the river. She placed Liam on her back, the bundle on her head and crossed the river without incident.

Secretly she was pleased to bathe and wash her hair, even though she had to accept the leash and Snow Wolf's leering eyes. As Liam lay safely on the riverbank, she suddenly felt the noose tightened and saw him stand and strip naked. He came to her in the river and again satisfied his lust.

As he rested on the riverbank he allowed Becca to bathe Liam and later change all the padding inside the backboard.

Sitting by the campfire afterward, she hopelessly combed through her hair with her fingers, under the watchful eyes of her captor.

The little blue bird awoke and moved, surprised to find that he was alive, he chirped, *No broken bones or feathers. It must be a sign that my job isn't finished.*

# Chapter 62

As Sadie brushed Grace's long red curls she quietly said, "I can keep your secret."

Grace looked at her in the mirror and laughed, "And what secret could that possibly be, young lady?"

"The one about you being half Indian."

Grace's whole insides jolted, but she kept her composure. "Oh that is so silly. What would make you think something like that?"

"I heard that old man."

"What old man?"

"The one that came and said he was taking you home and he called you…Geegee."

With her mind silently screaming she reached for any answer she could think of, "Oh, him. He was just a crazy old man that had me mixed up with someone else."

"But you called him 'Papa', I heard you. You were mean to him. He said he loved you and you were mean to him."

Shaking inside, Grace asked with a smile, "Have you told anyone about this?"

"No. I said I can keep your secret." Shrugging with one shoulder Sadie added, "Maybe you will give me the doll Master Wadsworth gave you for your birthday?"

Realizing the girl's knowledge left her position in society vulnerable, Grace locked eyes with her blackmailer. Forcing a smile she said, "Oh, Sadie, if I had known you wanted the doll, I would have given it to you long ago. Of course you can have it."

Filled with power, Sadie shifted her body and said, "And I think *you* can brush *my* hair now."

Mustering up all of her control Grace smiled and responded, "Oh that would be fun. Just like the girls who come to visit. You can be my best friend!"

The little girl's eyes sparkled as she danced around the room and said, "Maybe we can play on the swing and even pack a picnic and go to the pond for a swim. You know I can swim a little. I'm learning fast."

Grace pretended to be excited, "That would be marvelous. I'll change into my swimsuit while you go ask Tilda to make us a picnic basket full of good things to eat."

"Well, alright this time, but you just might have to start *taking* orders instead of *giving* them," threatened Sadie.

"Oh, who's giving orders? I *asked* you to talk to Tilda… not ordered you to…right?" countered the smiling Grace.

"Alright, I'll go get my swim dress and meet you out by the swing. We can swing awhile before we go to the pond."

"It's so hot today. Maybe we should go to the pond first and then swing. In our wet clothes, the air swooshing by will cool us even more," ventured Grace.

Sadie decided, "Yes, I suppose you're right. We'll meet in the backyard and go together."

Grace's mind raced as she changed into her swimwear. It was flannel knee-length bloomers with a jersey flounce top, belted at the waist and a puffy hat to match.

When they met in the backyard, Sadie was wearing a simple one-piece cotton dress. "When I grow up I'm going to have a swimsuit like yours," stated Sadie.

"Of course you will. And probably all different colors too!" exclaimed Grace.

Looking at the picnic basket Grace was offering, Sadie said confidently, "*You* can carry the basket."

"But, friends share carrying the basket, just like holding hands. That is...*real* friends," lured Grace.

Sadie responded quickly, "That would be fun. And it would show the other workers that we are truly friends and I'm not just a handmaid."

"And to let them all see we are real friends; let's sing a song as we go. Do you know the song, Old McDonald Had a Farm?" asked Grace.

"Yes. I've heard the others sing it and it is funny."

They sang it loud, "Old McDonald had a PIG...with an oink, oink here and an oink, oink there..." then they would laugh as they walked slowly to the pond, making sure that all the workers around and about would hear them and see that they were friends, sharing a picnic down at the pond.

After standing knee deep in the water and splashing each other, they emerged from the pond and Grace casually edged the laughing Sadie over to an area with less visibility. They spread the blanket and placed the picnic basket down on a grassy area, but close to a rocky bank lined with a curtain of cattails.

"We can pretend we are hiding out from monsters here behind the cattails," coaxed Grace.

Getting into the game, Sadie answered, "Alright My Lady, I will defend you!"

"Can you see if there are any monsters out there? Can any of them see where we are hiding?"

Checking through the cattails and all around, Sadie answered, "NO. We are safe here!" She turned with a smile as a large rock slammed into her forehead, shattering her skull.

# Chapter 63

Sashay had gotten ahead of Zeus and the chasers but knew he would shortly find her scent mixed with the original ones and realize that she didn't go home, which made her push on even faster. Following the now familiar smells, she came to where they overlapped each other with some smells separating from the group and veering off to the left. Determined to make Zeus proud of her, she continued the pursuit which lead her to a hollow tree and to a pungent padding of moss that had been deposited nearby. The ground was disturbed, but this group had continued until they reached a riverbank where she picked up all the scents again. This site also showed a few drops of blood. Following the latest scent, she found herself right back at the hollow tree. She stood, looking around, totally confused. Still set on gaining Zeus' approval she followed the trail and found herself back at the river's edge. She ventured along one bank and then back and along the other, with no success....there was no more scent...the trail ended. Feeling a total failure, she found a soft place to lie down. Placing her chin on her front paws, she watched in the direction she knew Zeus would be coming.

She was more tired than she thought and dosed off, not seeing the chasers until Zeus' shadow crossed her half-closed eyes.

*What are you doing here, Sashay? I thought you were going home,* said Zeus.

*I wanted to find them for you...my way of an apology.*

*No, you wanted to find them before me so you could feel superior,* he scolded.

*No, Zeus, really. I wanted to make you proud of me. But their scent has disappeared. It's all around here, but not up or down the riverbank.*

*Sashay, didn't you ever play with your humans along the river that runs near the fort? If you had you would realize that scent does not linger over water. If a human crosses it, we have to cross it too and pick it up on the other side.*

She rose to a sitting position and said, *I should have known you would have the answer. You are so smart, Zeus.*

*Don't start that now. I know you too well.* He turned and walked back to Gabe.

*I'm serious. Oh, forget it. Be bullheaded, who cares anyhow.* She muttered as she lay back down and pouted.

Zeus had followed the same route as Sashay. Answering Gabe's demand to "Find them," he had left the initial trail to followed Becca and Liam's scent to the hollow tree and then to the river, then back again.

Gabe encouraged Will, "The blood is not enough to worry about, but with that complete circle that Zeus just took us on, and finding that wad from Liam's padding, I'm pretty sure Becca made a run for it and Snow Wolf caught up with her, brought her back and crossed here. They can't be too far ahead. Once we get across the river Zeus can find their scent again."

"Yes, I agree. I think we are closing in on them. Becca just bought us a little more time. Let's make the best of it."

# Chapter 64

Grace immediately set the stone down near Sadie's head. She walked closer to the edge of the water and made a skid mark with her shoe, lining it up with the rock and the dead girl. Then she began to scream as she ran up the hill to the mansion. "AUNT OLIVIA! UNCLE FREDERICK! HELP, Help!" The older couple came on the run with Tilda close behind. Grace acted hysterical, "It's Sadie! She's fallen and struck her head! Help her! Oh, my goodness, she was by the water and turned to come to the blanket for the picnic when her foot slipped in the mud and she fell, hitting her head on a rock! Oh, it's horrible, just horrible!" She held both hands over her mouth and searched through her fake tears for assurance that they believed. She was relieved to see Olivia reach out and take her in her arms, while Tilda and Frederick ran to the child.

Olivia shielded Grace's eyes from the scene as workers carried Sadie's body up to the house. "Now, now my dear, I know this is tragic for you to see, but you mustn't let it scar your loving memories of the times you had with her. You were both such dear friends."

"Yes, yes, very dear. She meant the world to me, Auntie. Oh I feel so terrible. I should have been more careful and picked a different spot away from those awful rocks! I just didn't think anything this terrible could happen." She wailed and sank to her knees, feigning unconsciousness.

Frederick came to her side and picked her up and carried her to the house and laid her on the parlor sofa, "Tilda, fetch some smelling salts and a cool damp cloth for her forehead. The poor child is traumatized by what she saw."

"Yes, Ma'am. The poor thing. It's terrible…just terrible for Miss Grace to see such a horrible thing."

Peeking through her lashes, Grace watched as the adults scurried around in their attempts to comfort her.

She tightened her lips to fight back a smile as she secretly gloated; *That will teach her. How dare she think that I would give her my doll and do her bidding! She deserved to die! She caused her own death by blackmailing me. Now I can rest easy knowing that I have eliminated the one person threatening to expose my darkest secret.*

Later that evening Frederick went to Olivia. "I'm worried about something… about this afternoon."

"What is it, dear?" Olivia asked.

"I went back to the spot of the accident and the story Grace is telling is contrary to the scene."

"What do you mean? What are you talking about?"

"Well, Grace said the girl slipped in the mud and fell on the rock. But the rock had been moved. The spot where it came from was a little farther up the bank. Things just aren't making sense."

"Frederick! You can't be saying…you can't be accusing poor Grace of killing that child! You know she wouldn't do such a terrible thing as that. They were good friends and you know Grace loved her like a sister!"

"Yes. That's what is so confusing. I wonder if there were someone else out there that could have…no, Grace said she *saw* the child fall head-first on to the rock. It couldn't be someone else there that she didn't see..."

"I'll go get Grace and we'll get to the bottom of this. But let's do it here, in our room, where it is private. No need for the staff to know our private matters," said Olivia.

When Grace entered their room she still wore the fake distraught look, "Aunt Olivia says you want to talk to me about something, Uncle Frederick."

He told her of his concerns and she began to panic. Keeping her composure, she thought fast. "Well, I have to confess. I told a little white lie. I was letting Sadie play in the water by herself and I lay down on the blanket to relax...just for a minute. I must have drifted off to sleep very fast, because when I awoke I saw her lying there, already dead. I said that I saw her fall, but I really didn't." Looking at them both she acted scared, "Do you think there could be someone else out there that did that dreadful thing to poor Sadie? Why...it could have been me too! I wonder what makes a person do such a thing. It's just too frightful to think that I could have been next!"

"I think we might better call the constable and look into this further. The culprit may still be lurking around on the plantation...or perhaps it was one of our own workers!" said Frederick.

"What would any of our staff have against that poor child? She's lived here all her life. I think it must be an outsider, and perhaps he saw Grace waking up, before he could...you know." Olivia dropped her voice.

Grace grabbed at the story and reacted as if she were about to faint again, just thinking of what horrible things might have happened to her.

# Chapter 65

Becca and Snow Wolf caught up with Angry Frog and Anita. Snow Wolf immediately backed down, knowing he was facing a superior fighter. As he reclaimed his status, Angry Frog felt even more superior and began to think he could have whatever he wanted from this young loudmouth. As they made camp that night he looked over at Becca, still wearing the torn and dirty night gown, with even more of her body exposed.

"You want to share?" he asked Snow Wolf.

"Share what?"

Pointing with his chin he motioned to Becca, "Your squaw. She could use a real man for a change."

The enraged Snow Wolf knew he had to hide his anger, fearing another altercation with the bigger man. His nostrils flared as he grew furious with the thought of someone else touching her, but he tried to act casual. "Not yet. I'm not finished with her, but soon…real soon."

Running his eyes over her body, the older man licked his lips, "Not soon enough for me. But I'll wait…for awhile. I'm tiring of Sparrow. She's old and has no passion."

Trying to dissuade his enemy, Snow Wolf stated, "Blue is the same, she just lies there all frigid."

Angry Frog laughed, "That's because you don't know how to warm her up."

Snow Wolf thought *Then why can't you warm up Sparrow?* but quickly changed the subject and blurted out, "Did you find any meat for the pot tonight? I'm starved."

Angry Frog was not fooled by the interruption and smiled as he slowly returned to Anita, glancing back at Becca one more time.

Snow Wolf looked at Becca and realized the torn night gown was the cause of Angry Frog's lust. "It's time for you to change. Go over there, behind that rock, where he cannot lay his eyes on you."

Becca took her bundle and reached for Liam.

"Not the boy. He stays here," said Snow Wolf

Knowing there was no use to argue and not wanting to anger him, she took the bundle and did as told. As she untied the straps and laid out the clothing, she gasped. There sitting on top of everything was her little blowgun! *I forgot all about this. Yes, the darts are here too! I wonder if the poison has lost its power being packed away for so long. I'll just have to chance it.* She smiled, knowing that now all she had to do was wait for the right time, and she and Liam would be free. She just had to be sure Angry Frog was nowhere around when she used it. When she was fully dressed she took the weapon and small tube of darts and tucked them inside her wide belt.


Gabe froze as he saw Zeus wag his tail, fully attentive to something ahead. Will followed Gabe's stance as Sashay joined Zeus. Gabe edged his way to the wolves and peered through the brush. The campfire was small, but still held flickering embers, giving off a soft glow upon the area.

He grabbed the scruff of Zeus' neck so the wolf would not lunge forward, anxious to prove he had found 'his quarry. Whispering close to the wolf's ear he said, "Good boy! Now Stay! Stay Zeus!"

Zeus didn't understand. He had played the game and answered the command, "Find them." Now he was held back from playing with those he found. But Gabe was to be obeyed, so he lay down and was still, watching as his humans advanced slowly forward.

Sashay came to him. *What are they doing? I thought this was a game and you would jump out and pounce on the ones we've been tracking these past few days.*

Zeus answered, *So did I, but this seems to be serious. Perhaps not even part of the game. All I know is we must be very quiet and still.* There was something very different in his command.

*There you go with that word again…* sighed Sashay.

*Stop it! Haven't you learned anything these past few days? Just lie down and be still. If he wants us he will call.*

The men circled the outskirts of the clearing. When they were sure of who and where each person was, they moved closer. Each man saw that his wife was tethered to her captor with a leather strap around her neck. Knowing that things could go horribly wrong, Will decided to remove Liam, who was cuddled in his mother's arms. Gabe understood Will's gestures and nodded.

Liam was wrapped tightly in his blanket, so Will was able to lift him by grasping the fold at his chest. The baby made a slight noise and Becca was instantly awake. Seeing Will, she froze then glanced at her still-sleeping captor.

Will held a finger to his lips as he cuddled his son in his arms and moved him out of harm's way; laying him beside Zeus and Sashay.

Becca rose only slightly to see where her son was being taken, but it was enough to alert Snow Wolf who, upon seeing Will, jumped to his feet, brandishing a knife in his right hand and tightening the tether around Becca's neck by twisting his left wrist.

The scuffle woke Angry Frog. He sprang to his feet and came face to face with Gabe, who quickly slashed Anita's tether, setting her free. Angry Frog fought to clear the sleep that fogged his brain and grabbed his knife.

Knowing that Liam was out of danger, Becca took her strap with both hands and jerked hard, off-balancing Snow Wolf and giving Will time to set for battle.

In all the confusion, the tussle found each Indian man fighting two opponents, with the white men in the center of camp but facing the wrong foe. Gabe kept his eyes on Snow Wolf as he asked Will calmly, "Want to change partners, Son?"

With intense adrenalin flowing, it struck Will funny and he laughed, "Yea, I think I do. Let's do a little do-si-do here and line up with the partners we want." Standing back-to-back they moved in unison and turned to face their personal enemies.

Snow Wolf tried to pull Becca in front of him as a shield, but she spun around and jerked again. He tried to remove the strap so he could face his opponent, but Becca was ready and jerked so hard that he staggered backward.

Anita ran to the fire. Grabbing a burning stick she struck out at Angry Frog.

Keeping eye contact with his foe, Gabe started to smile. "She's a feisty one. I'd better hurry or she'll kill you before I get my chance."

"Don't get ahead of yourself, you old cripple. I've defeated far younger and agile men than you."

"Then do your best because I'm getting tired of playing around with you. I'm going to end it here and you'll never bother Anita again."

"Her name is *Sparrow*, old man," spat Angry Frog. "And you aren't getting her back." At that, he crouched and began to circle his enemy. With his eyes off Anita, she made her move and rushed forward and pushed hard, which sent him stumbling headfirst into the campfire. Sparks and his screams filled the air as he rolled away from the fire, clutching his throat and gasping with wide open mouth.

Angry Frog choked on embers he had inhaled when the force of his body hitting the fire, bounced them up and into his lungs. He died, writhing in excruciating pain.

Horrified by what he saw, Snow Wolf was now intent on just getting away by frantically slashing the strap that now held *him* prisoner. The coward turned and ran but only gained a few yards before a dart hit him between the shoulder blades. He arched his back and tried to reach the imbedded needle…to no avail. He turned and stared at Becca in shocked disbelief.

She took a warrior stance and showed him the blowgun as he fell forward…dead before he hit the ground.

Will turned to Gabe in utter disbelief. "Well, don't that beat all?" Turning to the wives he said, "You girls deprived us of the revenge we've craved since we found you gone."

"It was *our* revenge to take. We can now live without fear of those two ever bothering us again," said Becca, with the nodding Anita standing beside her.

The men went to their wives and embraced them with warm hugs and hungry kisses.

Zeus slowly emerged from the bushes, dragging the still sleeping baby by his blanket.

Sashay followed him, *Zeus, humans are odd creatures."*

*"Maybe, but they are my humans and I love them."*

# Chapter 66

The news of a murderer that might still be on the plantation quickly faded and life got back to normal.

All Grace knew was that she had shifted the suspicion away from her and had renewed her status with her family and peers. She was back to being the darling, sweet and innocent that they all knew and loved. All the while she felt justified in her actions and that the blame initially landed on the victim. *Poor, poor Sadie. If you had not pushed so hard and demanded so much, who knows? You might still be alive and enjoying all the comforts you had for such a short time. Now I must get on with my life, as wonderful as it is...without a handmaiden. Tsk, tsk. How can I survive?*

Grace donned a light pink satin full-length dress, trimmed in Italian lace and after assuring herself that she looked the epitome of purity, grabbed her fan and went in search of her aunt and uncle. Finding them out on the back veranda, Grace swished and swayed her way over to them and using the names she used when she wanted something, "Aunty and Unky, how are the plans for my...what do you call it? You know...that party coming along?"

"Oh, my yes, I've all but forgotten about the party! Frederick, we will have to get right on that. I will speak to Tilda and get things in motion. Gracie, you and I can discuss what style and color of dress ..." thinking aloud she added, "There will have to be fittings...and time for it to be made...and Oh, yes...the invitations! My, my we have so many things to do!"

Grace smiled lovingly at her uncle and taking both of his hands in hers she swayed back and forth. "I know you will make sure that everything is just perfect for me. I'm so happy and I hope to make you both proud of me. You are, aren't you...proud of me?"

Frederick's face lit up in a broad smile, "Gracie dear. We have a surprise for you. We were going to wait and announce it at the party but we can tell you now. We couldn't be more proud of you...because you are now legally our daughter! The papers are all signed, sealed and delivered and everything is official. You know, your Aunt Olivia and I once had a daughter. She died young, during an Indian raid many years ago. Her name was Autumn so we are hoping that you won't mind being named after her. How does it feel to now bear the name, Grace Autumn Wadsworth?"

Grace jumped in the air and holding her arms as though she were doing a pirouette, she danced around the veranda. "OH Aunty, Unky...You have made me the happiest girl in Charlottesville! No...in all of Virginia! NO...in the whole...wide...world!"

Frederick and Olivia stood and Grace came to them, hugging them both. "Do I still call you Aunt and Uncle? Aren't you now my mother and father?"

He looked at his wife and said, "We didn't think about that did we?"

She said "No, I would love it, but, will our friends accept that, knowing she is adopted?"

He answered, "Who cares what others think. We love one another and that's all that counts."

"Then I shall call you Mummy and Daddy!" said Grace.

"Let's shorten it to just Momma and Dad," he said.

She spun around the veranda again and shouted, "I'm GRACE AUTUMN WADSWORTH!"

# Chapter 67

Becca was ecstatic. Looking at Will she smiled and exclaimed, "I know where we are now. We are so close. I can't wait to see the valley again."

"And I've explained to the clan to make sure to keep our tracks erased, just in case that commander was not telling the truth and sends soldiers after us." Taking her into his arms he was glad to have her almost back to her normal happy self. Amorously he whispered, "You know we will have to go back to that dug-out bed you made and try it out for real this time".

She laughed and gently pushed away and turning for him to see the bundle on her back, she stated, "Except we have to make it bigger; it must fit three now."

He turned her back around and they locked eyes, "Or maybe a smaller one beside it?"

Her eyes danced, "We shall see, but for now we must concentrate on *finding* that bed. So, search my husband, search!"

Watching her race ahead he laughed out loud and thought, *She is almost back to her old self after that horrible ordeal. I'm letting her choose when the time is right that she can willingly give herself to me. All those days of having that choice taken from her had diminished her former desire for intimacy. All those college classes of psychology are finally paying off. As long as I have her and Liam back, I can wait for the rest.*

Gabe was worried about Anita. He remembered his psychology classes too, but she seemed different. She went willingly into his arms, but later in the day he would find

252

her crying to herself. When she saw him she would quickly dry her face and put on a fake smile.

*So much has happened to her all at once. More than a lot of people could endure and come out sane; first the ordeal with Angry Frog, and then my news about Gigi. I don't know if it is her heart, mind or spirit that is broken. She tries to put up a good front but will not confide in me so I can help. I know these things take time…I know that, but she is hurting and I want to take away her pain.*

Thinking back to that fateful night, Gabe recalled how, after the fight, and death, of Angry Frog and Snow Wolf, he and Will had gathered all their enemy's belongings and tossed them into the pit with their bodies.

After clearing all traces of the ordeal, they lead their wives away from the campsite toward home, followed closely by the wolves.

They had made swift time getting back to the cabins and found everyone ready to move on and find the valley. He could tell by Anita's actions that she was anxious to find it and begin a new future without fear. All he knew was that he only wanted to make her feel safe but happy too, and whatever it took, he was willing to do.

Realizing that the new fort commander did not know Gabe or Will, or that they were married to Indian women, they returned to the fort, where they secretly asked Sergeant Wilson about the legalities of the document explained to Thomas.

"All I know, sir, is that the document looks real, is on government stationery and the envelope was postmarked from Washington. No one else has filed a claim in order for me to find out if it is real," said Wilson.

"Can a man apply without his wife present?" asked Will

"I don't know that either, but give me some time and I'll look into it," answered Wilson.

"That's just it, Sergeant, we don't have much time. We have to find a safe place for our wives, but it would be great if we could apply and receive the property that Will's family settled on years ago."

"That should be easy. Will's father must have filed a claim on that property, and so being, it remains in the family name. Will is heir to it, in his parent's demise."

"How many acres are we talking about?" Will asked.

"That would be determined by the size applied for...or if you find the boundary markers."

"What sort of markers?"

"It differs. Most people back then just stacked a pile of rocks in each corner, or perhaps drove a large stake in the ground...although the stake would probably be rotted away by now. Look for a pile of rocks, or something that he would have used to mark his boundaries."

Gabe said, "If I can apply for Anita one of those land grants, I would like it to be adjacent to Will's property. Is that something that could be arranged?"

"As long as no one else has claimed the property."

"You won't get into any trouble over this, will you?" asked Will.

"I'll be looking up a deed for someone that wants to set the boundaries of his inherited property. No harm in that. I'll have the answers by your next visit." assured Wilson.

# Chapter 68

The plans went well and the afternoon of the party found Grace anxious to have everything perfect. She checked the dress hanging on the back of the door several times, and practiced her curtsey in front of her full length mirror while wearing just her camisole and pantaloons. She posed with nose in the air and chin jutting forward as she peeked out of the corner of her eyes at her image.

With no Sadie for help, she called for Olivia, who in turn called for Tilda. Grace's hair was a mound of curls on top and with several curls hanging down one side. Tilda assisted by giving her balance while she first stepped into a tiny corset. She had Grace grasp the bedpost of her canopy bed as she cinched the drawstrings tighter and tighter until Grace could hardly breathe.

"You are going to have to get used to it, my dear. It's time to start molding your body." said Olivia.

Then Grace stepped into layer upon layer of petticoats followed by a hoop frame beneath it all. Very carefully the elder women lifted and slid the dress over Grace's head and Tilda closed it with the several satin-covered buttons in back. Again Grace hung onto the bedpost as Olivia brought the satin shoes to her feet, then Tilda handed her the matching gloves. After another long look in the mirror she turned and nodded with a smile.

As they opened the door, there stood Frederick with a small velvet box. "You're not ready yet, my dear. Momma and I have a gift for your turning twelve today."

Grace couldn't sit in the dress for fear of wrinkling it, so she asked him to open the box. Inside was a beautiful hair comb, inlaid with rubies and sapphires. Olivia stepped forward and taking it from the box, positioned it in Grace's curls, slightly above her forehead. It looked like a tiny tiara, "Rubies for your hair, and sapphires for your eyes, my dear. You are absolutely stunning. *Now* you are ready."

Grace enjoyed her new friends and all her tutoring paid off because what she learned convinced them that she was becoming a refined young lady. She was ecstatic at her very first birthday party when she found she was the center of everyone's attention.

Some of the boys crowded around her as others elbowed each other and whispered their desires, while others dared each other to make advances. Those accepting the dare found themselves engulfed in her young charms as well as her expensive perfume; all the way from Paris, France.

She had learned how to flutter her fan as well as her eye-lashes and every young man thought she was flirting only with him. Oddly, most of the girls were not jealous and wanted to emulate her. She was in the limelight and she loved every minute of it.

# Chapter 69

The men were trailing the clan and making sure there was no sign of their passing. Gabe took this time to ask Will about his personal concerns.

"Will, how's Becca since...you know?"

"She seems almost back to herself except for...night. I haven't pushed her. She has to decide when the time is right. I try to remember all the classes, you know, you must have had taken them too, at the college. I mean the psychology part. I don't think there is anything physically wrong, I haven't even ventured that far, but if there was, wouldn't she have said something?"

"I don't know, Son, but Anita is not the same either. It's the opposite for us. She's willing in bed, but I catch her crying when she thinks no one knows. She denies it and gives lame excuses, but I think this has affected her far more than she is letting on. I guess we'll both have to be patient, but I just want to ease her pain and I don't know how or what to do. It's a helpless feeling. At least when Nichols took the women we had a plan to go get them, but I'm clueless as what to do to help Anita through this."

"Gabe, she has the double hurt, not only about Angry Frog, but Gigi too. She has had a lot to deal with in a short amount of time and she may be dealing with it through silent tears. I don't know if it is a Cherokee trait, or just our women, but they aren't the type to whine and demand attention. So many times I've wanted Becca to open up to me and let me know something that I can do, but it seems as though she wants to pretend it didn't happen. I fear she will pull away and go off into her own little world again and maybe this time she won't come back."

"Yes. That's how I feel. But should we be the ones to start the conversation or do we just let it go? I fear that by *not* saying anything Anita will think that I don't care or that I don't want to talk about it. Maybe Ellen knows. The girls always seem to confide in each other. She may know what I can do. I don't think Anita would burden Becca with it, knowing the trauma she's been through too. "

"Maybe we could approach the subject in a way that they will feel talking about it would help *us*. They both have a way of always wanting to take care of us...maybe if they realize that we are hurting too, that they will open up."

"When did you get so smart, young man?"

"Oh, probably from being mostly raised by the most caring person I've ever known. You've been more of a father to me than my own. He was a good man, but I don't have much of a memory of him. He died too soon."

"Will, we have a stronger bond than most fathers and sons ever get, and if you ever have a hankering to call me 'Pa' you would certainly make me proud!"

Will's smile spread from ear to ear as he glanced over to Gabe, "I've wanted to for years but I wasn't sure how you would feel."

"That settles it. You can call me father, dad or pa...I don't care which, but I'd be mighty proud...Son."

The men faced each other and locked eyes; as Gabe's smile filled his face to match Will's, they stepped in and embraced. Then with a slap on each other's backs they separated and returned to sweeping away the travois' tracks, as well as Angel's hoof prints.

When Gabe caught up with Ellen he wasn't sure how to start the conversation, let alone get her away from the others to speak in confidence. He sidled up to her and asked quietly, "Ellen, could I speak to you in private?"

She frowned and looked at him, "What's wrong?"

He tilted his head and motioned for her to follow him. Her curiosity accepted his beckon and they began to walk and talk quietly. "I'm real anxious about Anita. I know she's been through so much lately, but it's been weeks and I still catch her crying to herself and she won't open up to me and I feel helpless to comfort her. Has she said anything to you that could help me, help her?"

"Gabe, she is in so much pain right now." Seeing the look on his face she quickly added, "No, not body pain...mind pain. She has to deal with so many things. First what she had to endure while with Angry Frog, then the news about Gigi, and then on top of all that her pregnancy...what can you expect?"

"Her WHAT?" he blurted.

"Oh, my...you didn't know? Oh, no. I thought you knew. She confided in me that she was pregnant and with the thought of carrying that monster's baby in her womb, she is thinking of taking the tribal remedy, to end it. It is a very dangerous medicine and I've tried to talk her out of it, but she has her mind set...Oh, I feel just awful. Now she won't ever trust me again. But why hasn't she told you?"

"That's what I'm going to find out. Thank you, Ellen. I'll try to get it out of her without letting her know you told me. Do you know where she is right now? I've been with Will covering our tracks and lost contact with her."

"If you don't find her in the group she may be out searching for the herbs that she will need. Stop her, Gabe. She is not thinking clearly."

"Where? Where do these herbs grow?"

"Near water. Along the banks of running water."

Gabe set out, running the best he could through the clan. He asked along the way if anyone had seen her and after a shake of their heads, he continued his search. Finally one of the women pointed away from the clan and he turned in that direction. His eyes were brimming with tears as he ran, calling out, "Anita! Anita!" Through the tears he saw her. She was bent over pulling on a wide-leafed plant.

Rising up, she answered, "What is wrong, husband?"

"Anita, my Sparrow. I thought I'd lost you again! You weren't among the others. What are you doing?" He pulled her into his arms and held her close.

"Just gathering food for our supper tonight. You not to worry. No one left on Mother Earth who wants to hurt me."

"Honey, it's time we had a talk. You have to be honest with me and tell me what you are thinking and how you are feeling. I can't go on seeing your tears and not know how to help you. Talk to me, my little Sparrow. I have to know."

At first she began to shake her head, then looking into his eyes she melted into his arms. "So many things, husband. I hurt. I try not to hurt you with them. They are my hurt."

"Tell me all of your hurts. I want you to share with me, so I will know. Not knowing is hurting me too much. I have no way of knowing how you feel about what you went through with Angry Frog, but if you talk to me we can deal with it together. I know, too, that Gigi has hurt you. She has hurt both of us. We need to share that hurt too… please, Anita, talk to me. What all is hurting you?"

She started softly, "Yes, Angry Frog had no right to do what he did to me, but he is gone now and I can deal with

260

it." Her voice began to rise, "But Gigi, and her turning her back on me...that *big* hurt." The tears started, "I blame white man's world! They stole her from me! You and other husbands are the only white people I care about, all others...NO!" Raising her voice even higher she doubled up her fists and arched her neck. "I never want white man's world again! And I not *Anita*... I AM SPARROW!"

Gabe reached for her and she returned to his arms. "Then you shall have what you wish. We will live in the valley, and you have always been my Sparrow...I like it better than Anita, anyway. But I have a feeling there is more hurt. What is it? Tell me."

She shook her head, and clung to him. He rocked her gently and said, "Come now, Sparrow. I said I need to know everything so we can work things out together."

"I fear you will hate me. You will turn away from me."

He lifted her chin to look him in the eyes, "There's nothing you can say that would ever make me turn away from you. Don't you know by now how much I love you?"

She crumpled to the ground and whispered, "I am with child. *His* child and I hate it! I want it out of me and gone. If I could cut it out of me I would."

"Are you sure...about the pregnancy?"

"It was time for my moon cycle before he took me. It has not come. These plants could kill it and I'd be rid of him forever. Besides, I'm too old."

He knelt down and took her in his arms again. Lifting her back to her feet, he eased her over to a fallen log and lifted her on to it. "Yes. You could be carrying his child, but you could also be carrying *ours*. Remember the night before he took you? Remember how we loaded the bed last so we could have one more night of love? And what about the nights before that? What if it is *our* baby? And as for you being too old? There is a story in the Bible about a woman that was way older than you who had never had children, and God blessed her with a mighty son."

"But it has been many years, you and I…and no other child but Gigi…"

"It doesn't mean that it can't happen. Have faith in our God, our Yowa, the God we share. We can't kill this child, Sparrow. If it turns out to be his…for *sure*…and you still don't want it…" Seeing the look on her face he raised his chin and finished, "IF it is his and you don't want it…we will offer it to anyone that might."

"No! Not in this clan. His spawn could be evil, like him and I would hate to be reminded of…no. You will take it far away so I will never have to think of Angry Frog again.

"Alright, I will. Is anything else hurting you?"

"No, my husband, I am empty of secrets."

"Then drop those plants and let's head on back to the clan. And from now on, when you are hurting, *tell* me, so we can work things out together. Do you feel better now?"

She smiled and took his hand and pulled it around her waist, "Yes, I now feel…good."

Gabe knew now that Sparrow would never take the oath to adopt the white man's ways as the land grant document demanded. He desired the property but wondered, *Should I pursue it? I dare not offend Sparrow by bringing it up now but it would be a security for her if anything happened to me. She could sell it to make her life more comfortable. After all, it would be in her name anyway. I'll talk to Will.*

# Chapter 70

"How can I be of service?" asked Commander Simmons.

"Uh...I would like to introduce myself. My name is Pastor Abraham Chandler and I wish to invite you and your men...to Sunday Service at my church...in town."

"Thank you, I will pass it along to the men, but you do know that we have our own Chaplin here. He conducts non-denominational services here at the fort."

"Yes, I'm aware of that, but our little congregation has a few empty pews to fill...and that way the soldiers could... mingle with the townspeople and perhaps help Fort Wells become...a bit more cordial, so to speak."

Looking at the little man over the top of his spectacles, the commander sized him up to be nervous and wondered aloud, "Have any of my men showed misconduct in town?"

"Oh, no, of course not," Chandler stammered, "I just...I meant...between the people. Perhaps make the soldiers appear friendlier and less intimidating."

"So you are saying they *have* caused trouble?" Simmons was enjoying toying with the little man.

Chandler was clutching the brim of his hat and one of his hands shot up, as he muttered, "No. You are misreading my words...or I'm coming across all wrong. It's my fault. I'm just here to invite you all...so let's leave it at that,"

"Very well, Pastor. We'll leave it at that. Is that all I can help you with today?"

"Well, uh, there is one other thing. I understand that the last commander...Wadsworth...retired and moved back to his home. Could you give me the address...so that I might visit with him when I travel that way?" asked Chandler.

"And which way will you be traveling?"

Chandler's hands were briskly circling the brim of his hat, "Well, nowhere in particular, exactly. I...uh...just enjoy looking up...old acquaintances when I travel...in my spare time, of course."

Commander Simmons' first impression of this man was not good. Even though before him stood a man of the cloth, there was something odd about him. *Why is he so nervous? What is his real reason for wanting to know about the Wadsworth family's whereabouts?* He stared long and hard at the man before answering, "Commander Wadsworth resides in Charlottesville, Virginia. I am not privy to his personal address nor allowed to divulge it if I did. For that you will be on your own...in your travels."

The pastor took his leave, bowing out of the room and thanking the commander profusely.

# Chapter 71

"There's the crevice! I knew we could find it, Will!" Becca cried out as she jumped into his arms joyfully.

Will welcomed the warmth of her embrace and held her tight. With Liam strapped to her back he swung them both around, then tenderly kissed her before setting her down to face him. Forehead to forehead they stood locked in each other's arms.

"Hey, you two, are you going to stand there all day? Do you think Angel can make it up the ravine pulling the travois?" Gabe asked.

Letting Becca go, Will turned to him and said, "I've been thinking…I know she can make it up and over, the way Becca and I came back that day. There is no path, but the crevice is quite visible and following it along, it will take you to the valley."

"Then up and over it shall be!" Then turning, he took his wife into his arms and asked, "Well, my little Sparrow, are you ready to see our new homeland?"

With a smile she answered, "I am ready, my husband."

Jumping Fox with Morning Star and Badger arrived, leading the clan who were all gathering in the small clearing, quietly waiting for instructions. He first spoke to Becca then turned to them, "There are three ways to get to the valley. Some of you were here before and know the way to the ravine. There is another that goes up and over the top for those with travois that might be hard to manage in the ravine, and the other that goes through the small crack here," as he pointed to it. "Becca told me that if this path is chosen it will have to be when the sun is straight over head to allow light to guide you through. But you will have to be fast enough to outlast that sunlight before it gets too dark to see. One person can carry a torch, but even then you could stray away from the path and get lost inside. There is already one warrior that never came out one day long ago. You must choose the path you wish to take and go in groups. It is even more important we cover our tracks so that no one can follow us to the valley."

There was a murmur of discussion before groups were formed and ready to advance. No one chose the crevice. As most chose the ravine, Gabe set out with Sparrow leading Angel and the small group to follow.

Becca and Will already knew the other two trails, and even though they had not gotten all the way through the ravine, they wanted to find out where it came out. As they proceeded to the base of the ravine, Becca froze. She stood as if in a trance with tears streaming down her cheeks. Will's stomach lurched as he realized she was staring at the spot where her mother was shot and killed protecting her father that day when the soldiers came.

In fear of her falling into her mental safety zone, Will gripped her shoulders, "Becca, honey, I'm sorry…"

She fell into his arms and sobbed, "I miss them both so much. Why, Will? Why did they have to be killed? They were so loving and caring and were good people."

Jumping Fox came to them and asked what was going on. Will started to explain, but Becca pulled away from him and embraced her brother as she relayed to him in Cherokee how and where their mother died.

Jumping Fox supported her as they approached the spot. They knelt and began to chant in Cherokee.

Ellen and Morning Star moved forward and knelt beside the other two. Many of the clan knelt where they were and they all joined in the chant.

Will saw Thomas watching from the sidelines and moved to his side. Before he could ask, Thomas explained, "They are singing a farewell to their mother, Shining Water, and the clan is supporting their grief." The men stood silently until the grievers had finished their ritual.

When they returned Will reached out and took both of Becca's hands and said softly, "I'm sorry, Becca Blue,"

Looking at him through her tears, she nodded and moved in to lay her head on his chest. He hugged her close until she straightened and took his hand and without looking back she headed toward the ravine.

Gabe and Sparrow led the small group single file up and along the crevice that brought them to a small animal path leading down to a very high ledge overlooking the valley. Silently they stood in awe at the sight before them.

The panoramic scene yielded vast green lush hills which formed walls that directed a crystal clear river flowing from the northernmost reaches of the valley. The curve of the river depicted that there was even more beyond.

Noise from below brought them out of their reverie. Scanning the area below, they saw Will and Becca's group surging out of the foliage into a clearing near the river's edge. At that level the group, too, was amazed by what they saw. The young couple leading them had found this sanctuary years ago and knew that the others would be overwhelmed at the view from where Gabe stood.

Gabe gave a shrill whistle, which brought an answering wave from Will.

# Chapter 72

Tilda stood at the door as Grace primped at her vanity. "Miss Grace, you have a visitor. Says he came all the way from Ft. Wells. That is where you came from, isn't it?"

Grace froze, with hairbrush in midair. Staring at her reflection, her mind began to scream. *Oh my, why did he come back? I made it perfectly clear how I wanted it! Now he's back here to plead with me once more and I don't want to go through that again.* "Show him to the parlor and fetch Momma. I need to speak to her on a separate issue which needs my undivided attention. He can just wait."

"Yes, Miss Grace. I'll see to both."

Tilda brought Olivia to the room and stood for further instructions. "Please see to the visitor at once and tell him that Momma will see him shortly," said Grace.

"Who, dear? Who is waiting to see you?"

Grace stared silently at Tilda until the servant received the message that she was excused. "Momma. Papa has returned! What should I do? Can *you* send him away this time? Why can't he just leave me alone?!"

"I'll see to it Gracie. Don't you fret. I'll go now and let you know what he has to say."

Just minutes later Olivia came back and said, "It isn't him, my dear. It is Pastor Chandler! He's come all the way from Ft. Wells to see you." Lowering her voice to a whisper she asked, "Does he know?"

Grace's eyes opened wide, then almost to herself she stated, "Oh, my heavens, I don't know. Some of our friends back there know, but now I'll have to deal with another..."

"Another *what*, honey? Why don't you see him in the parlor. Find out if he knows and why he's here."

Remembering Sadie's overhearing the conversation she had with Gabe, she frowned and said, "No, maybe I'll see him here, and make sure you have Tilda busy elsewhere. We don't want other ears hearing anything he has to say."

"But that wouldn't be proper...having him here in your bedroom. You must see him in the parlor. Tilda is the only servant in the house and I will send her to tend the garden. I will stay with you, if you wish...as a chaperone of course."

When Grace and Olivia entered the parlor, Pastor Chandler was seated with his hat in his lap. He jumped to his feet and reached for Grace's hand and bowing low, he kissed it, "How wonderful it is to see you again, Gigi. It's been hard to find you. You've grown into quite a refined young woman... an absolutely *stunning* young woman."

"Why thank you, Pastor Chandler. It's nice to see you too. Please, take your seat. You do remember my...Mrs. Wadsworth, don't you?"

"Yes, yes of course." He turned and repeated his hand kiss to Olivia, "I dare say I was stunned to hear that you were arrested by the fort soldiers, back then. And you, dear Gigi, It must have been traumatic for you to see your friends and father arrested and taken away like hardened criminals. I'm sure that all that nonsense got cleared up once you got to the fort."

Olivia answered, "Yes. My dear Frederick set that poor excuse for a human being straight and we were all released immediately. It's good of you to care."

Grace tried to smile demurely and asked, "Tell us, what brings you to Charlottesville?"

In his manner, Chandler began to twist the brim of his hat and stammered, "Well, I...uh, just wanted to find out...

how you are doing…with your piano lessons. You have been taking lessons from Mrs. Wadsworth here, haven't you? And then…uh, I missed seeing you… and…and your family…in church, and wondered…"

"Thank you for your concern, Pastor, but as you can see I…and…Mr. and Mrs. Wadsworth are doing fine. You needn't have come all this way…"

"Oh, it's no bother, Gigi. I feel it is my Godly duty to make sure that each of my flock is safe. I still consider you…" then turning to Olivia added, "And you too Mrs. Wadsworth, as part of my flock. Are you attending any specific church nearby?"

Olivia nodded, "Yes, we go regularly to the Episcopalian Church."

"That's good news…yes, good news," he searched his mind for more to say as Grace exchanged quick glances with Olivia.

Wanting the little man to leave, Grace flipped her fan open and began to lightly flutter it below her chin, "Thank you for coming all this way. That is very sweet of you. I'm sure you must have other flock to search for…"

Glancing from Grace to Olivia, he said, "Well, not at the moment. I uh, well, was wondering, if maybe, uh I might be allowed to uh, call on Gigi while I'm in the area."

Seeing the situation for what it was, Olivia stood and said, "You do realize that…Gigi…is only twelve, don't you? Not quite the age for callers."

"Oh my, yes. I just meant as friends," he lied.

Olivia saw right through his charade, "I'll speak to her in private and return with an answer for you."

When they were alone and out of earshot, Olivia asked, "Grace, I couldn't tell if he knows or not. Is he someone you might consider a suitor later on? Being a pastor's wife would heighten your rank in society, but if he doesn't know and finds out later, he could tell the world and you would lose everything. It's up to you dear, what do you think?"

"Momma, I think I will take a walk with him…down by the pond. Get that area clear of servants so no one can… hear our conversation and I will find out. Go tell him that I will see him shortly and that we will take a walk."

When Olivia left, Grace rushed to her closet and rummaged through bundles that had been packed away since she first came to live at Whitmore Plantation. Finding the one she searched for, she untied it and carefully rolled it out. *Here they are…my darts and blowgun! It's been a long time since I've used it but I was pretty good when I did. I don't know if the poison is still strong enough, but I will just have to hope for the best.* She quickly secured various curls high on her head and tucked the sleeved darts into three of them, using the feathered ends as decorations. She slipped the hollowed mouth piece over the bottom of the fan to make it look like part of the handle, and shook the fan to make sure that it stayed in place and would be ready when…or if…she needed it. Patting everything in place and looking long and hard into the mirror she thought, *I hope I don't have to, but if he knows anything, I will.*

She found him waiting. He sat with a stiff, straight back, knees together and hat in his lap, hands holding each side of the brim. Unconsciously she shook her head, stepped forward, popped open her fan and asked, "Shall we take a walk? It's real nice down by the pond…where we won't be

271

disturbed." Fluttering her fan and eyelashes she added, "The cattails there can create a private little refuge."

Jumping to his feet, he stumbled and almost knocked over a pillar holding a porcelain vase. He grabbed it with both hands and steadied both the pillar and himself as he set it back down, then turned to pick up his fallen hat.

"Yes, yes of course. That sounds marvelous. It might be a bit cooler there too. It seems to have gotten very warm all of a sudden…wouldn't you say?"

She only nodded as she turned and lead the way to the back door and the path across the lawn. He quickly caught up and followed close behind.

After they were settled on the bench that Mr. Wadsworth had erected in Sadie's memory, Chandler took Grace's hand, "Gigi, I haven't been able to get you off my mind and have been hungry to see you and know more about you."

Fluttering the fan toward her little breasts she asked, "Pastor Chandler, what exactly *do* you know about me?"

"Please, call me Abraham, or Abe. Remember you said it sounded like your father's name, Gabe. Your mother…I think I saw her once…I know you love music. And Ms. Evans, your teacher, said you are very smart…*gifted* is the term she used. I agree with her" Glancing at her growing breasts he continued, "you *are* gifted…in so many ways…and…and you are oh, so, beautiful. I know you wanted to know more about God and I would love to teach you. Just give me the chance, Gigi, and I will do anything."

*He saw Mother!* "Well, a few things you *don't* know are, I am no longer Gigi. My name is Grace now. Grace Autumn *Wadsworth*. My father signed adoption papers making it legal. He was not my real father anyway. He was my uncle who tried to raise me after my parents died. He didn't want me, so he gave me to the Wadsworths just as he would give away a litter of pups. No, wait. He *kept* the pup, and gave *me* away. He thought more of his precious wolf than he did me. That's okey though, you see he was mean to me and treated me badly. He had an Indian woman living with him…in sin. He also thought more of her than me, too, so you see I'm glad to be where I am now. About learning more about God…I DO have questions. I hear the minister at the church we go to preach that God is all love and wants us to love one another…If so, then why would a loving God let my parents die, allow me to be treated as if I were a burden to be cast off at the first chance? They say that God knows and sees all…his eye is on the sparrow…he is everywhere at all times…Well, then why does a loving God let bad things happen to good people? I've seen people gunned down without putting up a fight, I've seen hunger and cold and had little to call my own, Where was He then? He must not have thought much of me, to know what was happening and allow it."

"But Gigi…Grace, You must have faith…"

"Where does faith come from?"

"Reading the Bible will answer so many of your…."

"Yes, the Bible. I'm told that it is the 'Word of God'.

"It is."

"In church they said that God wrote the Ten Commandments. Did He write the Bible too?"

"No, it was written by followers and believers of God."

"Then why do they say it is God's Word."

"Because He has blessed the Bible to be true."

"How do you know that?"

"By faith, Gi...Grace...by faith."

"So we are back to faith. How do you describe faith?"

"Faith is believing something to be true, even though you have no proof. You can't see it with your own eyes or hear it with your own ears, but you *know* it's true."

"Papa tried to tell me that years ago...but that makes no sense. No one can KNOW something if they don't witness it themselves. They can imagine it, or hope for it or even be brain washed into believing it..."

"Oh, my dear, Grace. You must see that the Lord loves His followers..."

"Really? What about the story they told us about Job. He was one of God's most faithful followers and what did that get him? He was used as a pawn on a chess board between God and Satan."

"But God gave back to Job even more than he lost after Job proved to be faithful..."

"Did He give Job back the children...the *same* children he lost? No. They were all dead. Would you want replacements for your loved ones or the real ones back again? If God is all powerful, then why didn't He give Job back his original children?"

Chandler could see that his hopes of her becoming his "Pastor's wife" would never happen. He dropped his head and sighed, "I'm so, so sorry that you cannot comprehend. I have failed you in explaining the answers to your questions. I will pray that someday you will dance in the light of knowledge. I promise you that He is waiting for you. All you have to do is have faith...

"Yes...*faith.*"

He knew there could be no future with her as long as she defied God. He felt empty inside, sick about leaving without being able to set this beautiful girl on the right path to her ever loving God. But he would pray. Ever so fervently …he would pray.

She wasn't sure she had convinced him about her parents and knew that if he left, he could ruin her life with some small statement. She would be taken away and sent to a reservation; back to the filth and squalor that she had come from. She would never see this luxurious lifestyle again.

Sadly he took both of her hands in his and lifted her to her feet. "My dear, I do not have answers to your questions, but I pray that someday you will find them, and when you do the gates of heaven will open and God will be waiting with loving arms. He is patient, like most parents, so don't give up asking the questions because someday, someone smarter than I will be able to help you understand. I want that for you very much because, as beautiful as you are here on earth, you could make a gorgeous Heavenly Angel."

He dropped her hands, turned his back and started walking slowly back to the mansion.

Her eyes narrowed as she reached for a dart and slipped it into the gun. As she drew breath to blow the small puff that would send the dart through the tube and puncture her target, something…from somewhere deep in her heart, kept her from doing so.

He left, unaware of how close he came to never leaving the plantation alive.

# Chapter 73

After spotting much wildlife and wondering where the river came into the valley, the clan split up and went exploring.

On one trip scouts separated and followed different animal trails that went along each side of the river. They set out, only to find themselves back together at an opening at the far end of the valley…a tunnel. The valley's river was coming from this tunnel.

The tunnel was a tubular rock formation, about ten feet wide and ten feet high. Its opening was about five feet above the ground, which formed a waterfall above a small pond beneath, before spilling out to form the river. One of the scouts climbed to the tunnel's opening and found that he could wade through it. He reported that the tunnel was only about thirty feet long before coming out at a small meadow in a large steep and rocky canyon. The water's source was surging from underground, near the meadow's edge, which created its own pool that swelled until it spilled into the tunnel.

With this news the clan decided it was time to set up their government, and came together for the discussion. After first voting on their new name, it was unanimous that they be called *The Valley Clan*, with Jumping Fox as their new chief and Lame Elk, Ellen's brother, as Shaman. Necessary positions were filled and the first order of business was to plan a ceremony of thanks to Yowa.

It felt good to see the new leaders take charge and give each member time to express his comments or concerns. It was good to hear the old ceremonies revised and brought back to life. Another vote was to decide whether to obscure the opening at the tunnel, or venture out and explore even more habitable areas. Deciding on staying in the first valley, the new chief asked for volunteers to mask the tunnel entrance on the other side, without hindering the flow of the river. Then he asked for a volunteer to document and oversee the property claims that each of the clan had chosen on this side.

Another subject was brought forth. A way was needed to alert all clansmen of danger. What and how could that be arranged? Many suggestions and ideas were exchanged before they realized the size of the valley would be too large for one single alarm, so it was decided to create a series of instruments that could be heard and relayed from one camp to another. Will volunteered to make several metal clanging triangles that would resonate and be distinguishable, and set them at intervals throughout the valley to make it audible to all corners of the valley. When people heard the alarm, they were to gather at a central spot and be informed.

Many other discussions wore far into the night, but the members came away content that they were well on their way to becoming a solid clan again.

That night Will asked Becca, "Now that we are living closer to your folk than townspeople, what would you rather be called, Becca or Blue?"

"The clan all call me Blue again, but dear husband, you can call me anything you wish. It doesn't matter as long as we are together and we have our son and the valley." He held her close and this time she did not stiffen or pull away from his advances.

Gabe and Sparrow chose a site upstream a short distance from the river, under an outcropping of the mountain. The formation was unique in that it had a roof-like rock overhang that gave shelter from the rain and harsh sun with a good view. He began making plans for a two-story home, using the natural setting.

Knowing a trip back to Ft. Wells was needed, he spoke to Sparrow, "I am going to ask around and make a list of what tools and hardware others need. I'll take Angel to carry the load. But the lumber will have to come from here in the valley." Without saying more he thought, *while I'm there I can check on the authenticity of the land grant papers.* "Do you want Zeus and Sashay to stay with you?"

Sparrow turned and with hands on her hips she asked, "What enemy is here? The clan is close. I will be safe."

"Never safe enough," he said as he pulled her close, "You are my world, little Sparrow!"

Thomas approached Ellen, "Honey. You know I have to go back don't you? If I stay away much longer I could be classified as a deserter and dishonorably discharged. I would be unemployed, without pay and no way to support you."

"Yes Thomas, I know. I've been expecting this since we entered the valley. I knew you were waiting to get here, to make sure I was safe and to know how to find me again. But you will not be going back alone. I am going with you. I, too, wanted to see the valley for myself after hearing Blue talk about it for so long, but I don't want this kind of life any longer. I want to be a soldier's wife for as long as you wish to stay in the Army. When and if you choose to quit, we will survive on whatever else you wish to do.

Besides, remember I was doing well selling my crafts at Hamilton's. And I'm still learning to be an interpreter. If the papers from Washington are true and we can get that land, we can live away from the fort if you wish." She walked into his arms and laid her head on his chest, "You see, you aren't the only one that has been thinking."

Engulfing her in his arms, Thomas lowered his cheek to the top of her head, "But what if the papers aren't true and they take you away? I couldn't stand losing you again."

"Well, then we will just find a way for me to escape again. I am going to trust the white man one more time, and I'm putting my life on the line to prove it. Let's explain to the others our decision, then we can head back. Or do you want to claim a piece of this heaven before we go?"

"You know, that might be a good idea. It could be our vacation home when we come to visit…which I plan to do as often as the Army allows. Your people have become my people and I want to share our lives with them."

"I agree. Let's go find just the right spot, then we will take it to the clan for approval."

When Gabe heard their plans to return to Ft. Wells he asked to join them, and they set out early the next morning.

When they got to the fort they were nervous about presenting Ellen to the new commander, but he was gracious and understood their dilemma and eased the tension by offering her a chair. After the paper work was done to return Thomas to duty, they dove right into the documents that would claim the property for them. She stood and swore her citizenship promises as prompted and was even able to sign her own name where the commander pointed out to her. When she had done so, Commander

Simmons took her hand and said, "It gives me great pleasure to issue this document declaring that you have followed all the agreements and will live as a white American."

Picking her words carefully she stated, "It gives me great pleasure to know that I am safe and no longer have fear of being forced to leave my husband and my home."

Gabe later asked Sergeant Wilson if he had found out if Anita would have to be there to sign the same papers.

"I'm afraid so, Mr. Adams. It states the commander has to see her quote the oath and there have to be witnesses present during it and the signing. If she can't sign her name she can make her mark and witnesses sign that also. That's the way it's been done before," explained the sergeant. "I did find Mr. Hudson's deed and the description can help a surveyor locate the corner boundaries. When you do, I will have the surveyor verify the property lines and you can make a claim to the adjacent property. All is looking good as long as you get your wife to state the oath taking the white man's way and abandoning her old one."

"I understand. I'll bring her in the next visit to town."

"Mr. Hudson's wife could take the oath and claim another parcel adjacent to his if she so desired. With him already owning that property and her adding hers, they could come out with a pretty big spread," added Wilson.

Gabe nodded, "Yes, I see they could. That would be good for them, for sure. I'll explain it all when I go back. They'll be glad to hear it."

Thomas unloaded Ellen's belongings from Angel so they could settle back into fort life, which was much easier for both of them. Ellen immediately went to her sewing and crafts and Thomas to his army duties.

Gabe's list from the clan was long, so he first stopped at the lumber yard and gathered what he needed there, then went to Smithy's for a nice visit. Zeus and Sashay enjoyed the visit with Orphy and then later with Tory when Gabe went to the mercantile to finish off his list.

He hadn't shared with the Hamiltons all the details of his visit with Gigi. He couldn't trust his emotions, so all he told them was that it was the middle of her schooling and she was not ready to come home yet. They accepted it.

After his list was filled he added many packets of seeds to surprise Sparrow. When visits were over he loaded up Angel and called for the wolves. "Come on kids, we're heading back home to Mama."

As he headed back, leading Angel with both wolves quietly following, he thought, *How can I get Sparrow to come back and swear an oath she would have no intention of complying to? She will not give up her beliefs in her god and spirit world and I have never asked her to. I've got a lot of miles and time to come up with some idea. There has to be a way...there's just has to!*

# Chapter 74

Grace sat in front of her vanity turning her head back and forth to decide which side was the most beautiful, and wondered about the young lad at the party that had not seemed enamored by her. She decided to ask Olivia.

"Momma, who was that boy with the black curly hair and blue eyes at the party? I think his name is Garret?"

"Yes, Garret Alan Piedmont III, why?"

"He seemed to be more interested in Hannah than me and I can't understand why," pouted Grace.

"Well, she is a little pretty, with her blonde hair..."

"But she does not compare to me!"

Ignoring her daughter's outburst, Olivia continued, "His father is a wealthy lawyer and Garret is being groomed to follow in his father's footsteps. Someday he will take over the firm, which will make him even more influential."

"And that would make his wife to be among the most rich and powerful of all Charlottesville, right?"

Olivia's eyes glittered with the possibility of her and Frederick's status' also being raised, "Yes, she would be very prominent and her family would be sought after by the most prestigious of the elite."

"So you think I should pursue his attention?"

"Of course, my dear. He will be a very eligible bachelor and they say, 'All's fair in love and war'. You get young Mr. Piedmont's attention, and he will surely drop Miss Hannah Bowers."

"But how will I see him again?"

"My mother told me that if a person saves another person's life, he will always feel a personal bond for them, although the person saved can grow to even hate the one who saved him. Every plan has to have the five W's and one H. They are: Who, what, where, when, why and how. We know the *who* is also the *what* in this circumstance...Garret. The *why*, is your desire to have him. We have to concentrate on the *where, when* and *how* part of the scenerio. This will have to be between the two of us. Daddy will not understand the ways of us women when we go after what we want! Garret's family is competitive with both racing and jumping horses. I'm told Garret rides quite frequently where his family's and our plantation are separated only by a rail fence. It can be easily jumped...do you know how to ride, dear?"

"I used to ride Angel back...*there.*"

"Angel?"

"Yes, that was a horse Blu...Becca owned. Will worked to pay for it and gave it to her...."

"Never mind, just tell me, how *well* can you ride?"

Grace beamed with pride as she boasted, "Better than any of the others. I used to do tricks on Angel when no one was around. I could ride her bareback and not fall off."

"But, did you ever use a side-saddle?" asked Olivia

"What is that?"

"A proper lady never straddles a horse. She uses a saddle that has a hook on one side, above the stirrup, that allows her to sit with both legs on one side of the horse."

"Oh, I used to sit sideways when I was playing."

"How well can you *act*?"

"I've gotten by at school; no one knows...you know."

"We'll start immediately. You mention to Daddy tonight, at the dinner table...."

And their plan was set in motion.

# Chapter 75

Sparrow was concerned about her pregnancy. She was convinced the child was Angry Frog's, and it was unusual for a baby to be growing so rapidly and to be so active, unlike her pregnancy with Gigi.

Gabe noticed that she would stop her chores and grab hold of anything nearby to stabilize herself with one hand and rub her abdomen with the other. "What is it, dear?"

"It seems this one is bored and wants to play kickball. It's too soon for this much movement," she explained.

"Maybe he is impatient and wants to be outside to exhibit his prowess as an athlete to the world," he teased.

Sparrow laughed, "Fancy words, my husband. But maybe *she* is the one in a hurry?"

"Time will tell, my little Sparrow. By the way, how much longer do we have to wait?"

"You are wise and know there are many moons to go."

Knowing she was right and masking his concern with humor, he said, "If it is much longer you will soon carry a table for your dinner plate right in front of you!"

She smiled and patted her growing abdomen and nodded, "Not long before you speak true."

But as the months passed and with the time approaching, Gabe knew the baby was too large for natural birth and told Sparrow that they must go to the fort doctor.

She shook her head, "I not need white-man's doctor." But she agreed that there could be trouble with the birth.

"I'm not arguing about this. You *are* going to the doctor where you and the baby will be in good hands when the time comes. We can stay at the fort with Thomas and Ellen until then…which could be very soon."

Finally she consented, knowing it would be a long trip to the fort from the valley, and in her condition she could have the baby on the way.

Without hesitation he packed a bundle, and after getting word to Will and Blue, and leaving the wolves, they started off. Each day was a struggle with some days covering more distance than others, but they arrived just days before Sparrow's labor pains.

Ellen was in her glory having someone who needed her and took charge immediately. The fort doctor informed them that he was an army doctor and had very little experience with handling births, so when her time came, at two in the morning, she, Gabe and Ellen set off to the town's doctor.

"Dr. David Druitt, M.D." was the sign on the door above the sheriff's office. With Ellen in front, the railing to grip, and Gabe behind, Sparrow made it up the stairs. Gabe's pounding on the door brought a very old doctor, who took one look at her and called for his wife. "Get her to the table in back and prep her while I deal with the others."

"But David, she's an India…" she began.

Glaring at her, he interrupted, "She's going to have a baby and needs our help. See to her right away!"

Glaring back at him, she said coldly, "Yes, doctor."

Gabe saw the exchange and stated, "She's my wife!"

"Yes, of course, Sir. She is in good hands and we will call you…if need be." said the doctor. "You can wait either here, or …well, everything is closed at this time of day…,"

Ellen took control and ordered, "I'll wait here, while you tend to the horse and wagon."

The doctor left the room saying, "As you wish, I have preparations to attend to, so if you'll excuse me..."

Upon returning and hearing Sparrows whimpers become loud cries, Gabe couldn't stand it any longer. He told Ellen that he was going to get some air and ran down the stairs. Upon reaching the street he didn't know what to do. *I can't leave and I can't stay in there. I'll just sit here at the bottom of the stairs.* Trying to get his mind off Sparrow's pain he thought, *While we are here it would be a good time for me to ask Sparrow to sign those papers. I'll tell her that she doesn't have to mean the things she says, just say them in front of the commander so we can get the property.* Hearing another wail, he cringed and lowered his head, *Oh, God; it was only one woman that disobeyed you, why did you have to make childbirth so hard on the rest?* As he stood to get away from her cries, he heard another...a baby's cry.

He rushed back up the stairs, two at a time, and burst in to find Ellen on her feet and watching the door to the back room. They both stood there, waiting. Then there came another baby's cry, a little different and much louder. Confused, they looked at each other and realized...TWINS!

Ellen and Gabe hugged each other and laughed for not realizing the possibility. The door opened with the doctor's wife holding the first one, with light complexion and a head-full of bright red hair. Behind her the doctor carried the second, darker skinned with coal black hair, who would not stop howling and flailing its arms. The doctor said, "Mr. Adams, meet your sons."

Gabe was astounded. They were as different as night and day, in appearance and behavior. The redhead was sleeping contentedly while the other was screaming and stiffening his body with tiny fists flailing the air around him.

The doctor's wife looked at the baby her husband held and laughed, "I fear he was either not ready to be born or he wanted to be first. I'm not sure, but he sure is mad."

Gabe took the one handed to him as Ellen took the other. They both went in to see how Sparrow was doing. "How's my girl?" asked Gabe.

"Tired," whispered Sparrow.

"Of course, but we have two fine, healthy boys," he said.

Raising her voice she demanded, "I only have one son. Take the other one away."

"Sparrow, you can't mean that," scolded Ellen.

"I do. I will not have Angry Frog's seed in my home."

"We can't know that it is his. Honey, the baby could be ours. Paternal twins can be different. He has more Indian features, but that doesn't make him less than ours. One looks like you and one looks like me…"

"NO! I told you, and you promised. I will not have that thing to my breast, now or ever. Take it away. I never want to see it again."

Ellen stood in shock. Holding the crying baby, she looked at Gabe for instructions.

Gabe motioned with his head to follow him out of the room. "She is determined to not have anything to do with this one. I don't know what to do. It could be ours, but she won't believe me. All her fears have come true in her mind; that the baby would be *his* and not *ours*. I know Sparrow, she won't change her mind. If I lay this one down beside you, can you watch them both while I talk to the doctor?"

"Of course, this one is beginning to quiet down and might sleep soon. Go…find out what you can."

Gabe went back to the doctor and asked if he could speak to him privately. When they were alone he told him the story of Sparrow's kidnapping and her fear of who the father of the baby could be. "Can a woman have twins from two different men?"

"You know, there is a book in my office that deals with twins, and if memory serves me right we can find the answer there. Let's go take a look."

After locating his spectacles he searched through the various medical books and pulled one down and thumbed through it. "Here it is," and started reading to himself.

Gabe became annoyed and said, "Well?"

Looking up from the book and over the top of his spectacles, the doctor realized Gabe's anxiety and said, "Oh, it says here, 'Superfecundation is the fertilization of two or more ova from the same cycle by sperm from separate acts of sexual intercourse, which can lead to twin babies from two separate biological fathers. The term *superfecundation* is derived from *fecund*, meaning the ability to produce offspring.' So it looks like your wife's fears might have some validity."

"But how can we know for sure? What if the second child is ours and she won't keep it? What do I do?" asked Gabe.

"Sir, I can't answer that. This is something you will have to work out with your wife. In the meantime you are going to have to find some way of feeding that baby until you both come to a decision."

Gabe turned and walked back to Ellen. The second baby was quiet now but seemed restless and unstill. She looked up, "Gabe, I know this is hard on everyone, but I may have a solution. What if Thomas and I took this young man…just until you two can decide on what to do. You know I am unable to bear children and Thomas would love to have a child, no matter what skin tone it is. Can we talk to Sparrow about it?"

"Oh, Ellen, that makes perfect sense. I'm all for that. Let's go see what she has to say."

Sparrow shook her head, "No. Husband. You promised to take it far away so I never have to see it again." Looking at Ellen she added, "I not want bad things happen to you and Tome-us. *That* is from Angry Frog…and he is evil."

Ellen pleaded, "Sparrow, please. Angry Frog *was* evil, but that's not saying that this baby will be. Let Thomas and I keep him and show you how love and affection could make a difference. If he turns out to be anything like Angry Frog, we will send him away ourselves."

Looking at each of them, Sparrow said, "I not want him to know he came from me…ever. Never he be told he has a brother. Promise me, Husband, Ellen, you not tell him! I go back to valley. He stay here. I no have to see. But know that I have warned you…he has evil in him."

The doctor came in and coughed dramatically. When they looked his way he quietly said, "Could this wait until later? My wife and I would like to get some sleep."

Realizing the time, Gabe asked him, "How soon do you think it will be before Sparrow can travel?"

"She had quite a battle with this birthing, and lost a lot of blood. I will release her to be moved to the fort, but let her rest there for a couple of days."

"How much do I owe you, Doc?" asked Gabe.

Ellen broke in, "Don't worry about that, Gabe. Thomas and I will take care of it." Exchanging glances with the doctor, she added, "We exchange favors...don't we Doctor Druitt?"

Understanding the situation, he smiled and nodded, "Yes, Mrs. Thorton. I think I may still owe *you* a bit. Oh, and Mr. Adams, I will need the names for these boys to place on the birth certificates. Not much time is allowed to file them."

With that settled, Gabe got the wagon and helped Sparrow down the stairs and onto a pad in the back of the wagon. She held the firstborn as Ellen held the second and Gabe guided the horse back to the fort.

When the plan was relayed to Thomas he was delighted. He knew how much a child meant to Ellen and he wanted to make her happy. He was surprised to have a fatherly feeling sweep over him as he watched Ellen rocking the child. She sent him to the fort barnyard where he gleaned a little milk from the cow, and then she tied off a corner of cloth and dipped it in the milk. When she offered it to the baby he took it greedily and began to suckle.

Sparrow's warning meant nothing to Thomas. Nor did he care that he had not fathered the child, only that they had a baby and their lives would now be fulfilled.

Sparrow would not go to their quarters or the infirmary. She and Gabe stayed in a corner of the new addition that Thomas had requested when the clan had been captured and brought to the fort years ago.

Holding his son, Gabe looked up at Sparrow and said, "I think it's time to name this little fellow. Have any ideas? We'll have to let Thomas and Ellen name the..." As he saw her eyes narrow and her jaw tighten he stopped in mid-sentence. "What do you want to name our son?"

She smiled and shrugged. "It is tradition for father to name the child. It is your honor. If I no like, we talk."

"Well, I've been thinking. You know how William chose the last few letters of his name for Liam? What if we did the same?"

"Name him Liam?"

Gabe laughed, "No. Use the last few letters of *my* name, Gabriel, and name him Riel." Looking back at the baby he added, "He's so beautiful, so much like Gigi. It breaks my heart that he will never know his sister." Again he saw the change in Sparrow and hurried to change the subject. "Now for a middle name. Liam has a Cherokee middle name, but you were from the Anita Clan. Is there an Indian name you wish for him?"

"Not yet. He must earn the name as he grows."

"But something has to be written on his birth certificate."

"Then you choose. You choose good. I like Riel."

"Well, little man, it looks like this will take more thinking, so you might have to wait just a tad bit longer. Say, Tad...hmmm that's short for Theodore. He could use all kinds of nicknames, such as: Tad, Theo, Teddy...Yes, that sounds like a winner!" Holding the boy to his chest, he added, "Welcome to the world, Riel Theodore Adams!"

Looking up at Sparrow he said, "Tomorrow we need to go to the doctor's office to let him know so he can fill out a birth certificate for him. There might be some legal issues about the doctor filling out and filing the birth certificate because of the twin birth."

Sparrow's head jerked up and she glared at Gabe, "You not say that word in front of our baby...not now, not ever." Taking the baby from him and to her breast she continued, "You remember promise to me. He must not *ever* know." Her body shuddered and then she turned her attention to the child at her breast and began to hum an old Cherokee chant.

Thomas and Ellen chose the names for the second child, and relayed to Gabe, "His first name was from my father, Gilbert. Ellen chose his middle name after her brother Lame Elk. Henceforth his named is, Gilbert Lame Thorton and we shall call him Lame."

"We can both give the information to the doctor so we can get copies of their birth certificates." said Gabe.

The doctor would not comply, "I'm sorry folks, but I am sworn to accuracy about these certificates and must fill them out truthfully. It was a twin birth, mother; Indian, Anita Sparrow Adams; father; white, Gabriel...uh, sir, you never told me your middle name."

Gabe stuttered, "That's alright, I never use it."

"But sir, the document has to be accurate."

Gabe looked around and stepped up close to the doctor, and whispered, "It's Meredith."

The doctor stated, "That's a fine name. No reason to be embarrassed. Many men are named Meredith."

"Shh. I don't like it nor do I use it...if you will be so kind as to lower your voice."

Nodding, the doctor returned to his writing and murmured, "Father, white, Gabriel Meredith Adams."

Gabe cleared his throat, "Getting back to the second twin, is there no other way around this? Do you have the documents for adoption?? My wife is very adamant about not wanting the child she believes came from her rapist. The Thortons here are willing to adopt him, to give my wife peace and the boy a loving home."

"Yes I have those documents but they, too, have to be filled out truthfully." Feeling sympathy for Gabe and the situation, he weakened, "I can do this much. I can fill out the adoption papers stating that the child was abandoned with no way of knowing who the parents are. I will stretch the truth this time because your wife truly *has* abandoned him. It will be up to his adoptive parents to make up their own story about who, why or even where it came about."

The couples turned to each other as Gabe said, "That means that each of our baby's certificates will state that they are a twin, and have Sparrow and my names as the parents. Your adoption papers will not. Neither of the boys must ever see those birth certificates."

"I'll not tell. We can hide the papers and say they were lost in a fire, or something," said Ellen.

"I will burn it myself!" Sparrow snarled vehemently.

Gabe took her in his arms, "I know this is hard, Baby, but we must get through this and on with our lives. I promise you...I will never divulge any connection with you...or Riel, to Lame. Thomas, Ellen, will you also make a promise to her that this will remain between us?"

"I promise," said Ellen.

"Me too," said Thomas.

Gabe shot a look to the doctor, who spread his arms and said, "It's none of my business how you want to handle this. After I sign these certificates they are all yours to do as you wish. My copies will go to the state capital and be placed in the birth archives. No one will see them."

Raising Sparrow's chin, he made eye contact and said quietly, "You see? There's nothing to worry about. This secret will go no further than those here. Now let's head back to the fort for some dinner. We have a lot to celebrate tonight."

Sparrow grudgingly allowed Riel to be laid beside Lame on a table nearby as the four adults enjoyed a quiet meal. As they relaxed Gabe brought up the topic of the property and stated, "Do you know how we could give Riel a good security in the case of our demise?"

Sparrow eyes narrowed, "What is this...d- mys?"

"It means if we die. If you swore the oath like Ellen did, the property next to Will's could be Liam's someday. It would mean he would have security.

"You swear white-man's ways, Ellen?" asked Sparrow.

"Yes, we have been granted 640 acres of our choice in the Ft. Wells area. We plan on building and living there when Thomas retires."

"You swear against Yowa?" Sparrow asked in confusion.

"I believe that the Cherokee Yowa and the white-man's God are the same, Sparrow. We just use different names."

"Husband tell Gigi that. They talk a lot of it. I no like white-man's ways. They took my Gigi. Their chiefs lied to our people and killed many of our families." Looking at Gabe and Thomas she added quickly, "Only the white men who marry us, I like."

"We know and understand all the reasons you should not trust them, but could you...for me...for Riel...pretend to take the oath so that our son will have that security?"

Sparrow looked long and hard at Gabe before saying, "I do it for you and for our son, but I lie. I not sure about

Yowa have two names. Then we go back to the valley and I no come out again." Then she cried out and pointed to the boys on the table.

Everyone turned to see Lame's outstretched arm pushing Riel to the edge.

Everyone jumped and ran and caught Riel before he fell. "You see? I tell you! He is evil!"

Ellen spoke in Lame's defense, "Sparrow, dear friend, Lame was only stretching as babies do. He has no control of his arms or legs yet. It was just a coincidence that he pushed Riel."

"None of you believe, but someday you will. Husband, I will do as you wish for Riel, but I want to be away from here. We leave tomorrow for the valley."

"Are you sure you are up to it? The doctor said you must rest for a few days," questioned Gabe.

"I good enough to get our baby away from that one!" She gathered Riel into her arms and headed for the door.

The next morning Sparrow stood in front of the fort commander and repeated the words to the best of her ability, with one hand on the white man's book and the other in the air like she was shown. Thomas and Ellen witnessed as she made her X on the dotted line, and Gabe finished filling out the papers for the 640 acre land grant.

# Chapter 76

Life in the valley was as it used to be in a much older time. For the clan it was contentment, but for Sashay it was boredom. *Come on, Zeus. Let's do something. This is as boring as it gets lying around here day after day. We need to stretch our legs, take a run, DO something.*

He lay there, with his chin on his front paws, *My human Gabe told me to 'Stay'; you heard him.*

Sashay was pacing around him, *That was days ago. Let's go see Tory and Orphy.*

Without lifting his head he yawned and rolled over to his side, *We can't go all the way back there.*

She nudged his chin with her nose, *Why not, who's stopping us?*

*You don't have the same feelings I have for these humans. They are my family,* he scolded.

*Big news, brother; you are a wolf; they are humans. They are not your family...friends maybe, but not family.*

*Have you forgotten? They have taken care of you all your life with food and shelter and love...*

*What love? The humans that I lived with left me behind, without a care...and gave me away to your human. This is beside the point. If you don't want to go see Orphy and Tory, then let's explore this new land. See what's here.*

This piqued Zeus' interest and he rose to his chest again. *Well, maybe we could...*

Bouncing on all fours, Sashay expressed her excitement, *Yes, yes, let's go find all the new sights, smells and sounds and you know...explore!*

Zeus rose to all fours, *Alright, but we can't be gone for long.*

# Chapter 77

The valley brought back memories to the older clan members who lived in the time before all the running from the army had begun. But most of this new clan was younger. When they left the forced march toward Oklahoma, most of the older ones did not have the heart to run any longer.

The elders of this new clan were revered and respected and were often visited by the younger clansmen to relearn some of the old ways.

Game was adequate for the clan's needs. They respected the animals' right to life by only taking what was needed. As the animals replenished the valley, so did the clan.

Blue was pregnant again and looked forward to bringing three-year-old Liam a new brother or sister to play with. Peace and contentment was like a fine veil of protection that settled over the valley to keep evil away.

But true to life, the veil was torn one day when Blue's search for Liam failed. She knew she had left him asleep and it had not taken long for her bath, or had it? She had relaxed in the river and later enjoyed the warmth of the sun drying her skin…maybe it was longer than she thought…

It took a while before panic set in. After checking all areas she assumed his little legs could take him, she thought *Perhaps one of the older children picked him up and took him to play with the others.* She went from camp to camp and asked all the children if they had seen him. Then it was time to find Will. *Maybe he is teaching him boy lessons…*

Will was found, but without Liam.

"Where have you been?" Blue cried through her tears, "I've been searching for Liam for hours and can't find him anywhere."

"I was with the elders. They were teaching…"

"Never mind! We have to find Liam!"

"Where was he the last time you saw him?"

"Here, on his mat, asleep. I went to bathe and it might have taken me longer than I thought, but I…I…"

"Don't worry, Blue. We will find him. Let's go about this in the old way. See if he left any tracks to follow."

"Yes, Yes, of course…I…I didn't think…I mean I thought he would be found quickly and then…when he wasn't…" Her eyes widened as she screeched, "Oh, what if some wild animal snatched him up?" Her breaths came in gasps.

Will took hold of her elbows and made her face him. Shaking her gently, he said quietly but sternly, "Now, Blue, get a hold of yourself. You can't help him like this. Stop, breathe, get control."

When he saw that she was starting to breathe easier he stooped to check out the area around Liam's sleeping pad. There were vague tracks of little footprints leading away and up the hill from their campsite. He smiled up at Blue and pointed to them.

They both began to rest easier until the prints led them to the cleft in the mountain!

They ventured as far as they could see into the mountain, calling his name until they realized their voices were bouncing off the rock walls and echoing down tunnels, making it hard to tell where the sound came from. When they became very quiet they heard a tiny cry, coming from all directions at once. There was no way to follow the sound. Will turned to Blue, "Go, get Zeus. He will be able to track Liam by smell and lead him back out."

Blue ran to their camp, but Zeus was nowhere to be seen. Nor did he come when called. She mimicked the whistle Gabe used for him, but he still didn't come. She ran back and told Will. He stood silent for a few seconds, then spoke in a rush, "Go to the triangle and alert the clan. We must make torches and form a search party. Liam must have gone in when the sun was overhead. We don't know how far he got before it became too dark for him to see his way back."

Blue raced to the nearest triangle and began to beat on it frantically. When one of the women came running she hurriedly told her what happened and that torches and volunteers were needed to search the cave. When she heard another triangle, further down the valley, she knew the message was being relayed. Then she searched the area for anything that could be used for a torch. She was going into that cave to find her son!

# Chapter 78

Sashay was excited about this new adventure and ran anxiously…either leading, following or alongside Zeus. Each new scent or sound led her to stop and perk her ears or put her nose to the ground. On one of these stops she asked Zeus, *Did you hear that call? That sounded like Tory or Orphy, but different somehow.*

Zeus answered, *Be still. I think it came from the other side of this ravine…maybe up the canyon a bit.*

*There it is again, but it's not them. This is…more powerful. Answer the call, Zeus! Come on!* Not understanding the new sensation that came over her, she moved forward.

*Don't be in a hurry. There are dangers out here, Sashay! Not like back with the humans' protection.*

*What protection? We've had no threats for them to protect us from*, she said

He took a deep breath and tried to explain, *That's what I'm saying; this is a different world.*

*Yes, more exciting! Come on Brother, let's find out who is calling us.*

She barely had time to finish her statement before she looked ahead to see a massive male wolf, standing still and statuesque. He was staring at them from his vantage point higher up the hill. Behind him was his pack, waiting for their leader's decision on what to do with the intruders in their territory.

*Oh, Zeus, look at him*, she swooned.

*I am looking and I'm not liking what I see. Get behind me Sashay, I don't think he likes us being here*, he answered.

Zeus was right. This alpha advanced toward them stiff-legged and with bristled hackles.

*What are you doing here? This is my domain and you are not welcome. Choose to leave now, or try to claim it. I've fought bigger males than you, wanting my territory and females.* The alpha stated gruffly.

Sashay advanced a little and said, *My name is Sashay and this is my brother Zeus. What's your name?*

*Name? My name is the leader of the pack you see behind me and I intend to keep it that way. Are you ready to fight, 'Zeus'?* He snarled sarcastically.

Sashay snapped, *Now you just wait a minute, big boy. There is no need to be so rude. We just moved here with our humans and....*

The new alpha was circling the pair, but stopped and arched his neck, *Humans? You live with humans? What kind of wolves are you? Or should I call you dogs? Do you even know how to hunt for your own food, or are you being fed like a pup sucking on his mother's teat?*

Zeus was sizing him up just as Sashay had to get another word in, *Now you stop that mean mouthing us. You are just a bully that has not been shown manners...and Zeus is just the one to teach you a few!*

Zeus cringed, *Sashay...I think it would be a good idea for us to choose the suggestion he had about leaving...*

*Nonsense! He is not going to run us out of the valley. He is an impolite boor and he must apologize immediately.*

The alpha continued to taunt Zeus. *Nothing to say for yourself, puny one, or do you let this scrawny loud-mouth do all the talking? She seems to have a lot to say about your ability to fight. Look around you, all this valley and*

301

*beyond, and all those females waiting…just for you…If you are alpha enough to win the battle.*

*Zeus! Are you going to stand there and let him disrespect me? You show him who's going to be boss around here!*

Zeus shook his head, and knowing the outcome before it started, made a lunge. The alpha was ready and took control of the fight from the beginning. When Sashay saw that Zeus was quickly losing the battle, she dove in to protect him. The other wolves began to advance until their leader commanded them to stay back.

When the fight came to a standstill, Zeus was down and bleeding. Sashay stood over him, and facing the alpha, she growled fiercely, *Take one more step and I'll tear that handsome face to pieces!*

Stepping back the alpha sized her up and realized she meant every word. He smiled, *So, you think I'm handsome?*

Realizing what she had said, she kept her protective stance and snapped, *In a puke-ish sort of way. I hope you're happy. Zeus has never fought, so that makes you a bully.*

*And it makes you the loudmouth that caused him to defend your honor…or do you have any?*

She made a lunge and snapped so loud the pack behind him heard her teeth connect.

The Alpha backed a little further, and to save his ego, he turned and said over his shoulder, *Your brother is lucky that I chose not to kill him. Take him home and teach him to fight…If he is going to live out here, he is going to have to learn to survive.*

She watched him strut through his pack and lead them out of sight.

*Zeus, are you able to get up?*

*I think so, but I'm awful weak, and I hurt all over.*

*I see you have many gashes that need to be taken care of. Let's try to find a safe place for the night and see about heading back to the humans in the morning.*

He groaned as he tried to stand. *I think I'd better lie here a little longer. You go, see if you can find a place and come back for me. That way we won't waste time and effort.*

*Good thinking. You just rest and I'll be back soon. Howl if he comes back, or if something else…*

*Just go, Sashay, I'll be fine.*

He drifted off to sleep, but was startled awake by Sashay's nudge. It was dark and he realized he had slept for hours.

*Did you find a place?*

*Yes. A cave close by.*

Zeus followed slowly as he limped his tattered body to the cave. Once inside, he found a sandy spot and eased himself down. Sashay stood guard at the opening and thought of how right that male had been about her big mouth causing the fight that had left Zeus' body torn and bloody. Thankfully the bleeding had stopped, but too much movement could cause the wounds to open and start again. *My pride will be the end of me yet…or him.*

At dawn Sashay nudged Zeus awake. *Do you hear that?*

He listened then said, *Yes. It sounds like my small human.*

She said, *It's from deeper in the cave. Can you walk?*

With each movement he groaned. *Yes, but not fast.*

*I'm not going further in there without you. It's too creepy,* she said with a shudder.

303

# Chapter 79

As the volunteers gathered around Will at the cliff opening, two clansmen stepped forward. "We would like to help. We know the cave." It was Tsoi and Soqua, the scouts who ventured into the cave to find Will and Blue years ago.

Soqua spoke, "You must realize that the cave is immense. It has two large tunnels that lead off the main cave." He stooped, and with his finger, drew in the dirt. Looking up at Will he said, "*This* is the way I followed you that day, but I sent Tsoi *here* and Tali *there*. They each took a torch and were told to start back if the torch began to die."

Tsoi offered, "My torch did dim a little, but I could feel a wind and I kept following it. It came out at the ravine that we took to get here."

Soqua continued, "Tali took the one on the right..." then added sadly, "but he never came out. I suggest that due to the size of the cave just inside, and the two separate tunnels, we need three separate groups to search each one."

Will stood with his hands on his hips. Nodding he said, "I appreciate you both and accept your volunteering to lead a search party. But I want to be in one of them."

"Not without me!" demanded Blue.

He went to her and took her in his arms, "Blue, you must think of this baby you carry. You might fall, or we might run into...who-knows-what in there. Please, for this baby, for me, for Liam's sake, let me do it."

"It is for Liam's sake that I need to go. It was my fault that he is in there. He's all alone and like you said, with who- knows-what. Don't you understand, I *have* to?"

Blue could not be denied and was the first to enter the cave, but once inside she readily accepted Will's plea to stick close to him.

Liam's cries were different. They went from screeching in fear to soft whimpering and back again. The problem was that although the sounds could be heard, they were bouncing off the rock walls and echoing down the tunnels.

"Each man in the group is to carry a torch, but light only one at a time. This way if it begins to dim it can be used to light another and we can continue. If a group finds the boy it is to whistle. Just as Liam's cry is carried, so will the sound, and we shall all return here," explained Soqua.

He led a group including Will and Blue down the same tunnel he had sent Tali years ago. Will kept a tight grip on Blue's hand as the light from one torch was not always sufficient. When an opening sprouted from the main passage, a volunteer lit his torch and investigated while the others waited.

Liam's cries became fainter, causing Will to have to hold tighter to Blue.

The path first led around large stalactites and stalagmites, but by the time Soqua lit his second torch the cave began to narrow, and the formations became smaller, but jagged and sharp, causing each person to search for smooth footing.

At this point the guide called for another torch to determine what lay ahead. What they saw was horrific; it was the undisturbed skeleton of Tali. Punctured bits of leather still clung to the bones of his feet. He lay on his back, with sharp stalagmites protruding between his ribs; one arm was across his chest and the other toward his torch that lay only five feet away. The stunned party stood staring at the empty-eyed, wide mouthed skull. The gnarled hands showed that he had died in agony.

"That could happen to Liam!" cried Blue.

Added pressure to find the boy urged the group forward, until just moments later they came to a dead end.

Tsoi's search party found their tunnel much the same as he described it, with twists and turns, and walls becoming so narrow their shoulders would scrape or, so low they had to crouch to go forward.

They came to where their tunnel forked and waited for Tsoi to tell them which way to go. "I guess my torch was so dim that I didn't see this fork before. This means you three keep following this tunnel. It will come out shortly near the ravine. You other three, follow me."

Tsoi's group weaved around bend after bend in the new tunnel, when something caused him to halt abruptly. He had seen the flickering of animal eyes. His arm came up in a motion for the others to stop, "Light your torches from mine, I see the eyes of predators coming toward us. Make ready for an attack."

The torches instantly illuminated the area and exposed Liam clutching Zeus' fur as the limping wolf guided the child out of the darkness, with Sashay following close behind.

Turning toward the direction of the main cave, Tsoi gave a sharp whistle.

# Chapter 80

Grace had used her wiles and persuaded Daddy to get her a horse. The bright-sorrel mare had white stockings and a blaze face. She was a beauty and it did not go unnoticed that Grace's hair came close to matching that of the mare's.

She was quite aware of how the young man at the stables watched her. *That's how I want Garret to look at me, and he will. I will make it happen and soon. He will forget all about that Hannah!*

"Isn't that sight breathtaking?" Olivia asked Frederick as they watched from the veranda overlooking the stables.

Taking a deep breath and exhaling he said, "It certainly is my dear. Both of them are a perfect match, and she rides surprisingly well."

Olivia stated cautiously, "She never ceases to amaze me with all her talents and skills. She will certainly make some young man a perfect wife!"

He cleared his throat and tapped out his pipe tobacco into an ashtray, "Well, she has many years to go before we have to worry about who *you* are going to choose for her."

"Oh, Frederick, you are such a tease. I wasn't much older than she when I set eyes on you and decided you were the one. Besides, I wouldn't dream of interfering. Whoever she becomes interested in, we will, by all means, check his background to see if he is worthy of her…that's all."

"Your beauty overpowered me, my dear. And if you recall…it was *I* who made the first advance," he chided.

She smiled and fluttered her fan as she peeked over it, "If you say so, my dear."

Her action brought instant recall to the scene of that day long ago and gave him reason to sit back in his chair and smile. Shaking his head slightly, he thought to himself, *And all this time I've thought it was my decision.*

Grace glanced up and saw that the young man was blatantly staring. She was pleased, and might have pursued it but he was just a farm hand and she and Momma had their sights set on a much bigger prize.

Later that evening Olivia and Grace decided it was time for stage two of their plan. Dressing for the action was as important as her make-up and hairstyle. Everything had to be perfect to perform the most accurate façade, and both ladies were good at planning.

At the next Ladies Luncheon, Olivia singled out Garret's mother, Lady Piedmont, and opened a conversation with her. After listening to a long dissertation about the Piedmont ancestry, Olivia casually changed the subject to Grace's classes in horseback riding. "She is trying so hard to fit in with her peers, but some of the girls seem to be giving her some strife. She's a newcomer in these parts, and had a rough start in life, but Mr. Wadsworth and I are trying to give her all the opportunities that she missed growing up. She's come a long way and learns so quickly that I'm hoping that soon she will master the Equitation classes. Her form is correct, and her use of aids is sufficient, but her difficulty is in controlling the horse."

"Oh, all of that will come with time, my dear." She leaned in closer to Olivia and whispered behind her fan, "I know I was never at home in the saddle, but held my own until I no longer needed to show my prowess. We girls have to display diverse abilities that society deems necessary for *proper* wives...Balderdash! I've never ridden once, in all the years of my marriage!"

"Yes, I agree. Since the abolishment of slavery, why a woman has to know how to cook, clean, even sew…oh, it pains me to even think of it all. In our parents' day, women had it easy. All those things were done for them, free of charge. Now we have to call them servants and pay them. And you know…you just can't get good help these days!"

Lady Piedmont's head bobbed in agreement, "It is a sad, sad world these days. We are deprived of so many niceties. Did you hear that Mrs. Rhodes caught one of their maids and a field hand up in her hay loft the other day?"

"Oh, my goodness, what did she do?"

"I'm not sure, but I think she fired them both."

"As well it should be. Of all the nerve, and on pay time! Does your boy…Garret is it?... go riding these days?'

"Heaven's sake, we can't keep that boy out of the saddle! He rides every day. Why, you could set your grandfather's clock by him. He leaves at seven each morning and rides for hours. He has a long line of fence that he checks each day. We could have one of the field hands assigned to it, but he says he likes the quiet time to commune with God. He's such a blessing to me…and his father."

"I'm sure you have much to be proud of! He likes to ride the whole fence line along our two properties? That is a long ride…Oh, here's our tea and crumpets."

Returning home, Olivia sent Tilda for Grace, then sent her out to tend the garden. She watched by the window until she saw the woman with hoe in hand, before saying, "I learned a lot about your Garret today."

Grace quickly came to her side, "Tell me everything!"

"Well, his grandfather came here from a long line of the powerful Piedmonts of Yorkshire, England, and was a

Count. His two sons held titles of Lord. One was Lord Maxwell and the other was Lord Louis. Lord Maxwell is Garret's father. Sadly these titles are not passed down to the next generation, but the American Society still regards them in high esteem."

"So, I won't be a princess?" Grace pouted.

"No, dear, but you will be treated like one. The Piedmonts are the closest thing to royalty here and are quite revered. Garret seems to be the apple of his mother's eye, and she will see to it that he gets whatever he wants." Turning to Grace she said… "Which will soon be you!"

The next morning Grace dressed in matching white leather vest and skirt with a light pink silky blouse. A wide-brimmed straw hat held a scarf of the same fabric and tied in the back with tails hanging down between her shoulders. Her white riding boots finished off the ensemble and she stood looking at herself in the mirror, turning this way and that.

Tilda muttered to herself as she made her way to the stables, "Land to Goshen, I don't know what's come over that child, wanting to get up this early and go riding all dressed all up like some fancy doll. She seldom gets up before noon and here she is getting up and off to who-knows-where. Don't understand white folks."

Olivia had given Grace explicit directions as to where the fenceline was and what to do when she saw Garret coming.

Upon arriving at her destination, she found a small grove of trees where she watched and waited.

Peering through the branches, she saw him approaching and let out a scream as she kicked the horse's flanks. The horse jumped so abruptly that Grace was ill-prepared for its instant action and found herself in a true dilemma.

She tried to grip the side-saddle's hook but her left foot slipped into the stirrup. She was thrown off the horse, except with her boot lodged in the stirrup, she was being dragged and bounced along the ground; screaming in earnest. Struggling to loosen her foot, she saw treetops and sky above as her body careened off of mounds of dirt, only to land on nearby rocks...before all went black.

She awoke to an unbelievable headache and a circle of strange faces staring down at her. She reached up to touch her head and found it held a wet cloth. When she tried to rise the room swirled around and she collapsed back to the pillow. All she knew was that she was on a divan in an unfamiliar house, with all these strangers. She cried out, "Momma... Daddy...What happened?"

A lady's voice answered, "There, there, my dear. You're going to be fine. You took a nasty fall from your horse. Thank goodness my son was close by and saw it all. He was able to stop your horse and..."

A man's voice interrupted, "That's enough, Mother. She can be told all of it later. Doctor, will she be alright?"

Although the plan did not go quite the way Grace and Olivia anticipated, it seems to have worked out even better. She might not have been able to fake the injuries that she planned, but the cuts, bruises and the knot on her head, were very convincing. As she began to remember the details she thought, *Well, young lady, you wanted it to look real, and you got it. This must be Garret's home. Momma, we did it! Oh, no, my hair...my clothes...I must look a fright!*

# Chapter 81

Life was getting back to normal in the valley after Liam was found and Zeus was healed. Sparrow and Gabe brought Riel and explained everything to Will and Blue. Sparrow was content with Gabe, Riel and her garden.

Becca's baby was growing inside her and she looked forward to its birth, but she couldn't shake an unsettling feeling of dread. Will came smiling up to her holding a string of fish he'd caught, "I got lucky today. We can have a nice dinner tonight."

She looked up and forced a smile, but he saw in her eyes that something was wrong. "What is it? What is upsetting you? Liam? Is he alright? Blue, tell me."

"I'm not sure, Will. It's just an odd bad feeling that something isn't right. I feel quivery inside."

"Is it the baby? Is it alright?"

"The feeling is in a different place."

"How long have you been feeling this way?"

"All morning…but it isn't the regular baby sickness; it's different. I can't explain it."

"Do you feel the hair on your arms or the back of your neck standing up? That's what alerts Gabe to danger."

She lifted her arms and they both saw the goose bumps. Will immediately looked around for any sign of movement in the underbrush. "Get Liam and come with me. We've got to find Gabe."

"No need to, Son. I'm right behind you," said Gabe.

Will turned, "You too? With goose bumps? What do you make of it, Dad?"

"Not sure, but Zeus and Sashay are upset too. My gut is telling me to head for the cave."

"No. I never want to go in there again. Liam might…"

Gabe shook his head, "Not while we are with him. I'm getting Sparrow and Riel and we'll meet you there. Tell all the others. Ring the triangle if you have to. Grab blankets, firewood, anything. I have no idea what this is, but with Blue and I both feeling this, it's not going to be good."

Blue was standing her ground, "No! Not the cave! I saw that skeleton. Tali's spirit may be lingering in there."

But when she heard a twitter and looked up, she saw the blue bird frantically flapping his wings above her. This time she did not hesitate. She grabbed what she could find but did not take time to tie the bundle, like she would have.

Then came a loud rumbling sound that resonated throughout the valley and shook the ground. Trees swayed and boulders began to tumble from the cliffs above…and then came a torrent of rain, pushed by a strong wind.

Will returned from sounding the alert and grabbed Liam in one arm and the bundle in the other. As they were leaving, Blue turned back to the river and filled a vessel with water, with the blue bird scolding overhead.

They climbed to the ridge above the valley and found Gabe standing alone with a look of fear on his face. "I couldn't find them, Son. Zeus couldn't even find their scent..." His tears went unnoticed in the rain, as he scanned the area and added, "Whenever this is over, whatever it is…I will find them. I pray she has found shelter for her and Riel. May her Yowa and my God protect them."

"Dad, do you think it is wise for us to go inside the cave? If this is an earthquake the cave could collapse around us."

Looking up into the rain, Gabe answered, "We don't have much choice, Son. Did you bring any torches?

"I could only find three."

"That will have to do. Maybe others will bring some."

Many of the clan arrived and began to enter the cave. Some came with belongings and some empty-handed. It wouldn't matter, because this clan was a family and there was little that they did not share.

Gabe pushed Will and Blue inside the crevice but stood at its entrance, searching the valley. When a blindingly bright lightning bolt struck a tall pine nearby, with a simultaneous deafening clap of thunder, he grudgingly stepped inside.

One after the other came the flashes of lightning and earth-shaking thunder, but the cave walls and ceiling held and the people inside survived.

Blue was so wrapped up in making sure that Liam was safe, dry and close by, that she didn't notice what happened to the little blue bird, but suddenly she looked up and around. He wasn't there. She thought, *I wasn't sure he survived Snow Wolf's blow that knocked him to the ground. I'm happy that he lived and is still looking out for me.*

As soon as the storm was over Gabe was the first one out and on the run with Zeus beside him. He didn't take the time to see the vast devastation of fallen trees and large boulders that had dislodged and rolled downward. The river itself was flooding the area and well over its banks. He ran along its edge to their camp and searched the area. Her garden was a muddy swamp of fallen trees and their lean-to was in pieces and belongings scattered. Not finding her, he headed further upstream calling her name and throwing branches and limbs out of the way. When he heard a soft cry he tore frantically at the debris. He found a body, face down. *This poor woman is dead, but it isn't Sparrow...I* *know it's not her. This is someone's wife or mother, but not Sparrow. It isn't her, not my little Sparrow…*But it was.

When Gabe drew her limp body into his arms he found Riel unharmed lying beneath her. The cry became stronger and Gabe reached for him and cuddled him close. With one arm holding his son and the other his precious Sparrow, he pressed his cheek against hers and rocked them both. Tears instantly escapeed his eyes and flowed down his bearded cheeks. As he visualized the scene, the knot in his throat hardened, making it difficult to swallow, while his stomach constricted, threatening to revolt. He choked and raised his chin for fresh air; with his chest on fire his mind cried out, *If I would have been here…I should have been here.* As he faced upward he screamed, "WHY? WHY GOD? Why her? She was my everything, my reason for living…my Sparrow." He laid Riel down, then lifted Sparrow and carried her further up the bank and gently laid her in a grassy spot, then went back for the boy.

Will and Blue found him there, sitting between Riel and her body. Gabe smoothed a loose tendril of her hair that had come loose from a braid. He slid it away from her face and behind one ear as he continued to weep.

Zeus came and lay quietly beside him and put his chin on Gabe's knee. Unconsciously Gabe patted his head and scratched behind an ear. Sashay left them alone and chose a site close to the baby.

"I think I know how she died. When the storm hit she did like we did during that other storm, and took cover under the trees. That last bright bolt of lightning must have hit the trees she was hiding under and traveled down to the ground where she was. How Riel survived, I'll never know."

"Dad, I'm so sorry, we loved her too."

Gabe looked up to see Will and Blue both in tears, not knowing how to ease the pain of their surrogate father. He nodded, "I know. I know you did. Blue, will you help me give her a traditional burial? I know she would like that."

"Of course, the whole clan will. They loved her too."

"Then that's what we'll do. But let's do it as soon as possible. It hurts too much to see her this way," he said.

"Dad, let us do it. Blue can take the baby and find someone to nurse him. Take Zeus and Sashay for a walk. Maybe scout the area…to take your mind off this."

"Maybe I will. Yes, that would be best. I'll be back in a couple of hours. Zeus, Sashay, Come."

Upon returning he found that Sparrow was not the only causality of the storm. Four graves lay side-by-side with bodies wrapped and lowered into them. The clan had waited for his return before they began the ceremony.

"Dad, when Blue took Riel to find someone to nurse him, one lady did not hesitate. She cuddled him to her breast and even asked Blue if she could keep him. Of course Blue said no, but I think you should know that two of the graves beside Sparrow held her husband and infant child. The woman offered to be his nursemaid."

Gabe nodded, "Tell her I would be obliged and I will compensate her somehow…that is until I find out what I'm going to do. On that walk Zeus found Angel. She was glad to see us and came to us immediately. On our way back I realized I can't stay here. I don't want to leave you, but I must do what is best for Riel. He has to have the opportunities that the white world can give him. I know what it did to Gigi, but she compared the two lifestyles. He

316

won't remember this one. Who knows…maybe he and Gigi might even meet someday."

Blue stood holding Riel as Liam clung to her skirt. She looked at Gabe, then to Will. "Will, there is something that I've wanted to tell you. Almost since we got here, I've been miserable. I didn't say anything because I was the one that brought everyone here, thinking it was perfect. But I miss the cabin, and all the things we had there. I miss Ellen and Thomas…and many things. Would you hate me if I say I want to go back?"

"Becca Blue! Don't you know that you and Liam are the only reason I'm here?" Turning to Gabe he said, "You're not getting rid of us that easy, Dad. We lost everything but the bundle we took to the cave…the storm saw to that. If it's all the same to you two, I'm ready to go now."

Gabe took Riel from Blue and said, "The main problem is how I am going to feed this little guy for as many days as it will take to get there?"

"Maybe the woman will go with us," Blue suggested.

Will frowned, "But then how will she get back here?"

Gabe thought for a minute, then told Blue, "Ask her. If she is willing to go with us, and you two will keep Riel until I get home, I will bring her back here to the valley."

Blue was ecstatic, "Of course we'll watch him. Once we reach the cabins we can get milk from town. I'll go now and ask the woman, but I also have to talk to the clan…I owe them that much…and I must say goodbye to Jumping Fox and Moon Star. Pack what you can find on Angel and when I return be ready to go."

Blue convinced the woman that the trip would give her time to ease the pain of losing her family, and she agreed.

After packing her few belongings she followed Blue to the waiting men, where she immediately reached for Riel and spoke in broken English, "My name, Kawani."

Blue added, "Her family was in the larger group that the evil soldier gathered and brought to the fort. She speaks a little English but understands more"

"At least it will be enough to get through this trip. Hand me her bundle and I'll add it to Angel's load," said Gabe.

Blue turned to Kawani and said, "It will be good to have a woman to talk to. We can get to know one another during the journey ahead."

"What are men's names?" she asked.

"Oh, I'm sorry." Pointing to each she said, "This is my husband Will and this is our son, Liam. The baby you are holding is Riel and this is his father, Gabe."

"And…where we go?" asked Kawani.

"Back near the fort where the soldiers…."

Eyes wide with fear, Kawani stepped back, "Soldiers?"

"No, no, no…We aren't going *to* the fort. It's a town near there. The people are good and kind, and treat us nice."

In fear of losing her, Gabe stepped in, "No soldiers…to a cabin in the woods near there. Then I will bring you right back here," pointing to the ground.

Kawani glanced from one to the other and then nodded.

Blue's face lit up in a large smile as she said, "Many surprises await you, my new friend, for we are going to introduce you to the white man's world!"

*Follow along with the lives of Blue Feather, her family and friends as they each struggle to survive their personal life journeys in...*

## *Blue Feather's Destiny*